NEVER FORGOTTEN

DI KAREN HEATH CRIME SERIES

JAY NADAL

Published by 282publishing.com

1

The rattle of a supermarket trolley broke the silence as he trundled along the road. With no stores nearby, the sharp sounds weren't a normal part of the street's auditory makeup. He pushed an old Tesco's trolley, rusted and full of discarded metal, carrier bags full of paper, clothes and oddments he'd picked up over the years. It shook as it passed over the uneven pavement.

Dressed in several layers, the smudges of exhaust-fume pollution left his coat dirty and tattered. His body bulged beneath it. An off-white beard travelled down his dark coat. He averted his gaze, not meeting the eyes of those who passed by. The harshness of street life taught him very quickly to stay isolated in every possible way. Even a stray glance could mean trouble best avoided. Under hooded lids, he watched them, disgust in their eyes.

The man doubled over and grabbed the lapels on his coat, the cough that had persisted since the end of last year becoming worse with every passing day. And with winter fast approaching, the dampness seemed to creep under his skin and squeeze his lungs as if they were in a vice.

At times he broke protocol and made eye contact with another person in the overstretched hope that someone kind might take pity on him and help. Each time he did, they recoiled worse than if he'd been one of the flea-infested coke addicts that lingered around day and night, their lips curled and heads moving away until they could safely redirect their eyes to the opposite side of the street or the person walking beside them. Their steps gathered pace as if about to break into a jog as they suppressed a tinge of guilt or horror, hastily beginning a vacuous conversation.

His body grew colder and his breath held a rasping rattle he'd only ever heard on the other homeless he'd seen. Those were the ones who didn't have much longer, and to think of it cast him into a blackness he couldn't fight. His mind searched for a happy memory, something to cling to, but every one of them was attached to a plethora of bad ones.

"Please," he croaked to those who walked by, "spare change," to others. Just enough money to buy a bottle of whiskey that could warm his chest, cloud his mind and numb the pain of life on the streets. That was all he needed, a couple of drinks to make the nights pass faster and the days to come quicker. Instead, passers-by avoided looking at his desperate face. Some looked sympathetic and concerned, but he saw through the facade to find their disgust and hatred.

It was the same route he followed every morning. Though his joints creaked, and his fingers were stiff, he walked around the perimeter of the abandoned building site. He rarely came up against another homeless person, most of those in a similar position to himself knew that this was his patch and offered him a degree of respect. This was the best time for him to be out. The overnight fly tippers would have been cruising the area looking for suitable sites to dump their illegal rubbish.

He grumbled to himself, his words incoherent at times. A sticky mess of thick phlegm rattled in his throat as a few words trip from his lips. "Wankers. The lot of them. Fuck you. All this for Queen and country, and what have I got left? God knocking on my door, waiting to collect me."

He rummaged through bins looking for any discarded morsels, searching in vain. He continued to push his trolley a few hundred yards before he spotted a fly tip directly in front of one of the boarded-up entrances to the site. As he neared it, he could see the usual pile of black bin liners, discarded pieces of wood, an old sink, and a few black tyres. Flies buzzed overhead, with many more crawling over the discarded waste. He had seen things like this before, restaurants unwilling to safely discard their rotten leftovers. For him, it provided an opportunity to have something more nutritious than a swig of beer and a used cigarette.

The flies protested at his arrival, as he kicked the bags and batted them away. Reluctant to leave, he waved his arms furiously and told them to fuck off as he leant down.

He tore open the first few to find nothing more than broken bits of polystyrene and bubble wrap. Disappointed, he pushed them to one side to discover what appeared to be some uncooked meat.

Leaning in, he brushed aside the leaf matter and plastic coverings before he froze for a moment, his mind desperately trying to play catch-up with his eyes. He shook his head and stared, unable to register the grizzly sight. The searing pain rose in his throat as bile reached the back of his mouth. He tried to make sense of why it was here, who it belonged to and what he should do.

It was a human hand and arm, partially wrapped in a black bin liner. The limb was almost devoid of skin and pitted by burrowing insects. The man turned away as his stomach heaved, his nostrils filled with the smell of rotting flesh.

He stumbled back and searched around, a mixture of disbelief and fear sending waves of panic through him. With his heart racing, he turned, colliding with his trolley as it toppled over, with him over it. He glanced over his shoulder once more. It looked as if the hand was outstretched, reaching for him, calling him.

The adrenaline flooded his system so fast that he almost vomited, the saliva thickening in his throat and beads of sweat trickling down his brow as his body became clammy. His brain had started to shut down, desperate to keep his sanity. His eyes widened as if someone was coming to deliver his own death as he turned on his heels and ran.

2

Detective Inspector Karen Heath stepped from Jade's car and took a moment to survey the scene in Hanover Street. Cold licked at her face and crept under her clothes, spreading across her skin like she had tiptoed into the sea on a winter's day. With her teeth chattering and an icy chill snaking down her spine, she pulled her thin coat closer and tugged the collar up.

The familiar rush of adrenaline that she always felt when turning up at a crime scene surged through her body. She knew from experience that it was all too easy to get swept away in a new investigation and miss vital information about her surroundings like any CCTV locations, unusual characters hanging back from any gathering of spectators and onlookers, or anyone sitting in a car watching the events unfold.

She joined Jade beside their vehicle, who glanced up the street to where blue and white police tape looped around lamp posts. The usual display of scientific services vans, police cars and an ambulance lined the road.

A strong gust of bitter wind whistled past them, causing Karen to draw in a sharp intake of breath. “Jesus, that’s enough to cut you in half. I hate cold weather.”

“Me too,” added Jade. “I’m sure my body was designed for the Mediterranean climate. In fact, I’m almost certain there must be Mediterranean blood in my background.”

“You reckon?”

“Definitely. Give me a Greek salad, freshly grilled fish, a glass of ouzo, and a sun terrace, any day. That will be me when I’m retired.”

Karen laughed and blew out her cheeks. “You’ve got a few years to go before you live that dream.”

Jade agreed. “Right, shall we crack on?”

They made their way towards the outer cordon where they both signed in with the scene guard who provided them with protective suits and foot coverings.

SOCO had erected a blue tent over the fly tip. A long line of wooden hoardings fenced off land beyond it.

“What’s behind there?” Karen pointed with her head.

Jade checked her notepad. “It’s basically waste ground, with a concrete shell of a building. Apparently, the offices or flats were supposed to have been built there, but work stopped on the site fourteen months ago. The developers ran out of money.”

The black hoardings had long been used by local gangs and graffiti artists to display their tags and murals. Karen wasn’t sure how she felt about that. Was it vandalism? Or street art? The jury was out as far as she was concerned. But as she looked around, it added a degree of vibrancy to grey drab and dreary buildings that surrounded this former building site.

"Who found the remains?" Karen asked.

Jade pointed over towards the ambulance, which had its rear doors open with a man wrapped in a red blanket sitting inside it. "The homeless fella over there. He lives in the concrete shell on the other side of the hoardings."

"A bit of a shocker for him, I think?"

"He's definitely suffering from shock. He discovered the limb and panicked. Mind you, anyone would do the same in that situation," said Jade.

"What was he doing?"

"He trawls the area every morning, apparently this is a common place for fly tippers. He scavenges for knick-knacks that I think make his life a bit more comfortable."

"Has any more of the body being found?"

"Nothing as yet."

Karen glanced over her shoulder to see a line of uniformed officers searching the immediate area. She noticed the first signs of media interest arriving beyond the outer perimeter. Reporters aimed cameras in their direction, whilst they searched for a better vantage point.

"We'll have a chat with… Have we got a name for Mr Homeless?" prompted Karen.

"Bobby McCreath."

"With Mr McCreath in a moment. Let's see what SOCO has found."

"Morning, Mason."

"Morning, Karen. I figured it wouldn't be too long before you arrived. I thought I'd hang around to give you an update."

"What have you discovered?"

Mason's protective suit rustled as he bent down to grab his notepad. "We have a left arm and hand; the hand is still attached. IC1. We're unsure whether it's male or female. A lot of the skin has been chewed off already, and has insect infestation, it's at an advanced stage of decay."

"Cleanly dismembered?" Karen asked.

Mason shook his head. "No. Quite an untidy cut."

"Any other evidence?"

"At the moment, no. The team is still going through all the discarded rubbish. We'll be arranging for it to all be recovered back to the lab. It will be a ball-ache of a job, but you never know. There might be a receipt, or a letter in all that pile which may give you a starting point."

Karen knew council inspectors often looked for that kind of evidence in an investigation. "We also have to consider the possibility that the limb may have been there before the fly tip or thrown on to it sometime later. The fly tip may not be connected. Mind if we pop into the tent?"

Mason nodded his approval. "We've done most of our examination, we'll be arranging for the limb to be removed."

"Thanks, Mason. We'll only be a minute, anyway," said Karen, as they made their way towards the tent, and lifted the flap. The first thing that hit Karen was a small swarm of flies that buzzed frantically around them, their bodies bouncing off the blue walls.

The crime scene officers looked up from their work and offered a nod in acknowledgement as Karen and Jade stood towards one edge. In front remained a huge pile of rubbish, but a limb had been placed on an evidence bag to one side. Pale grey. Some skin remained, but the red rotten flesh lay visibly exposed.

"Gross," was all that Jade could offer, as she watched maggots crawl through the flesh.

Mason was right. It was hard to determine whether it was a male or female, nor could Karen tell the age. But from where she stood, the size of the limb suggested it belonged to an adult rather than a child.

Jade stepped out of the tent, followed by Karen. "I'll organise for uniform to do the door-to-door enquiries. Do you want me to organise anything else, Karen?"

"That would be good, Jade. Though if it happened at some point during the night, or very early this morning, I doubt anyone would have been around. From the looks of it, most of these buildings are office blocks, and a few sandwich bars and coffee shops at ground level. We might get lucky with a bit of CCTV. But this area shuts down at night and doesn't get much footfall. Before we head off, let's have a word with Mr McCreath," Karen said as they stepped out of their protective clothing and handed it back to be bagged up by the scene guard.

Karen surveyed the crime scene one last time before she muttered under her breath, "Where's the rest of you?"

3

Karen made her way to the rear of the ambulance and peered in through the open doors. A paramedic glanced up from her note taking and offered a small nod from behind her face mask. “Do you mind if I have a quick word with Mr McCreath?”

“Of course not,” replied the paramedic. “You need me to be out of here?”

“No, it’s fine. What’s this in aid of?” Karen asked, pointing to the surgical mask on Mr McCreath.

“Possibly displaying signs of pneumonia. Brown mucus being coughed up, difficulty breathing, rapid heartbeat, and a high temperature, despite it being cold outside. All classic signs. We’re going to run him in to get checked over. I would keep your distance.”

Karen loitered towards the back door, reluctant to step inside the cab. From where she was standing, he certainly looked unwell. His matted hair hung loosely down to his shoulders, and his off-white dirty beard disappeared beneath the red blanket. He looked washed out and pale. His eyes carried a yellow tinge, and she was drawn to his hands which sat on his lap, thin bony fingers, with longer fingernails than she had, each with an accumulation of black dirt beneath them.

Her heart went out to the man. She imagined that more than anything else, he needed a warm, hearty meal, a hot bath, a change of fresh clothes, and a haircut and shave. She wondered how he would feel to rest his head upon a pillow and experience the warmth of the duvet cocooning him in on a cold winter's night. She shook away the melancholy.

"Mr McCreath, I'm Detective Inspector Karen Heath. I understand it was you who found the severed limb, so can you spare me a few moments?"

The man's soulless eyes bore into her, nothing but sadness and destitution were reflected within them. He nodded and then stared at the blanket, lost in his own world.

"I imagine you had a bit of a shock with what you discovered. Did you see anyone in the area within the last few hours?"

McCreath thought for a minute before shaking his head.

"Did you notice any vehicles, a car, perhaps a van, or even a lorry? Because that pile of rubbish came from somewhere."

"I… didn't… hear… anything," McCreath whispered, his voice cracking as each word exhaled on an out breath.

"What about any heated discussions, the raising of a voice, an argument, maybe screams? Anything like that?"

McCreath shook his head and then started to cough

violently, causing the paramedic to lay her notes down, and reach across and remove McCreath's face mask, before placing an oxygen mask in its place. The hiss of air filled the cab.

"You should start to feel a little better. It has steroid medication in there to reduce the irritation in your lungs, and make it easier for you to breathe," she said.

McCreath spluttered a few more times as the oxygen pushed through, crawling its way to the deepest parts of his lungs.

"How long have you lived around here, Mr McCreath?" Karen asked.

McCreath shook his shoulders. "Dunno, nine or ten months."

Karen couldn't glean much from the conversation. It was a homeless guy, clearly unwell, who hadn't heard or seen anything. Maybe he was being genuine, but from experience, many homeless mistrusted the authorities and society in general. They wouldn't ask for help, wouldn't snitch on each other, and preferred to keep to themselves.

Karen sighed and stuffed her hands in her coat pockets. "Thank you for your time, Mr McCreath. You've done really well, and you've been very helpful. I'll arrange for another officer to pop along and see you a little later in case you remember anything else. But in the meantime, I'll leave you in the capable hands of this lovely paramedic." Karen offered the man a reassuring smile.

It was hard for her to tell whether McCreath was genuinely shocked or felt a degree of remorse for what he'd seen, even though on the face of it, he didn't appear at fault.

Jade made her way over to Karen, glancing at the gathered entourage of reporters. "Karen, do you mind having a word with a very *persistent* reporter. We found him peering through a hole in the hoardings just a few feet away from the crime scene. He keeps pushing for answers, and he wants to get something back to his editor before the other reporters. Uniform cut the chain on the gate and entered the building site to nab him. He heard us talking. Would you believe it, he even tried to bribe me with some wine gums he was eating? As if that was going to work!"

Karen groaned and shook her head as she looked beyond Jade to the small cluster of reporters and photographers who stood eagerly waiting like a line of obedient dogs, anticipating their next treat. "Where is he?"

"We've got him in one of the vans. I threatened to arrest him for trespass on private land."

Karen followed Jade towards a nearby police van and found an overexcited and eager reporter hemmed in by a burly police officer. She recognised him at once as Chris Wallace, a man she'd clashed horns with on several occasions over the years.

"Wallace, you are like a bad smell. I don't have time now to deal with your questions."

"Come on, Detective Inspector. You and I go back a few years, so at least give me something to go on, anything I can use before the other vultures get to it."

Karen furrowed her brow. "Vultures? And you don't fit into that description, no?"

"No. All I'm after is getting a good story to the public, especially one like this, where you've got an axe murderer on the loose!" He threw his head in the direction of the blue tent.

Karen rolled her eyes. "Axe murderer? Where the bloody hell did you get that notion from? That's your very vivid imagination playing a very risky move."

"Well, it's not that often that you find a severed limb – one that's being hacked off a body in the most grotesque and barbaric way, hey?"

"Listen, Wallace, you know as much as I do now. This is an active crime scene, and we're still gathering evidence, and talking to eyewitnesses."

He flicked his hand towards the ambulance. "What, like the dirty tramp? I've already checked out his gaff. It's a pigsty."

Karen felt her blood boil. Not only had he annoyed her, but the man had trespassed on private land, and had invaded the only place that McCreath could call home.

"Wallace, I will say this only once. We'll be doing a press conference later. Come along to that, and you'll get as much information as I can give you and every other reporter at the time."

"But…"

Karen raised her finger to silence him, and narrowed her eyes, staring down Wallace. "There is no but. I'm quite happy to have you arrested for trespassing on private land. If you would prefer for us to do that now, then that's fine with me. It would mean that you'd miss the press conference later. Your choice."

"That hardly gives me the scoop, does it, Detective Inspector?" he spat.

"Wallace, we've not been on the scene long. I'm trying to get my head around it. The last thing I need is you jumping to conclusions, or worse, misquoting me. As the investigation progresses, if I find anything meaty, and I think it's in the interest of the public to know about it, I'll give you the first shout. Do I make myself clear?"

Wallace nodded reluctantly as Karen walked away, instructing the uniformed officer to release Wallace and escort him to beyond the outer perimeter cordon.

Karen reconvened with Jade, and they compared notes, checking the list of action points that needed to be carried out whilst the cordon was in place. Even though her uniformed colleagues had interviewed McCreath and taken his statement before she had arrived, Karen nevertheless wanted to hear it for herself, though the disappointment of not discovering anything of substance tempered her mood.

4

A chilly breeze cut through Karen's clothes as she stepped out of Jade's car. The onset of winter wasn't far away. With temperatures in the past few days cooler, the clouds were heavier and angrier-looking, and a dull greyness seemed to smother her surroundings. Thankfully, the rains hadn't arrived. One thing she hated more than anything else, was rain. The winters in the UK were long, dark and drawn-out. She could just about cope with that, but when rain was added into the mix, the country seemed to dip into depression.

As she made her way through the office, her thoughts turned to Bobby McCreath, and how he spent his life living outdoors, sleeping in doorways, and empty buildings, a sheet of cardboard for a mattress, and a few ragged blankets for warmth. Now he was in the care of the hospital, she hoped they could make the necessary plans to find him shelter, especially knowing the temperatures in January and February could be brutal. Sadly, homelessness was a problem up and down the country, with no city or town unaffected by it. What upset Karen further was knowing that Bobby McCreath was an army veteran and had seen active duty. Post-traumatic stress and divorce had seen him spiral out of control, drink being his saviour.

Karen threw her jacket on the back of an empty chair and made her way towards the front of the incident room, which buzzed with activity. Steve had taken the lead in Karen's absence, and set up a whiteboard, along with extra computer terminals, files, and the necessary paperwork. Additional members of the team would conduct much of the legwork, including the reviewing of witness statements, data inputting and cross-referencing on the HOLMES2 system. The details of every phone conversation, interview, evidence record and all lines of enquiry undertaken would be catalogued. Steve had organised an exhibits officer to log every item seized or recovered such as mobile phones, keys, items of clothing, and weapons.

Though there was an excitement that rippled through the assembled officers, Karen's mind turned to the thought that someone had died in horrific circumstances, and their job was to find out who and why.

Karen glanced around the team. All the usual suspects were there, including members of her extended MIT who had proved invaluable in her last investigation. A few civilian staff as well as a couple of uniformed officers were dotted amongst her assembled audience.

Turning towards a noticeboard, Karen took a moment to glance over the map pinned to it. A red pin confirmed the position of this morning's crime scene. Further close-ups of the area had been printed off and attached to one side. Most of the officers had already become familiar with the scene, having examined the bodycam footage. Further photographs of the crime scene would arrive soon from SOCO.

"Thanks for organising all of this, Steve. It's much appreciated and gives us a chance to get cracking on with this as quickly as possible."

Steve nodded, appreciating the sentiment.

"Okay, team. We've just returned from a location where a severed arm and hand were discovered by a homeless man. Most of you have seen the footage that was recorded at the scene and are up to speed with it."

There was a consensus of nods and grimaces in reply.

"As there was a large press contingent gathering, and watching our every move, it's wise that we do a press conference as soon as possible, so that we can put out the facts as we know them before the press distort them. I think it also helps to allay any fears that residents may have."

"But we haven't got much to tell them, guv. We don't normally run a press conference until we have more information." Brad pointed out.

Karen agreed, but knew that they needed to lead on this before the Chinese whispers started.

"As far as I know, none of the photographers had an opportunity to take any photographs before SOCO arrived. I imagine we won't have photos being circulated. Although, our favourite reporter, Wallace, did find a way to evade the cordon, and get close. I'm certain he hasn't got anything, but again it makes sense to get out there first in case he does have something."

Jade chipped in and gave the rest of the team an update on

the discovery. "As yet, forensics can't confirm whether the arm belongs to a white male or female, nor age, other than it's probably an adult."

"And until we can identify the limb, and who it belongs to, finding a motive is going to prove difficult. I'll attend the mortuary tomorrow, and hopefully we'll get further insights, but don't hold your breath," Karen added.

"Where do we start?" asked an officer.

Karen paced around in a small circle as she gathered her thoughts before pausing in front of the picture of the limb. Her eyes travelled up and down the length of the arm, down towards the fingertips. The advanced stages of decomposition turned Karen's stomach, forcing her to look away.

"We need officers to conduct door-to-door enquiries. Some are commercial offices, but considering it's a Sunday, I doubt they're open. They will need checking, and perhaps followed up again tomorrow. Whilst we are down there, look for any CCTV installations, especially those overlooking the construction site. I couldn't see any, but there may be some positioned inside those buildings, looking out on to the streets."

As Karen retrieved her jacket, Jade confirmed that they would run a misper report to check for any recent cases.

"Okay, you lot, get on with it, I will update the DCI, and liaise with the press office to organise our press conference for later today or tomorrow. If any of you need me, I'll be in my office."

And with that, Karen watched the team disperse in different directions, some grabbing their coats to head out, others gathering in small groups to divide the tasks. It felt like a well-oiled machine, everyone knowing what they needed to do. A sense of pride washed over her, and her lips curled upward.

There was a common goal amongst them all. Someone had been on the receiving end of a possibly brutal and nasty attack. She wondered whether the victim had been alive or dead when the arm had been severed. She hoped it was the latter. One thought did cross her mind. What had the victim done to deserve this? Which only led her on to another question… What kind of person would inflict such a horrific injury on someone?

5

Having moved away from the main incident room, Karen noticed that the corridors appeared quieter than they had been for a while. She made her way towards Skelton's office, unsure if he was inside. She had tried his internal line several times without response. But she knew if she didn't track him down, he would find some reason to have a go at her later for not keeping him in the loop.

Karen peered through the open door to find the lights on, his chair pushed back, and Skelton nowhere to be seen. She chewed on her bottom lip whilst deciding what to do. She could send him an email providing him with an update, so at least then there was an official record of her notifying him.

She was about to turn and head back to her office when she heard footsteps behind her. Turning to look over her shoulder, she saw Skelton making his way back from the men's toilets, shaking his head, sniffing loudly, and wiping his nose with a tissue.

With his eyes fixed wide, his pace slowed as he saw Karen loitering.

"Got a bit of a cold?" asked Karen.

Skelton grumbled something incomprehensible, shook his head as if to wake himself up, and breezed past her back into his office.

Karen rolled her eyes as she followed him in. *His usual charming self.*

Skelton cleared his throat as he planted himself in his chair and cleared his throat again. He grabbed his mug and took a swig of cold coffee, which contorted his features even further.

Karen noticed that Skelton appeared more dishevelled than normal. His hair was untidy. The man had loosened his tie, and it hung low on his shirt, and his suit jacket appeared crumpled. She spotted his attempts at shaving. Patches of stubble were more prominent in areas where he hadn't taken a second swipe with his razor blade. As Skelton looked up at her, Karen couldn't help but stare at his sunken eyes, and his fixed stare. If she wasn't mistaken, his pupils were dilated, and his complexion looked washed out.

"I thought I'd give you an update on the case, sir," she began.

Skelton nodded, whilst his eyes travelled around the room. "What have we got?"

"A severed arm and hand. We've been unable to locate any further body parts, despite an extensive search of the area. I'll be in attendance tomorrow to see what the pathologist has to say. He may be able to give us an indication as to how long the limb has been severed for a better age profile, and perhaps the type of weapon used."

Karen continued to fill him in on who had discovered the arm, and the general layout of the location. She also went into detail to explain the action steps she had put into place, which Skelton didn't appear to object to.

There was something about Skelton's demeanour that bothered Karen. As she was debriefing him, she couldn't help but notice how his eyes kept tracking around the room, appearing unable to fix on one thing. "Sir, are you sure you're okay? I don't mean to offend you, but you're either distracted, or not feeling great?"

"I'm… I'm fine. Have you got enough in the way of resources?"

Karen nodded. "I think the press are going to have a field day with this, which is why I wanted to stay one step ahead of them and get a press conference organised for today, but it's just too late," Karen added, checking the time on her phone. Noticing that it was seven twenty p.m. "Our best bet is to do the conference tomorrow after I return from the mortuary. I can liaise with the press office first thing tomorrow and send them an email this evening just to give them the heads up?"

Skelton checked his online scheduler on his monitor. "I'll be around for that tomorrow. I'll be in and out of short meetings here and there, but just give me an indication nearer the time."

Karen rose from her chair and confirmed she would update him tomorrow morning and copy him in on the email to the press office this evening.

KAREN STOOD ALONE in the communal kitchen stirring her black coffee for a few minutes, deep in thought. Her mind seemed to float from one idea to another, odd thoughts with little interconnectivity. It was one of those rare moments where she allowed everything and anything to invade her thinking. The need to visit her sister, getting home to feed Manky, McCreath's homeless plight, and the beginning of an investigation. Layered upon that was Skelton's random and erratic behaviour. She'd seen it countless times in her career. The dilated pupils, sniffing and inability to focus all suggested one thing to her, he'd taken something, and her hunch was a class A substance.

She pushed those thoughts to one side as she washed and dried her teaspoon. The day shift had left all their plates, stained mugs, and dirty knives and forks in the sink, knowing that night-time cleaners would clean up their mess. She shook her head in disbelief. *These were grown men and women who couldn't do the most basic of chores.*

She cursed her rumbling stomach and the closed canteen, the vending machine offering little more than crisps and chocolate as she passed by on the way back to her office.

She shivered in response to her frigid office as she lowered herself into her chair and wiggled her mouse to awaken her screen. Perhaps it wasn't a cold office, and more a lack of warm food that left a chill inside her body. With nothing more than a banana and a yoghurt after returning from the crime scene, tiredness and fatigue were robbing her of any energy to continue. Karen leant over her chair and opened her bottom drawer to rummage through her emergency store of multi-high-energy naughty treats that she relied upon when she hadn't planned and picked up something from Tesco's. Tonight, her meal would be a cup of coffee and a Toffee Crisp.

Karen fired off an email to the press office with all the necessary details, ensuring she copied in Skelton, before she sidetracked once again as random thoughts crept into her awareness. The dream she'd had not long ago bothered her. The hijack had been replayed in her thoughts as she'd slept, and for the first time, she'd heard the voices of the hijackers. It was still sketchy, random obscenities, with aggressive and threatening words firing over her head in volleys. They were all London accents, that she could be sure of, though she hadn't been able to distinguish between North and South London. But then again, was there really a disparity between the accents that bordered each side of the Thames?

Karen froze and stared at her desk as she furrowed her brow. Something else bothered her that hovered just outside of her awareness. She tried desperately to focus, willing her unconscious mind to release more valuable nuggets of information, more pieces of the jigsaw that would help to make sense of the living nightmare that followed her around every day. It felt like that extra piece of information that she needed was just outside the grasp of her fingertips, and yet it was there, goading her, teasing her, and highlighting her weaknesses.

Her palms began to sweat, and her face flushed as she gritted her teeth. It was there, she knew it, but for whatever reason, her mind wasn't willing to give up all its secrets.

She rocked back and forth in her chair, pleading with the demons to give her the breathing space she needed to think clearly.

A random voice screamed through her mind. "Shoot the fuckers, shoot the fuckers!"

Who said that? Which one of the masked attackers said it?

The sound of gunfire sent her heart racing, pounding in her chest as her head spun. She felt the first waves of another panic attack taking hold, as her breath came in short, shallow gasps. Karen tilted her head back in her chair and closed her eyes, trying to get a grip on her breathing, puffing out her cheeks, and trying to inhale deeper, as she gripped the armrests on her chair.

Control... Control... Control! You've got this!

"This wasn't part of the plan!" came another voice as more images flooded back into her awareness. That voice. It was the same voice in her dream. It sounded familiar but muffled. It wasn't clear enough,

"Fuck... Fuck!" Karen muttered as a damp sheen coated her face.

And then, as quickly as the voice and images had appeared in her mind, they disappeared. Blankness replaced the pictures of bodies lying on the floor, the screams of horrified passers-by, and the screech of tyres as they faded into the distance.

It took a few minutes for Karen to open her eyes again. Tears threatened to overwhelm her as she readjusted to being back in the room. Her sense of isolation and vulnerability made her want to lock the door and hide under her desk, desperate for someone to rescue her from the living hell that played out in her mind.

One way or another, Karen needed closure. She was certain that seeing a shrink wouldn't help, nor did she want that on her record. That would only give the powers that be more ammunition to consider her unfit for active service and pension her off on the grounds of ill-health. Everything she had done so far to uncover the truth had led her down blind alleys. Information that she knew she had seen before on the system had been erased, and someone was always one step ahead of her. The fact that Skelton kept getting the alerts of her snooping bothered her even more. But she truly believed that the first place to start would be to find out *who* was responsible for removing the data and evidence that she was reviewing.

Karen sat back in her chair, exhaustion willing her to sleep, and her mind crying out for space to rest undisturbed. But she couldn't. Not whilst the horrors of the hijack kept pulling her back to a dark place that she was fed up with.

She spent the next hour going over what she already knew, searching for ideas on how to take this forward. It was then that a random thought appeared. For that, she would need someone's help.

6

Karen wove her way through the officers on the morning shift. Many had congregated around the kitchen, the sound of random conversations and spoons clinking in cups filling the air. The energy levels were up amongst her team, if only she could have felt the same. The events of last evening had left her exhausted, and with delays on the Central line, she had got back to Epping just before midnight.

A long hot soak in the shower this morning, followed by a breakfast of cornflakes and toast had helped, but she still felt deflated. The vibe and energy of those around her were what she needed to pick her up.

"Coming through, coming through," Karen announced as she squeezed through them, keen to put her lunch in the fridge. With a Costa coffee in one hand, her handbag slung over her shoulder, and a sandwich in her other hand, she cursed as her job phone rang in the back pocket of her trousers. In her attempt to reach her phone before it rang off, she slammed her coffee down a little too hard on the work surface, causing some hot liquid to splash out of the spout and burn the back of her hand.

"Bollocks," she cursed. She retrieved her phone from her pocket to see a missed call from Wallace, their roving reporter nemesis. *If it's urgent, he'll call back.*

"Morning, boss," Steve said as he grabbed the kitchen towel and handed her a sheet.

"Thanks, Steve. Oh, morning, by the way." She smiled as she dabbed the back of her hand, before picking up her coffee and heading to her office.

Steve and Jade followed Karen, both sipping their coffee and grabbing a seat.

"How are you both this morning?" she asked, switching on her computer monitor, and straightening out her desk.

"I'm good, thanks," Jade replied. "I got an early night. I picked up the shopping for the week, put a load of washing on, had a bath, and I was out sparko by ten o'clock. I feel quite refreshed today." She smiled with a shrug of her shoulders, looking pleased with herself.

"And you, Steve?" Karen asked.

"I'm more conscientious than Jade. I stayed a bit longer to do *my* job, and then stopped by the garage to pick up a few parts for my bike."

Jade's eyes widened, and she formed an O with her mouth in mock disbelief at Steve's accusations. "You cheeky bugger. I put in the hours as well. You stayed because you're going through a dry spell with the women!" she teased.

Karen smiled, she loved moments like this where they

could forget about their work and share the kind of banter that took place in offices up and down the length and breadth of the country. She was about to chip in when her phone rang again. She peeked at the screen and saw it was Wallace's number. Karen rolled her eyes as she faced Steve and Jade.

"Heath," Karen answered. She nodded her head and continued to roll her eyes and bob her head as she listened to Wallace drone on. "Can I just interrupt you there? As I said to you yesterday, we would be organising a press conference. Unfortunately, we ran out of time last night…"

Karen was interrupted in her explanation as Wallace cut in. She tapped her fingers on the desk listening to him plead for useful insights he could offer to his editor.

"As I was saying before you butted in, we tried, but it was too late to get things sorted in time. We'll be arranging the conference for later today, and the press team will contact you in due course."

Wallace, unhappy with being stonewalled, continued to harangue Karen on the phone.

Karen took in a deep, sharp intake of breath, choosing to count to ten. "It's not my concern whether your editor fires you or not. You will be invited to attend like everyone else. If you have an issue with your editor, I suggest you take it up with him," she replied firmly before hanging up.

Jade raised a brow. "Pushy little git, isn't he?"

"That's one way of putting it, I guess," Karen replied as she tossed her phone on to the desk. "Besides, I've got more pressing issues," she continued, crossing her arms and staring at both of her officers in mock anger. "Someone has been helping themselves to my Percy pigs in the kitchen… I wonder who that could be?"

Steve and Jade began to blame one another.

Karen intervened, "Jade… If I find that you have been sneaking my Percy pigs… Again! I'll put you down for the Christmas Day *and* Boxing Day rotas."

She threw her hands up in the air. "It wasn't me. I haven't got a sweet tooth."

"Jade, you are such a liar. Whenever someone brings sweets, cakes, or chocolate into the office, you are one of the first in the queue," Karen replied.

Jade looked incredulous, desperate to hold back a laugh that threatened to give the game away.

"Only you two, and Brad, know that I hide my Percy pigs in the old hot chocolate box which has my name on it. And everyone out there knows not to touch it. One of you lot would have the balls to sneak a few. And sorry, Jade, but you are at the top of my list of suspects. I bet you if I took that box down to forensics, your prints would be all over it."

Before Jade could spring to her own defence, Karen ushered them out of the room as she made her way towards the incident board, Jade's protestations still echoing in Karen's ears as the banter and blame game continued.

KAREN STOOD beside the incident board, as her officers gathered around.

"Good morning, everyone."

There were murmurs of responses from those gathered.

Karen began the briefing by instructing all her officers to make certain they were up to date with everything that went on yesterday. For a few officers drafted in, it was their first day on the investigation.

"I'll be attending the post-mortem straight after this briefing, and I'll make sure that the database is updated with the findings. Hopefully, it will give us a starting point. In the meantime, what else do we have in terms of statements and any CCTV footage?"

Craig, one of her officers, waved his pen in the air. "We're pretty thin on the witness front, to be honest. There were a few of us knocking on the doors yesterday afternoon, but as you suspected, they were nearly all offices."

Another officer towards the back of the group chipped in with further information. "Guv, we found a couple of apartments above the commercial premises. We've managed to speak to them, and they didn't hear or see anything. They commented that they hear the odd lorry, but mainly taxis and couriers passing by."

"Thanks. Our job today will be to visit offices that overlooked the crime scene. They should be open. I need as many of you as possible to get down there and start asking questions."

The officers scribbled notes as they listened.

"These offices must have CCTV security systems. If you locate any, analyse any footage for Saturday night, leading into Sunday morning. If there's anything of interest, give me a holler straight away."

"Anything else that we need to focus on?" Brad asked.

Karen shook her head. "Not now, Brad. We need to gather as much information as we can. The witness statements and CCTV must be our best bet. That'll be all for now."

The assembled officers filtered off in different directions, as Karen made her way back to the office to grab her handbag, asking Steve to go with her to the post-mortem.

WAINWRIGHT PEERED over the severed limb as Karen and Steve entered the examination room. The limb, and the plastic bin liner that had been wrapped around it, had been placed on a stainless-steel table. He glanced over his shoulder as they joined him.

"Good morning to the pair of you," he said with a warm smile.

"Morning," they replied in unison.

Karen still couldn't get over being fascinated by Wainwright's Adam's apple as it bobbed up and down in his bony neck. For someone considered tall and gangly, he carried a robustness in his voice, and a commanding authority.

"How have you been getting on?" she asked.

Wainwright put his tape recorder down and took a step back. "Well, the forensic team have taken anything resembling prints from the black bin liner. On the face of it, seems as if there's only one set of identifiable prints, and my guess is that they belonged to the poor chap who discovered this grisly find."

"What can you tell us about the limb itself?"

"Well, what I can say, Karen, is that the arm definitely belongs to an adult. The growth plates are fused, which confirms that identification. I would also say that this arm belongs to a white female based on the hair distribution and muscle mass present."

"There's not a lot of skin tissue left is there?" Steve asked, looking at the exposed flesh.

"I'm afraid not. She has not been skinned or anything like that. The lack of skin tissue is due to the maggot infestation and what appears to be bites and`tears. I'd say rats, based on my experience. But there are small patches of skin which allowed me to do the detailed examination of the hair distribution."

"Is there an estimation on how long this limb has been separated from the rest of the body?" Karen knew she was clutching at straws.

"It's hard to be completely certain, but I would say between two and six days based on the stages of decomposition and decay. Much depends on where this limb was before being discovered. Was it indoors or outdoors? The temperature ranges that it was exposed to. Other factors such as how long it was exposed outdoors before being discovered? And so on."

Karen nodded, accepting the difficulties in ageing the limb.

"But I'm sending some sample tissue away for further examination. That may reveal a more correct time frame," Wainwright added for reassurance.

"Was it surgically removed?" she asked.

Wainwright grabbed the metal probe and leant in towards the upper part of the arm. "No, this wasn't surgically removed. This was far more brutal. There was more of a chopping or hacking motion. If you look at this section here," he said, pointing the end of the probe towards the top end of the humerus, "you can see that there is no clear cut through the bone,"

Karen leaned in closer, even though she didn't want to. She noticed what appeared to be step marks in the gradient of the bone, which suggested it had been severed after repeated attempts of hacking through it, each impact of the instrument causing a different score mark.

She grimaced, pulling away, exchanging an uncomfortable glance with Steve who had chosen to stay towards the foot of the table.

"Can you give an indication on the type of instrument? Are we looking at a machete, or an axe or a butcher's cleaver? Something like that?" she asked.

Wainwright nodded enthusiastically, confirming that an instrument of that nature would have been needed to cut through such a large bone.

"Okay, thanks, Wainwright, that's all we need to know now. We'll check in with forensics and see if they have been able to extract a DNA profile. Anything else for us to know?"

Wainwright shook his head apologetically, wishing he had been able to help further.

Having left the mortuary, Karen and Steve split in different directions. Steve said he wanted to follow up on a couple of calls that had been made into the incident room.

7

Karen hovered outside the meeting room for fifteen minutes, waiting for Skelton to arrive. She paced impatiently up and down the corridor, watching the various reporters and photographers arrive in dribs and drabs. "Where is Skelton?" she mumbled under her breath, checking her phone yet again. There were no missed messages, and with only ten minutes to go until the press conference was due to begin, Karen felt the first twinges of apprehension twist her insides.

She peered in through the doors and noticed that the room was almost packed to capacity. A few additional reporters and photographers lingered towards the back and along the sides of the room. From experience she knew photographers would often stand to get unobscured pictures of the officers conducting the press conference.

Karen glanced over her shoulder to see Skelton moving at pace towards her. He was busily texting, looking perturbed. By the time he reached her, not only was he out of breath, but his face was red with exertion. Either that or something was bothering him. His eyes had narrowed into an intense stare as he reached her.

"Are you okay, sir?" she asked.

"Yes… Um… Yes. Just another pressing issue that I need to deal with. Shall we get on with this?"

Karen shrugged and opened the doors and walked in, hotly followed by Skelton who continued to stare at his phone. They were joined at the front of the room by a press liaison officer, Sally Marchant, who had organised the press conference. The three of them stepped up on to the stage and took their seats, Skelton seated in the middle.

Karen glanced around the room. The noise of dozens of muted conversations rippled around the room and raised the ambient sound levels. Photographers trained their lenses on the three of them and clicked away. She recognised a few faces, and taking pride of place was Wallace, sitting in the front row with a gleeful smile, like that of a child who was about to receive the best pupil award at the school assembly.

Even though she hated press conferences, and hated reporters even more, they were a necessary evil that she had to put up with in her line of work. At times they had proved useful but had also been a thorn in her side on just as many occasions.

Skelton exchanged hushed words with Sally Marchant behind his hand, which he used as a makeshift screen. He knew from experience that several of the reporters were adept at lip-reading, and he wasn't about to fall into the trap many officers had fallen into, by saying things that weren't meant to be shared in public.

Karen turned towards the notes prepared by Sally and cast her eye over the main points. Skelton as usual was going to take the lead, and she would only chip in if Skelton needed to talk about the finer details of the investigation.

Skelton cleared his throat and asked the gathered audience to settle down in order for him to begin. The request had an instant effect as the various conversations muted to nothing more than a whisper as all eyes trained on him.

"Early yesterday morning, the Metropolitan police were called to a location in London where remains were found. Upon attendance, and with the support of the scientific services division, it was confirmed that the remains were indeed human."

Skelton paused for effect, checking his notes before continuing.

Karen noticed a nervous energy amongst the gathered press corps, many shuffling towards the edge of their seats, desperate for more information.

"At present, we are in the early stages of the investigation, and keeping an open mind as to what happened. Following a post-mortem this morning, we can confirm that the remains belong to a white female."

Skelton glanced at Karen for a moment before continuing, "I'll be leading the investigation, and the day-to-day running will be conducted by Detective Inspector Heath to my right. Do you have anything extra to add, Detective Inspector?"

Karen cleared her throat before saying, "All I would like to add is that if anyone has any information relating to this incident, or anyone in the local area who saw anything suspicious, please contact Crime Stoppers where your call will be treated confidentially, and all calls to that line treated anonymously."

"Any questions?" Skelton added.

A sea of hands shot into the air, and Skelton began to pick them off one by one.

"Have you identified any suspects?" asked a woman towards the back.

"I'm afraid not. As I said, we are in the very early stages of the investigation and are still piecing together the circumstances as to how human remains ended up at the location."

Wallace stuck his hand up in the air and glared at Karen with a smile. "Is McCreath the homeless man who *apparently* found the limb a suspect? Or has he been ruled out?"

Karen's anger boiled at Wallace's mention of McCreath's name. She knew that there was a strong possibility that McCreath would now be tracked down and hounded by the other reporters in the audience.

Skelton gritted his teeth and glared at Karen before returning his steely gaze in Wallace's direction. "As I said at the beginning, we are in the early stages of an investigation, and we haven't identified *any* suspects."

Wallace barged in again, cutting another reporter off who was in mid-sentence. "Should the public be worried that an axe murderer is targeting people at random and chopping off their limbs?"

"No," Skelton replied sternly.

Wallace continued to hound him. "But you've only discovered a severed arm and hand, so surely the public have a right to be concerned. We have to question where the rest of the body is, or body parts are. Are we expecting them to be scattered across London? Is this just the start, or could there be other bodies out there?"

The questions were relentless, and Karen wished she could fit a muzzle to Wallace's face to stop his drivel. The interest she noticed amongst the faces of the others, and what they were hearing from Wallace, only raised their curiosity further. Not only could they smell blood, but they could smell a great story. There was a risk that the conference would end in pandemonium if they didn't move on.

Sally Marchant shifted in her chair, glancing across to both officers, willing them with her eyes to close this line of questioning, and either move on, or bring the press conference to an end.

Karen didn't wait for Skelton to intervene. "That's merely speculation on your part. I can assure each one of you now, that as soon as we have more information, you will be the first to know. At present, there is no risk to the public at large. We are taking this as an isolated incident and are following all lines of enquiry."

"That's all for today," Skelton ordered as he rose from his chair, signalling that the press conference was over.

It didn't stop the questions coming as Skelton, Karen and Sally Marchant made their way through the throng of reporters and out into the corridor.

Skelton blew out his cheeks and ran a hand through his hair. "Well that was a fucking shit show. That Wallace needs to be knocked down a peg or two. He hasn't moved on from the days of the gutter press, wanker!"

Karen glanced at Sally, and they both looked relieved. "I think that's the best we could do, sir. It's given us breathing space. Sally, are you and the team happy to field any questions that come through on email?"

Sally said she was more than happy to, as both she and Karen watched Skelton storm off, glaring at his mobile phone.

"Where are you going, sir?" Karen shouted after him.

"I've got to be somewhere. I'll be back later, not that I want to be," he ranted as he disappeared down the stairs and towards the car park at the back.

"Good work, Karen. You handled that last bit well. I thought Wallace wasn't going to stop."

"To be honest, Sally, I didn't think it was going to stop either. He was like a dog with a bone. All he's looking for is sensationalism. Keep an eye on him. We might need to suppress his exuberance a little," Karen replied as she said goodbye and headed back to her office.

SKELTON MADE his way to the address he had been given and paused outside the front door. He glanced up and down the street, pedestrians and shoppers passing by, oblivious to what lay behind the door. To one side, an Indian mini mart had a regular flow of customers coming in and out with bags full of fresh vegetables. To the other side of the doorway was a print shop, with window graphics detailing their photocopying and printing services.

A thickset man, dressed in black jeans, white T-shirt, and black leather jacket opened the door just as Skelton was about to press on the doorbell. He looked up to see a camera positioned above the doorway and knew straight away that they had seen him lingering outside, puffing away nervously on a cigarette.

"Inside," said the man, in a hoarse voice, his bald head, and stubbly beard, making him look even more menacing.

Skelton stepped into the darkened hallway and followed the steps down into the basement. Yet another illegal gambling den owned by the Connells, it was empty at this time of day, but for Sally Connell and her two brothers, Terry and Steve, who flanked her. They stood by the bar, watching Skelton's every move. Sally Connell was dressed in a black two-piece suit, with a white blouse, and had her arms crossed across her chest, her face expressionless.

The text messages that he had received from Sally this morning had put him on edge. Even though he had tried to focus during the press conference, all he could think of were those messages, and his futile attempts to pacify her as he made his way to the briefing. Normally, he looked forward to seeing Sally, but some of these recent clandestine meetings had left him a nervous wreck, and afraid of his own shadow. He tried everything to stay on their good side but was fast running out of excuses.

"What's this all about, Sally?" Skelton asked, desperate to keep his composure. He stuffed his hands in his pockets to hide the shaking.

"I've been in touch with the Manchester firm. Yildiz is ready to move. The consignment is coming in a few days, and the hit is going to go ahead. Once this deal is done, we'll be moving in different circles altogether. We need to start clearing up loose ends."

It was the news Skelton wasn't hoping to hear. As far as he was aware, this was the biggest job that the Connells had been involved in, but the financial rewards would push the Connells into being one of the biggest criminal organisations in the country. His bowels began to twist, and his mouth felt as dry as a bag of sawdust. What he wouldn't do to knock back a glass of Scotch right now.

"What do you mean loose ends?" Skelton asked tentatively.

"Well, you're getting a decent whack out of this, so it's up to you whether you want to remain on our payroll or go on the run? You could still be of use to us."

Of course, Skelton wanted to remain on their payroll, but there was a part of him that yearned for Sally so much, he wondered if he could survive without her. He'd had plenty of women in his time, so many he couldn't remember most of their names, let alone what they looked like. But Sally was different. She was his equal. Tough, gritty, and oozed sex appeal like no other woman he'd ever seen.

"I'm here for the long haul. As long as it's mutually beneficial to both of us." Skelton sneered.

Sally's lip curled up. "We need you to do something for us. We've put up with your DI for far too long. She is a loose end. I need you to set up a fake lead for her in the hijacking job. We need her alone."

Skelton didn't like the sound of this. "Alone?"

"Don't be a fucking dick. Alone! Surely you don't need me to draw you a diagram of why we need to get her alone," she spat.

"I can't. I can't be responsible for the deaths of any more

police officers. We've already done away with two, and I carry the blame for that."

Sally's eyes narrowed, and her bottom lip twitched. "You can't? You bloody well can't? I'm not asking, Skelton. I am fucking telling you. You need to make sure that we get her alone so that we can deal with her. We've given her a warning before, and she didn't listen."

"I can't, Sally. I work with the woman. I will find a way to get her to stop. I'll even find someone to take the fall and admit to being i volved in the hijacking. There are plenty of crackheads I know who would quite happily take a bunce from me."

Sally shook her head, disappointment etched in her features. "Skelton, you've had so many opportunities. We'll look after you and let *us* deal with Heath. You won't have any blood on your hands. I'm giving you twenty-four hours to think about it. Either you set her up so we can deal with her, or we'll just take her out in front of all your lot. Your decision. Now fuck off."

Skelton swallowed hard and stepped backwards out of the room, scared to turn his back on them. Panic and fear raged through his veins, and his head spun as he raced up the stairs, desperate for fresh air.

Sally picked up her phone and dialled a number and waited for the person on the other end to answer. "It's me. We tested Skelton, and he didn't buy it."

8

Karen's head spun as she made her way back to her team. Though the press conference hadn't ended long ago, the activity in the incident room had gone up a notch with officers busy making calls, gathering in small groups to share information, and dozens of fingers tapping away on keyboards across the floor.

She shook her head to refocus as she darted through the desks towards Jade, who looked up as she approached.

"I heard the press conference went well?" Jade said with a hint of sarcasm in her tone.

"Good news travels fast then."

"Don't you mean bad news travels fast?"

Karen nodded. "Something like that. Any updates at all?"

"Nothing yet. I'm chasing up the officers who are doing door-to-door enquiries. They've drawn a blank so far. The problem we've got involves a road directly opposite the crime scene. There aren't any buildings overlooking the location where the remains were discovered. That particular entrance into the building site was chosen specifically because it allowed larger lorries a greater turning circle and the ability to reverse into the site."

"Are any cameras trained on that spot?" Karen asked.

Jade shook her head. "But the good news is we have identified one camera based at a law firm that overlooks their reception, and the road beyond. We are retrieving the footage as we speak."

The conversation was interrupted as Karen's phone buzzed in her back pocket. She retrieved it and checked the screen. The number wasn't in her contact list. "Hello, DI Heath… Hello… Hello." She pulled the phone away from her ear and looked at the screen to make sure she was still connected, before continuing. "Hello," she asked once again before tutting.

"Problem?"

Karen shook her head. "I don't think so. Whoever it was hung up at the end. Maybe a wrong number."

"It might have been a sales call," Jade suggested. "The sales team dial thousands of numbers through automation software all the time, and as soon as one connects and someone answers, that number is placed on another list, and the number's called again by a sales rep. It's their way of checking to see whether a number is live or not."

"Yeah, I've had those before. I absolutely loathe sales calls. Especially the silent ones. Haven't they got anything better to do?"

They both laughed as they imagined the caller not knowing how to respond.

"Okay, keep me informed if anything comes up, Jade," Karen said as she headed left. What she needed to do now was more important than worrying about who was trying her number.

Karen made her way down two flights of stairs, making a detour by the canteen, before pushing through the doors of the high-tech unit. The atmosphere was quieter down here, with serious faces staring at screens, and plenty of intense thinking and analysing. She scanned the room and spotted Charlie leaning back in his chair, his fingers interlocked behind his head, as a perplexed look flitted across his face.

Charlie Whitworth was as good as they got when it came to forensic computer analysis. Karen had relied on him on several occasions for enhancing footage and retrieving lost data. If there was one person she could trust, it was Charlie, especially because he carried a secret torch for her.

"Uh-oh, here comes trouble," he said as soon as he spotted Karen making a beeline for his desk.

Karen greeted him with the biggest smile she could muster. "I come bearing gifts," she offered, placing a Cadbury Flake and can of Coke on his desk.

Charlie viewed her with suspicion. "You never bring me gifts. Either you've come to your senses and realised that I'm the man for you, or you've got one hell of a favour to ask of me. Even though I live in hope of the former, my money is on the latter."

"Don't be like that, Charlie. You've helped me out on lots of occasions, and I feel bad that I've never said thank you properly. Here you go," she said, nudging the chocolate and can across the table to him.

"This *really* must be bad. Is this your way of letting me down gently?"

"Charlie. I've never said that I would go out with you, nor… Have I said I wouldn't go out with you?" Karen flushed, realising what she had said.

Charlie choked on thin air and burst out laughing, causing his colleagues to put their heads above their workstations to see what was happening.

Not wishing to dig herself any deeper, Karen pressed on. "Listen, Charlie, I need a really, really big favour from you."

"Here we go…" Charlie replied, tossing his pen on the table and crossing his arms. "Let's hear it."

Karen grimaced in mock embarrassment. "Well… I've been researching an old case. And I *don't know* what I've done, but a lot of the information that was once in the files, has disappeared. And I'm wondering if I've pushed the wrong buttons? Or if… someone else… was also researching that case and pressed the wrong button?"

"I don't like where this is going!" Charlie's voice rose in concern.

"I was hoping you could check the database to see if it was me, or someone else who caused the data to disappear, and whether there's a chance of retrieving it from an old backup?"

Charlie covered his face and shook his head in disbelief. "I can't do that, Karen. Firstly, I don't have access rights, and secondly, that's way above my pay grade."

"I know, I know. But maybe it's a systems bug, and no one spotted it. If I've deleted that information by accident, I'm going to be in so much shit. I might even get sacked!" Karen pleaded.

"Yes, Karen, and I could get sacked for doing what I'm not supposed to do. Do you not understand that?"

"I do. Honestly, I do. But I don't know who else to ask… unofficially. Come on, you and me go back. I need you to do a simple check."

Karen was about to continue when her phone rang and she picked it up from the table to see that it was Jade. "Yes, Jade, what's up?" Karen listened intently, her interest peaking as the conversation unfolded. "Right, I'll be there in two secs," as she hung up. She looked at Charlie once again, pleading with him silently to reconsider.

Charlie shook his head. "Nothing is a simple check when it comes to systems and databases, Karen. Listen, I would love to help you, but it's just way beyond me. I can't do that for you."

A knot formed in Karen's stomach. The plan had crashed at the first hurdle. She felt despair and frustration as hope slipped away.

"Okay, Charlie. I'm sorry to have put you in such a difficult situation. I didn't mean to. I just thought it was something simple to sort out." She squeezed his shoulder, before turning and hurrying away.

Jade's call had her rushing back to the incident room. Following the press appeal, they had received a call from an office which may have captured something on their CCTV. That was a small breakthrough as far as Karen was concerned, but what interested her more was that PolSA, the Met fingertip search team, had discovered a right leg and foot in bushes at a nearby car park.

9

Karen raced through the building following Jade's call, bursting through the doors of the incident room to find the activity levels had reached fever pitch with the new discovery. The moment she stepped inside, phones rang off the hook, her officers shouted across the terminals and the photocopier hissed as it churned out reams of paper.

By the time she got to Jade's desk, Karen gasped for breath as her temples throbbed.

"What have we got, Jade?" Karen asked as Jade finished a call.

"Karen, it's gone crazy. We've just had a call come in from a member of the public. They found what appears to be the top half of a body floating in the Hertford Union Canal." Jade could hardly get her words out fast enough.

Karen's mind felt like it was banging off the walls of the incident room. They had gone from nothing, and the early stages of an investigation, to three significant finds in the space of twenty-four hours.

"This is better," Karen said, rubbing her hands together. "Who discovered the torso?"

"A female out walking along the canal path. She saw what she thought was a black bin liner full of rubbish that had been dumped in the water, but as she drew closer, part of the bag had split, and she saw flesh. At first, she wondered if it was a mannequin, God knows how many times those things have caused a false alert, but this time it seemed to have been the real thing."

"Have we officers down there already?"

"Yes, Karen. We have uniform on scene. Do you want me to do anything else?"

"We need a full statement from the witness and check it over in case we need to go back and speak to her again."

"Consider it done."

Karen rolled her tongue around her mouth, deciding on the best course of action. "Okay, make sure uniform create a large enough cordon around the scene, and deploy a search team to comb the towpaths in either direction for five hundred yards. Also organise the underwater search team to do a trawl of the canal in case other body parts have been discarded."

"Will do, boss."

Karen clicked her fingers to jog her memory. "What about the limbs that were discovered? Where are you with that?"

"We've heard from the crime scene. PolSA have been doing a fingertip search of the area and widened their scope to include adjoining side streets. It turns out there's a small open-air car park squeezed in between two buildings about a hundred and fifty yards away. You can't really see it from the street, and it's just about wide enough to get a 4x4 down the dirt track which then opens into a car park that holds about ten to twelve cars."

"Is it on private land?" Karen asked.

Jade nodded.

"Any CCTV?" From experience, she knew that the small pop-up car parks had little in the way of security and experienced a higher rate of car crime than the larger NCP car parks, which had control barriers and CCTV in place.

Jade's brow furrowed. "I'm not sure. I've taken the liberty of getting SOCO down there to do the forensic recovery, and I'll get uniform to check the location."

Raw adrenaline coursed through Karen. "Good stuff, Jade, thanks for organising it."

"I bet they're linked to our victim" Jade said.

"Bit of a coincidence, don't you think? Left arm and hand, right leg and foot, and now a torso. And they're all less than a mile apart."

Karen let those details settle as she considered the repercussions and consequences. Her thoughts turned towards Wallace, and the field day he would have as soon as he got wind of the new discoveries and his "axe murderer" angle. With the discovery of the torso in the canal, it was there for the press and public to discover. Karen would need to rely on Wainwright and forensics to tie in these three grisly discoveries, and confirm what she suspected, that they all belonged to the same victim.

JADE SPED BACK towards Hanover Street, the location of the first grisly discovery. With winter fast approaching, the nights were drawing in quicker. Karen glanced out of her passenger window. The dark clouds loomed overhead, casting eerie shadows between the buildings and alleyways. She knew that PolSA could continue their search well into the night, even if it was under torchlight.

Darkness posed a problem for any police investigation. So much relied on visual assessment, spatial awareness, and creating a mental picture of each crime scene, and the location of the evidence upon discovery. As a result, extra care and vigilance were needed to make sure nothing was missed. Karen had known of other investigations that had missed vital evidence like bloodied footprints, or a discarded weapon because initial searches had been conducted in the dark, the later discoveries only being made during a second daylight sweep.

"Do you think we'll get lucky with this footage?" Jade asked, as she looked ahead, her eyes darting from left to right, and occasionally glancing in her rear-view mirror.

"I don't know. We could do with a break, but so much depends on the camera angle, the sharpness of the image, and more importantly the time anything was captured. Did you do a check on the law firm before we came out?"

"I did, Karen. Herbert and Shaw. A small legal practice that lease out the first and second floors of this building. They primarily focus on commercial law. There's nothing on the system to flag up any issues with them."

Karen hummed to herself as she pulled out her mobile

phone and thumbed through her text and WhatsApp messages. The majority could wait. Her mum had sent a text message asking her to get in touch as it had been a while since she had heard from her. She'd reply to that one later. There was another message from her friend Debbie confirming that she was still on for a bite to eat that night, if Karen was free. Karen smiled at the long line of question marks. She fired back a reply saying, "Hopefully, and will confirm later."

Debbie had been badgering Karen about a girl's holiday next summer, something they had spoken about often. The problem was, they couldn't agree on where. Debbie wanted to go to Italy, Karen liked the idea of somewhere quieter, like one of the small Greek islands. She had heard great things about Zante but had yet to convince Debbie.

Karen tucked her mobile back in her handbag as Jade pulled up outside Herbert and Shaw. Karen stepped out of the car and paused for a moment, weighing up the proximity between the crime scene, and the offices where she stood. She presented her back to the front door of the building and looked across the street towards where a PCSO stood guard. In her estimation, the cordoned off area was at an angle of about thirty degrees from her position. They clearly didn't overlook the crime scene, so her only hope was that they caught someone or something passing by.

Karen and Jade waited in reception, a solitary receptionist tapping away on a keyboard who looked up occasionally to give them a polite smile. They were joined a few minutes later by a man in blue overalls, and another distinguished-looking man, in his late forties, smartly dressed in a perfectly cut grey suit, brilliant white shirt, and red tie.

"Good afternoon, Detective Inspector. I'm Maxwell Herbert, the senior partner here," said the smartly dressed man, extending his hand.

Karen and Jade introduced themselves and presented their warrant cards.

"We are following up on a call from you about an ongoing investigation. We believe you have something that may be of interest to us?"

Herbert shook his head and rolled his eyes. "Yes, terrible news, terrible. And to think something like this just happened across the road from us. It's quite shocking, really. After your officers came by earlier on, we checked our CCTV footage." Maxwell pointed up towards a camera positioned behind him overlooking the reception area, and the front door beyond.

Karen followed the line of sight to confirm that it had an unobscured view.

Herbert continued, "And we believe we may have something of interest for you. This is Robert Jones, our facilities and maintenance manager. I'll leave you with him and he can show you what we've discovered. Unfortunately, I have another meeting to attend," he said in a hurry, checking his phone and saying his goodbyes before rushing off towards the lift.

Jones led Karen and Jade into his office, situated behind reception. His office certainly didn't carry the calm and contemporary tones that the reception offered. Paperwork was piled in stacks on his table, tools lay scattered on shelves, and a box of cables sat on the floor by his chair. The bookshelves above the desk were stuffed with manuals, procedural booklets, and files about various topics such as health and safety, alarm systems, sprinkler systems, and electrical contractor receipts. Jones settled himself into his chair and blew out his cheeks as he pulled his keyboard towards him and moved his mouse around the screen.

"Sorry I'm dressed like this," Jones said apologetically. "I only wear this when I'm doing maintenance. And I've been changing a couple of ceiling lights. Anyway, it might be nothing, but we checked the tape a few times, and we noticed something. There was nothing during daylight, but over the course of Saturday night, what appeared to be the same, or similar car passed four times within the space of an hour." Jones shrugged his shoulders. "As I mentioned, it might be nothing, but it certainly looks like the same vehicle," he added, scratching his head.

"Well anything you've got might help us," Karen replied, positioning herself to one side of Jones, as Jade moved around to the other side.

Karen leaned in closer as Jones brought up the video on his monitor. He fast-forwarded to the relevant bits and paused the tape when the silhouette of a car appeared in the footage.

"There you go," he said, jabbing the screen with his dirty, stubby index finger.

Karen glanced across at Jade, before both leaned in to get a closer look. They couldn't make out the model, or a number plate, but could see it was a saloon. They continued to watch the recording as Jones whizzed through and paused on the other three time frames where the vehicle was spotted.

"Now I'm no expert, but to me that looks like the same motor? A dark saloon."

"Did you see a commercial vehicle during the night? A van, a lorry with a cage on the back, anything like that?" Karen asked.

"I'm afraid not. I understand from your officers that a load of discarded commercial waste was dumped there. If that's the case, then they don't necessarily have to come past us. It's happened a couple of times. They reverse from the opposite end of the road, so they can just tip their load and drive off again."

"And if that happens, they are out of view of the camera in reception?" Karen asked.

"Correct. It's quicker for them to exit from the other end of the street without getting seen. They can be in and out and around the corner and into main traffic in under a minute. If they go past our building, they can't turn off for a good few hundred yards."

Karen gritted her teeth. Most CCTV footage struggled to capture fine enough detail during the night, and she wondered if digital forensics could do much with the recording.

10

After leaving Herbert and Shaw, Karen had covered the short distance to the car park to assess the other scene before making her way towards the canal. No more than a few hours ago, daylight illuminated her surroundings, but the colour had faded, leaving a matt black canvas. The darkness was thick, and the torch she carried did little to light her path.

Karen hated autumn and winter; it pulled her mood down. She groaned as the chill crept through her coat.

The closer she got to the canal, the more frenetic it appeared. Divers bobbed up and down in the water like seal pups. Uniformed officers hurried up and down the towpath, and the white outlines of SOCO were clearly visible as the flashlights from cameras lit up the area. A row of arc lights set up along the towpath at thirty feet intervals kept their brilliance trained on the murky waters beneath.

"I hope we're not down here too long. It's bloody freezing," Jade said as they both signed in the scene log and grabbed a set of overalls and foot coverings.

Karen agreed. After leaving Jade's car, her body willed her to race back to its warmth.

The stretch of water ran parallel to Victoria Park, with the towpath either side of the canal, and tall imposing brick walls that led up to the streets surrounding it. Their Victorian elegance had been replaced by urban graffiti sprawl in lurid colours that saddened Karen. A row of canal boats remained shored on the opposing towpath – some were unoccupied, others offered a faint yellowish glow that crept around the edge of curtains that covered their windows.

Karen dropped in line behind Jade as they walked along the towpath, stepping on each plate laid down to avoid contaminating the ground and the crime scene. Her eyes were drawn to the cold murky waters and what potentially lay beneath. Her pace slowed as an avalanche of thoughts tumbled through her mind. She was jolted when she walked straight into the back of Jade who had stopped.

"Oops, sorry Jade. I was miles away," Karen apologised, and then realised why she had stopped.

In front of them on a sheet of tarpaulin lay the partly covered torso that had been fished out of the water. Blue tarpaulin sheets had been erected around the discovery, shielding it from prying eyes. From what Karen saw, the victim was white and female. A small saggy breast had been exposed where the bin liner had been torn away.

Karen and Jade exchanged a glance as Steve joined them.

"What have we got, Steve?" Karen asked.

"Divers pulled this out within the last hour and are looking for more. It's an IC1 female. I don't hold out much hope. They said it's murky and clogged up down there. They've waded through discarded bicycles and shopping trolleys."

The three of them turned towards the water. Speckles of light from the arc lights bounced off the surface as ripples formed from the bubbles that rose to the surface. Ghostly illuminations danced in the water, fanning from left to right as divers searched the gloomy darkness.

Karen turned to face the brick walls that lined the canal. They were at least ten to fifteen feet high. She looked along the top edges and saw nothing. She doubted if anyone in the buildings above could see the canal from their vantage point.

"Have you questioned any of that lot?" Karen asked, nodding towards the row of riverboats parked on the opposite towpath.

"We've just started, boss. Some are permanent moorings, and others are passing through. From those we've spoken to so far, no one heard or saw anything. The first they knew about it was when officers turned up responding to a call from the public."

"No suspicious activities, the revving of the car, the heavy splashing of water, nothing at all?"

Steve shook his head.

"Typical," Karen replied, glancing up towards street level. "I doubt anyone saw anything from up there either but get a couple of officers up there just to have a look around and get the lie of the land."

The three of them spun on their heels when they heard the commotion behind them. Local reporters and photographers had arrived. Several PCSOs were ushering them backwards.

Karen groaned. "That's all we need. If Wallace isn't there already, I'll bet you a fiver he'll be here within the next few minutes. Do me a favour, Jade. Go back up there and get the PCSOs to push the cordon further back. I don't want any of them near the scene."

Jade nodded and marched towards the commotion.

Excited media was only half of Karen's problem. If any of them managed to find a way into the space beyond the tall walls, they would have a perfect vantage point over the whole scene.

Karen and Steve walked up and down the path for a hundred yards looking for any entry or exit points and came to the conclusion that the only way down to this part of the canal was from the very steps she had taken. They had crossed under two road bridges that travelled over the canal, so there was a possibility that the torso had been thrown into a canal from one of those, but it was all speculation.

"Surely, trying to carry a torso wrapped in black plastic down the stairs would challenge most people? It's both a cumbersome and heavy object. Whoever managed to do it must have been pretty strong…" Karen speculated as her eyes tracked down the stairs towards the canal and back. In her estimation, she thought it was at least twenty yards from the street to the canal, possibly even thirty.

Steve agreed. "I think anyone would struggle to carry that weight. What happened if there were two of them?"

They both exchanged a glance, knowing that if a pair of killers were involved, their job of finding them would become even harder.

Karen and her team spent the next hour processing the scene, comparing statements, and crunching through several theories. The full resources of the Metropolitan Police were deployed at the scene, with divers, SOCO, PolSA officers, and within the last thirty minutes, a police sniffer dog, that was being guided up and down the canal path by its handler. Karen watched as the white and brown spaniel raced in and out of bushes searching for anything of interest.

"I could do with a cup of tea, and a chocolate biscuit," Karen muttered as she stamped her feet on the spot and wrapped her arms around her chest to keep herself warm.

Jade remained with her, whilst Steve had gone up to street level, and was walking around the adjoining streets looking for any other vantage points, cameras, or backyards.

"If these body parts belong to the same person, why scatter them in so many locations?" Jade questioned. "Surely if you dismember a body, you dispose of it in one place. Using different locations adds to a greater chance of being discovered or seen?"

"Possibly. Maybe it's part of their ritual. If you think about it, none of the body parts were particularly well hidden. They weren't buried or anything like that. It was as if they were discarded in a way that they would be found. In the perp's twisted head, it's a game. They knew that the parts would be discovered, and that we would start an investigation, but they're leading us on a merry little dance." Karen shrugged. She understood what Jade was thinking, but she was none the wiser and just as confused.

When Karen checked her phone, it was gone nine p.m. She cursed under her breath, knowing it was unlikely she would be away from here any time soon and would have to let Debbie know. She fired off a quick text to apologise but promised to call tomorrow morning to reschedule. She signed off with half a dozen kisses. Though she knew it was lame, and hoped that her friend would understand, Karen nevertheless felt guilty for letting her down yet again. That was the biggest bugbear that she and the other officers felt. Their role so unpredictable, the hours so erratic, that just holding down a social life let alone a personal, or married life was always challenging, and not always successful.

A whistle and the call from a police officer alerted Karen to some activity further down the towpath, beyond the arc lights and into the darkness. A solitary light from the torch bounced off the floor and zipped left to right. Karen and Jade made their way past the current crime scene and followed the new hub of activity. By the time they arrived, the dog handler was praising his dog, who jumped for joy when its favourite ball was tossed into the air as a reward. A member of the SOCO team knelt beside them on the floor, inspecting an object on the ground.

"Guv, I think we found something of significance," the dog handler offered as he stepped backwards to avoid contaminating the scene further.

Karen paused about six feet away, waiting on feedback from the scenes-of-crime officer, who gingerly set about making a small incision in the black plastic with a small surgical knife.

It was only when the plastic was peeled away at one end that Karen's eyes widened.

The toes of a left foot peeked out from the opening.

11

Karen stifled a yawn and arched her back as she sat in Wainwright's office. They'd gone through two cups of coffee and several croissants that Karen picked up in Costa coffee on her way to the mortuary. Thankfully, Wainwright had finished most of his assessment by the time Karen arrived. Alongside tiredness, simmering hatred and anger boiled inside her after seeing the news that morning.

News of last night's discoveries flashed across most of the local news channels. The reporting was professional and considerate. That didn't bother her. It was the reporting in the local press spearheaded by Wallace that left her seething. He'd sensationalised the discoveries, by claiming the axe murderer had struck again overnight. Wallace's article only added further fuel to the fire that burnt within with its headline screaming, "**MANIAC AXE MURDERER STALKING VICTIMS AT NIGHT**".

The press office had been on to Karen first thing this morning after receiving countless calls from media agencies searching for a story or the latest updates. If Karen had crossed paths with Wallace that morning, she would have had more than a few choice words to say to him. A photographer who tagged along with him to the press conference had run images taken from the canal. From the angle of the photographs, they had been taken from an elevated position, and Karen assumed the photographer had sneaked into the backyard of one of the premises at street level to get a good vantage point.

Sally Marchant from the press team had sent over screenshots of the clippings that she had seen. Wallace had gone into detail about the grisly find, and how the police appeared to be on the back foot, with no leads, nor suspects. Wallace had gone further by naming Karen and the lack of police cooperation being offered to them and the wider public, despite repeated requests from him.

The article didn't paint Karen in a great light, and she knew it would only be a matter of time before she was marched into Skelton's office for another roasting.

"Chin up, Karen," Wainwright offered, throwing her a sympathetic smile after Karen had told him about the events of this morning. "Sadly, that's their job. I don't think they would sell many newspapers if they didn't throw in a dash of sensationalism. You'll be hard-pressed to find a news agency who presents an unbiased opinion. The mainstream media generally are the better ones of the bunch, but the local press have a much harder time of it, so they need to… shall we say… invoke their creative licence."

Karen threw her hands up in frustration. "I know. I know what you're saying. But they really are the fucking bane of my life."

Wainwright raised a brow. He wasn't one for profanity, and didn't like hearing it either, but didn't pull up Karen because he empathised. "Well, as far as I'm aware, I don't think there's ever been a single case handled by the police as far back as I can remember that hasn't been under the media spotlight and been the centre of criticism. I wouldn't worry about it. You're better than that. Don't let him get under your skin."

Karen gritted her teeth and narrowed her eyes. "I think he already has."

Wainwright waved away her frustration and leant back in his chair. "Let's move on to things that are more relevant, shall we?" he suggested, opening the folder in front of him. "We can wait for your friends in forensics to confirm this, but in my opinion, it's highly likely that the torso, left arm and hand, the right leg and foot, and the left foot all belong to the same victim." He passed over a set of photographs taken by his assistant.

"As you can see, we've taken close-up photographs of the marks made when each limb was severed from the body. And in my opinion the pattern of the cuts appears to be consistent. Your nemesis, although I hate to bring him up, might be right. The way in which this person has been dismembered would suggest that an instrument like an axe, or a large butcher's meat cleaver, may have been used. Each limb has been hacked at several times."

Karen spun the photographs in her hands, looking at each close-up in more detail.

"That doesn't give me enough to go on, but it at least gives us an idea of the brutality and level of force that the victim suffered."

"True, it doesn't give you much to go on, but there is good news. The right leg was severed at the top of the thigh. And examining the torso, the right hip has an implant."

Karen's eyes widened as she rummaged through the pile of photographs and pulled out the close-up of the implant.

"The implant has a serial number, and if the implant was performed in the UK, we can check the serial number against the National Joint Registry, and voila, you have the identity of the victim. I'm not a hundred per cent sure, but I'm fairly certain that it would have been done in the UK."

Karen felt a ripple of excitement course through her veins.

"And there's more for you, so don't say I'm not nice to you. I would say that the woman was approximately five-foot four inches tall, and over the age of sixty. She was well-nourished, and her last meal was probably porridge, because remnants of oats remain in her stomach."

"Over the age of sixty?" Karen said with a shake of her head.

"More than likely. The implant tells us a lot. The victim has a small-head cemented metal-on-polyethylene implant, which was the most cost-effective treatment for men and women older than sixty-five years of age. The presence of an implant gives you more information, because it informs us that the victim had a disease or medical condition which necessitated an implant. This kind of implant gives us a clue to the age, and often, implants are generally made of metal alloys these days and used in about seventy per cent of cases."

"This is fantastic, Wainwright. You're a bloody genius," Karen said, excitement bristling in her voice.

"I try. It's also worth noting that there were no signs of sexual interference, nor any historical injuries."

"Could you find out a cause of death from what you've got?" Karen enquired.

"Strangulation. There were injuries to the skin and sub tissues, and the lower part of the trachea had been crushed. Ideally, I'd like to have the head as well to be absolutely certain."

Karen nodded. "Nope. That's good enough for me. That gives me plenty to go on."

"The only thing that bothers me is why dismember the body? She was an elderly woman, perhaps a bit fragile in her movement, because of her hip. Over the age of sixty, and then a nutter hacked her to pieces. I don't get it."

Wainwright discussed the possibility that the killer was trying to hide the victim's identity or that the act of dismemberment excited him in some way. Both were plausible, in Karen's opinion. They both concluded that neither of them knew enough about the reasons behind dismemberment to make sense of it.

Wainwright continued, "I've got an idea. We could talk to a forensic psychologist. I'm sure there's one or two in my list of contacts. They would be best placed to give you an insight into the mind of a killer who dismembered their victims. What do you think? I can see if we can get a meeting for later today."

Karen shrugged, but agreed. Any input into the case would be helpful, and this was clearly beyond her understanding. She left with Wainwright's words ringing in her ears. What if the act of dismemberment excited the killer?

12

Once back inside her office, Karen stared at the incident board and the map of the area pinned alongside it. Three locations had been mapped out with red pins to confirm the location of each find. Geographically, they were located within a small area, which suggested that the killer knew the area well, and perhaps lived close by. There was no discernible pattern to the locations. From where she stood, nothing jumped out at her.

The body parts appeared in a specific area, and as she moved in closer to examine the finer details of the map, she couldn't see anything that suggested they had been deposited near any crucial landmarks, or places of interest, but the fact that they were disposed of in a certain area had to carry significance. What it was, she wasn't sure.

Brad rose from his desk, and joined Karen, his bulging eyes even larger, as he scanned the map. "What do you make of it?"

Karen shrugged a shoulder and shook her head in uncertainty. "I don't know, Brad. I'm staring at this map, hoping something will jump out at me, but nothing has so far. There must be something behind these locations. If you're going to dismember a body, then surely you would dispose of the body parts, so they weren't found?"

"Maybe the killer wanted them to be found. Or was too blasé to worry about hiding them?"

Karen knew that that was a possibility as well. Often killers believed that they were invincible, and beyond the long arm of the law. They would hide out in full view of the public, going about their lives as normal as if they hadn't committed any crimes. *Short-sighted mentality on their part*, Karen thought.

Craig, one of Karen's officers, interrupted the conversation, and handed Karen the printouts that had been received. They were still warm as Karen took hold of them and flicked through the latest updates from the forensic team. It wasn't the news that Karen wanted to hear, as they had been unable to find a matching DNA profile on the database from the first limbs that had been discovered.

Under any other circumstances, discovering the identity of the victim would prove extremely difficult without a DNA match or dental records. And without the head, the victim would have remained unidentified, like they had never existed. Whilst forensic services continued to run tests on the recent discoveries, Karen's hopes rested on finding the victim's identity through the National Joint Registry. Officers from her team had already requested a copy of the records matching that serial number, and now they had to sit back and play the waiting game.

"Brad, I've got a couple of calls to make. In the meantime, can you run a misper check for any women over the age of sixty reported missing in the last…?" Karen thought for a moment, "start with the last four weeks, and see what it throws up. Let me know, and if we draw a blank, we can extend the time frame."

Brad nodded, gulping down the last of his coffee from his mug before heading to his desk.

Karen stopped at various desks along her route, checking in with members of her team. She wanted to make sure that the data inputters were updating the HOLMES2 database with the findings from forensics, and her visit to the mortuary this morning. She also asked them to run a search for any crimes that had been committed in the last twelve months where victims had been hacked to death, or dismembered.

Feedback from Wainwright led Karen to entertain the idea that perhaps the killer had started off by hacking their victims but had progressed to dismembering them to get the same buzz. She wasn't entirely convinced by the notion but had chosen to keep an open mind and explore all potential motives.

Karen spent the next hour clearing the email backlog that cluttered her inbox. Despite her valiant attempts at deleting all the internal memos and circulars, there didn't appear to be an end to the number that remained. With so much going on, she'd hardly thought about her own investigation into the hijacking. The trail had gone cold, and she wondered if there would ever be closure for her.

"Bloody hell!" Karen screamed, as her phone sprang into life, and vibrated across her desk, startling her. She grabbed it and glared at the screen. Wallace. Mr Dickhead. She let it ring off before tossing the phone back on her desk, choosing to count to ten instead of answering and giving him an earbashing. The phone rang again several times in the following minutes, and each time Karen glared at it, in two minds whether to switch it off, or answer. Curiosity got the better of her when she answered on the fourth occasion.

Karen opted to stay professional. "Detective Inspector Heath."

"Inspector, this is…"

"Yes… I know who you are. What do you want, Wallace? I'm rather busy." Karen tried her hardest to avoid the explosion of abuse that threatened to escape from her mouth.

Wallace sighed at the other end. "Inspector, it doesn't have to be this way. All we need is a little cooperation. You have an ongoing case which threatens the safety and security of the public. We have a collective responsibility to make sure there is adequate sharing of information, whilst reassuring society who are terrified there's an axe murderer roaming the streets."

There he goes again, sensationalising.

Karen put her fingertips to her temples and rubbed. "At what point did you choose to believe that there was an axe murderer roaming the streets looking for unsuspecting victims? Or was it your way of getting extra brownie points with your editor?"

"Well, I don't hear you denying the claim. You have body parts turning up over the city, and we haven't got a clue what you're doing about it."

"Wallace, off the record?"

Silence fell between them, and all Karen heard was tiny pants of breath on the other end of the line.

"Wallace? I haven't got all day."

Wallace sighed. "Okay, off the record."

"If we have anything of value to say, we will release a press statement, and you would be one of the first to hear about it. But what I read this morning was inaccurate, deliberately aimed at causing panic, and frankly piss poor reporting."

"Well, I don't like being stonewalled, Inspector. I was there last night; I saw what was fished out of the canal. I could have said more."

A curse clung to her lips. "You didn't have to. Your fantastic photographer friend decided to get a few sneaky pictures and post them online. I think that says it all. Don't you agree?"

"He was just doing his job. Besides, you had pushed back the press so far, we couldn't see anything."

"That was the intention. It was to give us the space to concentrate on gathering evidence and not be distracted by your lot. What you fail to recognise is that the victim has a family somewhere. She might be someone's sister, aunt, or even a granny. And until we find her identity, we're trying to be respectful. Unlike you, who see it as another story."

Wallace raised his tone, his frustration increasing. "I need more than that. You must have active lines of enquiry and motives that you're investigating."

"Wallace, until I know more, that's all I can say. I suggest if you have any further questions, refer them to the press liaison officer, Sally Marchant. And we'll discuss each and every one of your questions in the right way. But for the time being, stop hassling me," Karen replied firmly before cutting off the phone, and throwing it on to the table as she rocked back in her chair, closing her eyes in a desperate attempt to quiet her mind.

13

Karen shuffled her way to Skelton's office, her feet reluctantly dragging her there. She felt weary and tired after her last conversation with Wallace, and probably hadn't handled it as well as she should have. He was an annoying sod in her opinion, like a mosquito bite, that itched and irritated you for days.

Skelton sat at his desk, his fingers interlocked and resting on the table as Karen appeared at the doorway.

"Sir, have you got a minute?" Karen asked.

Skelton nodded towards the empty chair across the desk from him.

Karen dropped into the seat and felt the first signs of awkwardness. As usual, her boss offered no pleasantries or smiles, but something else seemed to have changed in him. His desk was clear, all the paperwork neatly stacked in piles to one side. From where she sat, it appeared as if his computer was off, and he carried a pensive look on his face. The crease lines on his forehead dug deeper than usual, his lips were strung tight into a thin pencil line, and she watched as his thumbs circled around each other.

"Everything okay?" Karen asked.

"Yes. I've just got a lot on, and I'm being pressed for decisions. It doesn't matter," he said, unlocking his hands, and now tapping his fingers on the desk. "How are we getting on with the case? Any more parts showed up?"

Karen shook her head. "No. We've not found the murder weapon, a motive, or even the victim's identity as yet. But I'm hoping that's about to change. We should be getting information any minute now from the National Joint Registry, regarding the name of the patient who received the hip joint that was discovered in the victim."

"That would be a good start," Skelton replied. "I saw the press reporting on the case. That Wallace seems to be a bit of a tosser. He was at the press conference, wasn't he?"

"Yes, sir."

"The chief super wants us to get a move on. He doesn't appreciate the media attention that we are getting. Have you got enough resources; do you want me to get more bodies to help out?"

"I think we're ok for resources at the moment. Unfortunately, the media attention can't be helped, but we'll be able to pacify them when we have a name and inform the next of kin. I'll let you know when we know more." Karen rose from her chair and saw herself out.

Skelton remained seated as he watched Karen disappear through his doorway. Without moving his head, his eyes turned towards his phone sitting on the desk. It had bleeped three times to alert of an incoming message in the five minutes before Karen's arrival. And each time, it had been the Connells pressing him for a decision.

They'd backed him into a corner, the choice far more difficult than he had anticipated. Whichever decision he took, the consequences would be catastrophic. The question was, who would be the victim, him or Karen?

Skelton took a deep breath as he grabbed his phone and pressed the redial button.

KAREN MADE herself a cup of coffee and headed back to her office just as a desk phone rang. She quickened her pace, determined to put her mug down without spilling anything, whilst also answering before it rang off.

"Heath."

"Heath… Wainwright," he laughed. "Have I called you at a difficult time?"

Karen smiled. "No. Sorry, I was just holding a hot mug of coffee when you rang, and I was desperate to put it down and not give myself third-degree burns by spilling it on myself."

"Ah right, I see. Well, I can't talk for long anyway, I'm just about to start another examination, but I thought I'd let you know that I did indeed have a forensic psychologist in my contact list. Unfortunately, they can't see us today, but we can go tomorrow, does that suit you?"

"That's fantastic, yes. I look forward to that."

"Excellent. I'll send you the details later, must dash." And with that, Wainwright hung up.

Karen was looking forward to the meeting, and with Wainwright in tow, that would just be a bonus. He had a knack of making her feel happy, centred, and somewhat calm. She wasn't sure what it was about him, whether it was his deep commanding voice, or his laid-back demeanour. But he was certainly someone she could rely on both personally and professionally, and for that she was grateful.

Karen logged in and checked the case file to see the latest update. The digital stills they had captured from Herbert and Shaw were with the digital forensic unit, and they were still in the process of enhancing the footage. Karen made a mental note to chase that up. Footage from the surrounding area in proximity to the canal had also been recovered and was now being reviewed by members of her team. Though they had been unable to find any cameras trained on the canal and the location of the discoveries, footage from the streets either side of the canal and the bridges that crossed it could prove invaluable if they were able to find any suspicious vehicles or persons of interest, especially if they appeared more than once.

Reviewing CCTV footage was a time-consuming and laborious process. Hours, days, and sometimes weeks of footage would be reviewed just to find those few seconds of vital information that could progress a case. Karen reminisced about how she had done her fair share of that as a constable in uniform, and then as a trainee detective constable, or TDC as they were known, when she joined CID. She always looked back fondly on a time as a trainee detective constable. The role was complex and detailed with lots of ongoing training and exams. They'd been the most challenging times for her, but she'd loved it. It had really tested her as a person mentally, emotionally, and psychologically. The variety of the work was far more in-depth than anything she had experienced as a uniformed constable, but she wholeheartedly believed that it was the making of her.

"Are you free for a bite to eat?"

The question made Karen jump as Jade appeared in her doorway. "Jesus, I nearly shit myself. I didn't even know you were there."

"Sorry, was I interrupting something?"

"Don't be daft. No, I was just thinking about… stuff. For some reason, I started thinking about my time as a TDC, and how I ended up here."

Jade's face twisted in curiosity. "Aw, missing your time as a newbie?"

"Less stress than what I've got now, that's for sure."

"And less money," Jade added.

Karen looked at her watch and weighed up the options. "You know what, sod it. I'm definitely up for a bite to eat. Let's do it."

"Cool, I'll just grab my bag and meet you back at your office," Jade added as she turned and shot back to the incident room.

Karen started to log off and tidy her desk, unsure as to what time she would return this evening, if she returned at all. Her phone sprang into life, and Karen grabbed it to check the screen. She recognised the number as being one that had called her on several occasions, and each time the caller had remained silent.

If this is another sales call, I'm going to tell them where to get off.

"Hello, Detective Inspector Heath." After a silent pause, Karen rolled her eyes. "Hello?"

Karen was just about to hang up and then froze.

"Erm… Erm… Detective Inspector Heath?" a woman in a soft timid voice asked.

"Yes, this is Detective Inspector Heath, how can I help you?"

There was another lengthy pause, but Karen could hear intermittent breathing at the other end.

"I'm Barbara Murphy. I need to speak to you. I need help."

The woman's voice was jittery and intermittent, the words tainted in fear and panic. It took a few moments for Karen to realise who Barbara was, her eyes growing wide as she continued to listen.

"I've got information, and I need to talk to you about the attack on the police cars."

Karen tensed; she could feel her body go rigid. Her hand slowly tightened around the phone, her knuckles turning white in response. Her heartbeat accelerated, almost thrusting forward through her ribcage as her mouth turned dry.

"Of course, Barbara. We can arrange a time for you to come and see me. Are you free now?"

Karen's heart sank when the line went dead. She pulled the phone away from her ear and checked the screen in case she had pressed something inadvertently. But the call had been disconnected. Karen hit the redial and pleaded silently for Barbara to answer again. She waited thirty seconds, forty seconds, and nothing. She redialled again, but after another lengthy pause, Barbara didn't answer. Karen willed her to be there – hoped that she would be there, but Barbara didn't answer.

Karen's mind swirled as the past and present collided in her brain. She needed to speak to Barbara again. But when would Barbara call back?

14

The restaurant still had its fair share of customers as Karen and Jade were seated at a small table to one side. Pizza Express was their go-to place. The food was good; the atmosphere was lively, and they could just sit, talk and take their time to enjoy a normal meal like those around them. In their line of work, it was a rare luxury, as they often found themselves having take-aways, or going without food for most of the day.

The waiter took the drinks order before leaving them with a menu.

“It feels like ages since we’ve done this,” Jade said, with a tinge of excitement in her voice as she glanced around at the other diners.

“You’re telling me. I wasn’t hungry when we left, but my stomach started to rumble the minute I walked in here. Pizza places always have this smell that makes you feel warm and fuzzy and completely ravenous.” Karen smiled and tapped her stomach.

"I know. I'm normally quite careful with my food, but whenever there's a pizza in front of me, I can literally polish off the whole thing."

Karen and Jade spent the next few minutes poring over the menu, exchanging ideas about what they wanted. Karen had already moved on from choosing a pizza, to casting her eye over the dessert menu. She felt good having the opportunity to enjoy time to relax, and a few light-hearted moments after the past few days. The events of today had been enough to stress her. No matter how hard she tried, her mind kept dragging her back to the phone call with Barbara, as the conversation played over in a loop.

She glanced across at Jade, who had her face buried in the menu. Karen so wished she could tell Jade. She needed someone else to talk to about it, but the last thing Karen wanted to do was get Jade involved as well. Then she'd have to tell her everything, the nightmares, the threats when she was attacked in her apartment, her suspicions about the Connells, following Skelton, and her unauthorised database searches and following up with witnesses from the hijack. The more she thought about it, the crazier it sounded in her mind. Jade was a cracking officer, and a good friend. But she wasn't prepared to hear what Jade may say, in case it was something she didn't want to hear.

Karen leant over and rummaged in her bag between her legs on the floor. She fumbled around in it to find her phone, before pulling it out and checking the screen beneath the table. There were no missed calls, no text messages. And nothing from Barbara.

"Everything okay?" Jade asked.

Karen dropped her phone back in and righted herself with a smile. "Yes, I had a missed call from my mum. I felt my phone vibrating again."

The waiter returned with two bottles of Peroni beer, offering a smile, and telling them he would be back in a few minutes to take their order.

"That reminds me, my mum and dad want to visit next weekend." Jade rolled her eyes. "But I haven't confirmed anything yet. I thought I'd wait and see what happened with our investigation before confirming anything with them. And to be honest, it drives me mad when they turn up."

Karen's eyes grew wide as she sat back in her chair. "Why? I thought you got on okay with them?"

Jade put the menu down and folded her arms before leaning on the table. "I do get on with them. But I live in a small apartment, and the last time they came, even though they didn't stay, you could see my mum and dad casting a disapproving look around the apartment. They weren't impressed in the slightest."

"Oh, dear. Don't let that piss you off. What you've got is more than adequate. Besides, with the amount of time we're in work, it's a perfect place to go back and crash."

"Yeah, but I know my mum and dad. If you could see the house that we grew up in, it's positively palatial in comparison. I've lost count of the amount of times they've told me to get a better, higher paid job so that I can afford the better things in life."

Karen smiled sympathetically. "They've only got your best

interests at heart. Most parents would only want the best for their children, and your parents are clearly used to a certain level of comfort. If I were you, I would just make the most of seeing them and know that after their visit they'll be out of your hair for a few more weeks… or months."

"Or years…!" Jade chipped in, tossing her head back and laughing.

They ordered their pizzas, along with dough balls, marinated green olives, and calamari, and spent the next hour picking through the food, swapping stories, and talking about nothing in particular. Karen ordered another round of beers after realising that they were going down quickly. Feeling relaxed, she sensed the tension ease from her shoulders as the beer hit the right spot. Though she couldn't shake off the call with Barbara and the curiosity that followed. Her only hope was that Barbara could find the courage to call back in the coming days.

A flash of guilt ran through Karen's mind when she realised she hadn't called her friend Debbie today. Having cancelled on her the night before, she had promised to call her today. Karen made a mental note to text Debbie on the Tube back home and would pin down a firm date in their diaries to meet up in the next few days.

Karen excused herself for a moment to visit the ladies, and upon her return saw Jade had paused eating for a moment and was scrolling through her phone. She looked up at Karen as she returned to her seat.

"You're going to want to see this, Karen. Wallace has been a right idiot," Jade said shaking her head and handing her phone over to Karen.

Karen scrolled through a news article that had been posted

on a local news website. The article was accompanied by a short video clip that showed Wallace standing beside the first crime scene presenting to camera. Subtitles had been added to the bottom of the video clip. Despite the ambient noise around them of loud conversations between other diners and plates being rattled, Karen's curiosity turned to anger as she read the scrolling subtitles.

She glanced up at Jade, who cast Karen a disparaging look, and raised a brow before tutting.

Karen was incensed. Wallace had repeated the same accusations that he had thrown at her during their phone call, accusing the police of stonewalling, and keeping them at bay. He accused them of stopping the press from informing the public about the severity of the crimes.

"He really is a low life, isn't he!" Karen spat as she replayed the video clip. "I told him to liaise with our press team, and that he would be the first to know if we had any decent breakthroughs. And we literally had this conversation just a few hours ago. Damn, he works fast."

"There's nothing we can do, Karen. The more we have a go at him, the more he seems to fight back."

Karen listened with one ear to Jade's words, whilst she scrolled through the rest of the article. She stopped and read a few sentences several times before gritting her teeth and almost throwing the phone across the restaurant. There was a part of their phone conversation that she had stressed was off the record, but Wallace had repeated it in this article, saying that in a conversation this afternoon with Detective Inspector Karen Heath, she had accused him of writing inaccurate information that was aimed at causing panic, and was nothing short of piss poor reporting.

Karen knew the repercussions that would follow, and she shook her head in disbelief and stared down at her food. Anger now replaced the hunger she had had just a few minutes earlier.

If she wasn't careful, Wallace could seriously upend her career.

15

Skelton stood outside the address and looked up towards the signage above the door. McCarthy's Casino was all that remained of its previous owners. Liam and Cormac McCarthy had been murdered on the instruction of Sally Connell after a violent feud between the Connells and the McCarthys. Their bodies had been packed in crates and shipped back to Ireland, and emptied outside Coakley Funeral Home in Bantry, Co Cork, their hometown, as a warning.

The McCarthys were part of a bigger clan. Liam and Cormac had five other siblings. Sisters, Grainne, Orla and Aoibh, and brothers, Eamon and Darragh. Following the news of their brothers' killings, the clan arrived in London to seek revenge. The sisters were just as tough, violent, and capable as their brothers. What followed was nothing short of a bloodbath. The McCarthys had underestimated the stranglehold the Connells held on Northwest London. Off-licences belonging to the Connells were attacked and ransacked, the shopkeepers beaten to within an inch of their lives. The Connells retaliated by firebombing the illegal betting dens that the McCarthys had owned.

When the warnings went unheeded, the Connells stepped up their intention. Eamon and Darragh were captured, beaten and tortured. The brothers were bundled into a taxi and driven to a stretch of waste ground. They were shot in the head and their naked bodies thrown to the floor in an act of retaliation, mimicking the way two undercover soldiers were killed by the Provisional IRA in the spring of 1988 during the height of the troubles.

The sisters were equally valiant in their fight. The fact that they were women offered little sympathy in the hands of the Connells. Grainne and Aoibh were beaten to the point where they were barely alive, many of their fingernails had been ripped out with a pair of pliers, their teeth had been smashed in with a hammer, and their mangled bodies thrown into the back of a lorry and sent back across the Irish Sea. The Connells never said what happened to Orla. Rumours abounded that because she was the most attractive of the sisters, she was drugged and shipped off to connections in the Far East where her soft white skin, long flowing brunette locks, and brilliant blue eyes would command a high price as a sex slave amongst an underground group of high-rolling Chinese businessman.

There was a lot of history to this place. It was the last of the McCarthy empire, and another acquisition for the Connells. Skelton rang the door and waited. The fear travelled in Skelton's veins but never made it to his facial muscles or skin. His complexion remained pale, his eyes as steady as if he were shopping for shoes. He let out an understated sigh as he heard the bolts being unlocked, and the door opening just a few inches.

A pair of dark eyes appeared from the shadows and studied him, before the door opened further, allowing him to pass. In the hallway, three other men stood, each one twice as wide as Skelton. He knew the procedure and raised his arms above his head as two men moved in and patted him down. He kicked off his shoes and waited whilst they examined the insides looking for any concealed weapons. Skelton knew how to keep a poker face. All those nights spent gambling had paid off after all. So long as he appeared nonchalant, no pinkness in his cheeks to betray him, everything would be just fine. One of the men moved so close Skelton could smell his evening vindaloo on his breath.

Without any words being spoken, the men ushered Skelton further down the corridor which opened into a large room with a half-dozen circular tables, hard floors, and dim lighting. The back windows had metal shutters over them, keeping prying eyes at bay.

Sally Connell and her brothers stood to his left, propped up against the bar. Each brother took up a position either side of her, their hands stuffed in their bomber jackets, blank expressions, no emotions shown. Sally looked bright and dazzling, spotlights above her head illuminating her figure and making her blonde hair look like a glowing halo around her face. She stood dressed in a two-piece black suit, with a white ruffled blouse beneath, the buttons undone halfway. Skelton could just make out the outline of her inner breasts as they curved up under the opening.

Trails of smoke crept up into the air as Sally puffed on a cigarette. The three of them stared at Skelton for a few moments before Sally spoke.

"Why have you been avoiding my messages?"

"I've just been busy. We have a major case on at the moment, so I've spent all my time on the incident floor. It's a bit hard to message you back, or even call when I'm surrounded by twenty other coppers."

Sally nodded and offered a sly smile, not believing a word that came from his mouth. "Have you thought more about what we discussed?"

The anxiety swirled around Skelton's insides and felt like he was hooked up to a cattle fence – not enough voltage to kill but enough to keep things uncomfortable. He looked down at his shoes, tussling with his thoughts. "I can't do it. I can't set her up. I feel like shit already for the death of those two officers, and the countless other informants that I've told you about. I just can't do it."

"There's no can't about it, Skelton. You do it. No ifs, no buts. Just do it."

"I can't, Sally. I'm not living with that. If you're going to do something to her, I'll tip her off."

Sally's eyelids quivered as tension bristled in her face. "You aren't going to do anything like that, you fucking wanker. Who the fuck do you think you are talking to me like that?"

Sally's brothers didn't flinch, and continued to cast their cold, iron stares in Skelton's direction. Skelton knew he was treading a fine line and had no doubt that one if not both of the brothers were carrying a firearm.

The tense stand-off followed, the Connells maintaining the high ground, and Skelton squirming to get out of this situation. "Perhaps I can give her a false lead about the hijacking, something to keep her occupied and keep her off our backs. What do you think of that?" he asked with a plea.

Sally turned to retrieve something that was on the bar top behind her.

Skelton felt his insides squirm and twist. *Is this it? Have I lived my last day on this planet?*

Sally twisted around and threw a large soft white bag of substance in his direction. "Since the first time I met you, Skelton, I knew you were spineless. You're a roach, a parasite. All mouth and no trousers. You claimed to be a big man, but… you're nothing. Absolutely… nothing."

"I am something. I'm something to you. I've been useful, you know that? And I still can be," Skelton pleaded.

Sally raised a hand to silence him. "That bag is worth twenty-five grand on the street. Use it, sell it, do whatever you need. But as of today, we do not need your services any more. You are not welcome in any of our establishments, and I suggest you stay away from our business dealings. Do I make myself clear?"

Skelton recoiled at the venom aimed in his direction. "Please, Sally, I beg you. I'm still a valuable asset to you."

"You're not valuable to anyone other than yourself, and even that's questionable," Sally guffawed loudly, before hurling further abuse in Skelton's direction.

Skelton shook his head in defiance – a defiance heavily laced with terror – his mouth so dry that his words choked in his throat. "That's not true. I'm fucking putting my neck on the line for you. I've sacrificed my career and reputation for you."

She twisted her perfect lips into a sneer. “Don’t get all righteous on me now. Career? Really? You’ve always been a bent copper. You were born bent!”

His heart thumped against his ribcage as his pleas fell flat into the charged space between them. “Bollocks. This isn’t the way it’s supposed to be. For fucks sake, please, Sally.”

Sally’s eyes twitched with anger, as Skelton continued to plead, his words falling on deaf ears.

“Turn around and get out of here whilst you can still walk. And if I were you, sweetie, I would seriously think about a career change because I hear being a police officer carries a serious risk to your health. Know what I mean?” Sally said calmly, as she closed the gap between herself and Skelton, before leaning in and giving him a kiss on the lips.

The two brothers took a step forward to confirm the meeting was over. Several of the heavies that Skelton had met at the front door appeared in the shadows and took up their positions either side of him and grabbed him by his arms, before wrestling him through the hallway and ejecting him on to the street, his protests echoing in the darkness.

Sally looked over her shoulder towards the bar and then back at her brothers before smiling. “He’s fucked.”

16

The lorry bounced over the potholes as Gary Miller navigated the small side streets. Their day-to-day work took them all over London. They would go where they were sent, and most of the time Gary was fine manoeuvring the vehicle around busy roads. But the street he found himself in now was double-parked with residents' cars and left little room to dance around any oncoming traffic.

"This is just flipping ridiculous. They should stick double yellows around all the streets in Central London. That would stop the knobheads from parking. I mean, look at that one over there," Gary said, jabbing his finger in front of him. "Who the fuck parked that, Stevie Wonder?"

His workmate, Terrell Cullor, creased up in laughter, and then laughed more when his cup of tea shook uncontrollably in his hands, spilling over the sides. "Hey man, don't diss Stevie Wonder. The brother was a soul legend, man," Terrell shouted above the din of the radio that blasted out tunes from Kiss Fresh. His brilliant white smile, and his perfectly shaped teeth stood out against his black skin.

Gary looked across at his partner and sneered. "At any point did I say anything about his colour, you tosser. I meant that anyone who parked their car like that clearly had a sight impairment!"

The banter they shared got them through their days. Attending to blocked pipes, blocked sewers, and sucking out other people's shit, nappies, wet wipes, needles, syringes, condoms, and a multitude of other things affected them. Their clothes would often be stained with foul water at the end of each working day. The smells that surrounded them, seeped into the skin of their pores which meant that they had to shower twice at the end of each shift.

"Got a joke for you, what did the sewage worker say when he was working on New Year's?"

Gary glanced across at Terrell and rolled his eyes, "Not another one of your shit jokes!"

Terrell laughed at Gary's accidental pun, "Boom boom!"

"Fuck off, tosser."

"Well?" Terrell pushed, and raised a questioning brow.

"Dunno."

"I'm tired of last year's shit," Terrell replied, howling at his own joke.

Gary shook his head and stared ahead.

Terrell continued to chuckle to himself as he stared through his window.

"What have we got on the schedule for today?" Gary asked.

Terrell grabbed the clipboard off the dashboard and scanned the different jobs. "We're off to see a fatberg first."

"That's no way to talk about my Missus!"

Terrell rocked back in his seat, tears streaming from the corner of his eyes. "She ain't a fatberg."

"No, you're right. But if you see her in the bath, she looks like one of those giant icebergs that took the Titanic down."

Terrell choked and spluttered as an image of Gary's wife flashed through his mind.

"Mate, if your missus could hear you now, you'd be sleeping on the sofa for the next month. We both know that you're scared shitless of her."

Gary nodded and rolled his eyes, before dismissing Terrell's assessment.

After pulling up at the location listed in the incident report, they both jumped out of the cab, and assessed the scene, before identifying the right manhole cover and grabbing their heavy-duty manhole lifting keys. With difficulty, they lifted and slid the cover to one side, away from the inspection chamber, leaned over the hole, and stared into the darkness that disappeared beneath the pavement.

The first thing that hit them was the smell. Terrell took a half step backwards, squeezing his eyes shut in surprise. It reminded him of the Portaloos he'd used at concerts in his youth.

A second unit arrived as Gary and Terrell were kitting up. It called for serious equipment: a white protective suit over their normal clothes, a hard hat with a head torch, two pairs of gloves, glasses, and waders. For this type of job, at least two teams were needed for safety, as well as assessing the size of the task ahead, before calling in extra resources.

With a hoist now positioned over the inspection chamber, Gary was winched down first, followed by Terrell, both taking care not to cut their gloves on the rusty ladder.

Gary's boots found a ledge, and he transferred his weight off of the ladder to his feet, followed by Terrell. A thick, nauseating, cloying smell surrounded them.

"Jesus, it stinks to high heaven!" Terrell shouted as the beam of light from their head torches lit up the darkness ahead of them. They moved off and began to explore the subterranean underground that they called home. The water and sewage around their feet sat stagnating, a sure sign that there was a blockage ahead. Normally it would be free-flowing, and it didn't take long to find a huge yellowy white mass ahead of them that blocked half of the tunnel.

"That's the culprit," Gary indicated as they moved closer. Rats scurried and scattered in all directions, desperate to escape the spotlight centred on them, their bodies disappearing into the slimy mess around their feet and swimming off into the darkness.

Thankfully, they weren't there to begin the removal of the fatberg, as their job was to assess the scale of the job, and the problem it was causing. The job of removing it would be left to a team of "flushers" who would break down the fatberg into pieces and suck it out. Their job was far riskier than Gary and Terrell's. Each flusher carried an emergency airbag in a metal tin that provided clean air for up to an hour, just in case. The release of hydrogen sulphide was the one they really had to be careful of. It could overcome and suffocate workers in a matter of seconds.

Gary and Terrell had been offered positions as flushers, but both had declined due to the risks involved. For both of them, poisonous gases were an occupational hazard anyway, and both wore gas monitors to alert them to carbon dioxide, methane and hydrogen sulphide levels whilst they did their normal inspections, and that was more than enough for them.

Gary whipped out his tape measure and measured the size of the obstruction, whilst Terrell took photographs and checked his monitor for gases. It wasn't the biggest fatberg that they had seen, and they estimated it would take two to three days to remove it once they'd checked the other end of it. Despite the coolness at ground level, sewers were uncomfortably hot and sticky places, and the first signs of perspiration collected in the small of Gary's back, as his T-shirt clung to his protective suit. Terrell didn't fare any better as rivulets of sweat snaked down his face, stinging his eyes inside his glasses.

"Have we got everything we need?" Gary asked as he gathered his equipment together.

"Yep. Where's the next inspection hole?"

Gary waved an arm back in the direction of the fatberg. "I've checked on the map, it's over in the grounds of the decom pumping station down the road. We can go in from there and work our way back to the fatberg and then we'll be able to calculate the length before firming up a works schedule for the boss."

"Let's do it, homie," Terrell replied whistling to himself, as he turned and stomped back through the sludgy mess, each of his steps slurping and slopping against his boots.

17

"When are they going to listen," Gary moaned as he stepped from his cab and viewed the broken chain that hung from one of the gates. "Bloody kids again, I bet you."

Despite high fencing and the proverbial warning signs, such sites attracted more than their fair share of unwelcomed visitors.

He had been to a few stations like this and realised they tended to attract more nocturnal activity than during the day. Discarded silver canisters used as laughing gas littered the floor, empty beer cans lay in piles, and he'd even seen the odd syringe and used condom. How they managed to get into these allegedly secure sites was beyond comprehension as far as Gary was concerned. Chain or metal fencing at least ten feet high made it impossible for them to scale, and yet he knew the pesky brats still found a way in.

The decommissioned pumping station sat idle, its job done. This particular station had served the local community well since the twenties. But as London swelled in size, it had struggled to cope and was deemed inadequate and retired from service.

The grass around the building was knee-high, the concrete access road long fractured through a lack of upkeep. Weeds now crawled through the crevices where they spread to form a green patchy carpet. The building itself hadn't been touched in years. Despite its windows being boarded up with metal sheets, criminals still broke in and stripped anything of value that wasn't bolted down for scrap metal. The once ornate brickwork was now a scrawling mess of graffiti.

"Well, the security patrols are doing a fantastic job," Terrell said sarcastically, nodding in the direction of the large sign pinned to the fencing, which showed the silhouette of a security officer and his dog.

Gary tutted in agreement.

The pair donned their protective overalls and kitted up once again. This was a small inspection chamber, so didn't need a second team to lower them into the tunnel, as Gary, followed by Terrell, descended the metal steps into the darkness below. It took a few moments for their eyes to adjust to the gloom as their head torches bounced light off the brick walls. As they reached the bottom, Gary stepped off the rungs of the railings first, followed by Terrell. The foul water levels were lower on this side of the fatberg, but still came up to beneath their knees. Gary checked his gas monitor to make sure it was safe for them to go ahead before they ventured any further.

Debris floated on the surface. Wet wipes, drinks bottles, and nappy sacks were intermingled with human waste that lapped against their waders each time they took a step.

Gary was about to move off when his feet became entangled in some rope that floated beneath the surface.

"What the fuck is this?" he shouted, as he lifted a leg out of the water. The length of long, thick rope had looped around his ankle and made him stumble. Gary placed a hand on the wall to steady himself.

"How the fuck did rope end up down here?" Terrell muttered, as he used a metal pole to unhook it from his friend's waders.

It was a substantial rope, at least an inch thick in his estimation, and as he yanked it with the hook on the end of his pole, more evidence of the rope emerged from the darkened smelly swamp around them. Terrell followed the line of the rope as it disappeared a few yards in front of him beneath the water again. His torch caught something in the darkened space beyond and the sound of scurrying and splashing.

At first, he struggled to focus in the darkness, his eyes searching for an explanation. "Hold on a sec, Gaz. I think we might have an obstruction."

Gary tried to look over Terrell's shoulder but couldn't make out much. They had only travelled a few tentative yards before Terrell's torch caught sight of the obstruction again. It looked like a thick pile of clothes, perhaps even a bag of them. Terrell narrowed his eyes, trying to make out what it was. The nearer they got, the clearer it became, and that's when Terrell froze.

Confusion clouded his thoughts, panic tensed his muscles,

and fear made his stomach lurch. His breath came in short, sharp bursts.

"Fucking hell, fuck… fuck…!" he screamed.

Gary barrelled into the back of Terrell who had frozen, and now both sets of eyes were trained on what lay ahead of them.

The body of a man floated in the middle of the tunnel. Rats crawled over his body, consumed in a frenzied feasting on human flesh, oblivious to the two spectators who had joined them.

18

Karen stepped out of the car and surveyed the scene. The presence of the police had caused a crowd to gather in the street. A large cordon had been put in place, shutting off the entrance to the pumping station. PCSOs manned the outer cordon, which Karen estimated to be about fifty yards away. Jade had parked further up the road and was in discussions with local officers.

Steve had been on duty when the call had come in, so he quickly alerted Karen whilst he made his way over. The severity of the situation wasn't lost on Karen as a long line of emergency vehicles took up one side of the street. An ambulance had been called along with a fire engine, the forensic team, and half a dozen marked police cars. Various members of the emergency services stood around engaged in small discussions as Karen joined Steve.

"What have we got, Steve? Is it as bad as you told me on the phone?" Karen asked, her eyes travelling beyond Steve and to a large white tent that had been erected in the grounds beyond him.

Steve glanced over his shoulder in the same direction and nodded. "This is a bit of a tricky one. We've got a body down there in the middle of the sewer. It was discovered by two Thames Water employees investigating a blockage."

Karen flicked her hand towards the tent. "And the blockage was the body?"

"No. They were here in response to a report of blocked drains and discovered a fatberg further down the road. But to gauge the length of it, they needed to approach from the other end too. But they discovered the body of a deceased male. IC1. Age hasn't been confirmed yet."

"How are they doing?" Karen asked.

"Pretty shocked, to be honest. They've been treated and checked over by the paramedics, and we've also taken statements from them."

"Did they see anything else that might be of interest to us?"

Steve shook his head. "I think after discovering the body, they shot straight back up, called us, and then reported in with their bosses. I've let them go home to be with their families and told them that we may need to follow up with a secondary interview."

"We could do with getting down there to have a look. I'm not sure that forensics would be able to gather much evidence from down there, and in those conditions."

Steve shook his head. "I don't think we can. We've got officials here from Thames Water and they haven't let anyone down there as it's too risky."

Karen furrowed her brow. "Dangerous or not, we still need to have a look. Besides, I want forensics to take photographs of the scene for us to examine later. Who said that we can't go down there?"

Steve flipped open his notepad to check through his notes. "Don Barrett is their supervisor. He's the guy over there with the orange hi-vis jacket, and clipboard under his arm."

"We'll see," Karen replied, as she walked purposely towards Barrett. "Don Barrett?"

The man turned from the conversation that he was having with other officials and looked Karen up and down before nodding.

"I'm Detective Inspector Karen Heath, and I'll be in charge of the investigation surrounding this suspicious death. I really need to have a look for myself, and we need to get someone from forensics to take photographs of the scene. The sooner the better."

Barrett blew out his cheeks. "It's not gonna happen. It's way too dangerous down there for members of the public."

"Mr Barrett, I'm not a member of the public. I'm here to investigate a suspicious death. For each minute we spend discussing this, we could be losing valuable evidence."

"I doubt you'll get any evidence. If there's anything of value, it's probably been flushed away already."

"Well, that's for us to decide but we're hardly in a position to do anything about it whilst standing around talking about it. I really need to see down there, even if it's just for a few minutes."

"Detective, we are dealing with a range of noxious gases

down there, and to an untrained individual like yourself they could prove *extremely* dangerous. I'm not being awkward, trust me. But going down into the sewers is a dangerous job, even for my guys. It's so easy for them to be overcome in a matter of seconds if there's a release of gases. If that happened to you, I can't guarantee we'd be able to get you out quick enough."

"What are you talking about?" Karen asked, her mind swimming with conflicting thoughts.

"If the noxious substance monitor went off, you'd have to get out quickly or risk dying of sewer gas, that's not really what you want for your legacy, is it?"

Karen crossed her arms and contemplated the situation. "I'm prepared to take that risk, and if we go down with a member of your team, they can keep an eye out for potential risks, can't they?"

Barrett stared at the tent. "It's doable, but that's putting both of our jobs on the line here. You do realise that?"

"In and out before you know it."

After some moments of deliberating, and Barrett checking in with head office, Karen received the green light to go down with one member of the forensic team to do a quick assessment, but they would have no more than five minutes down there.

Barrett kitted up both Karen and the SOCO in exactly the same protective equipment that Gary and Terrell used. Karen found it hard to move with the waders being so heavy. It felt like she had lead plates attached to her feet. The hard hat felt uncomfortable and smelt of sweat that turned Karen's stomach. Having been given the all-clear, a member of Don's team had already descended into the sewer to receive Karen and the SOCO. Karen was the first to head down into the murky darkness. She scrunched up her nose as the smell assaulted her nostrils. Karen imagined it would be a lot worse had she not taken a tip from Don to spread Vick's nasal rub along her top lip and around her nostril openings.

"Oh God, this is fucking gross," Karen muttered, as her feet plunged into a sticky, black slimy mess that made every step challenging. The sound of the slops and splashes echoed around the Victorian chamber as she followed the Thames Water employee to the scene.

With the fatberg untouched further up the tunnel, there was an earthy, manure type smell which made her retch at one point as she looked at blobs of "mud" left on the walls from receding water.

Karen shuddered. The vile little globs glistened. Inspecting them in the queasy warm air hit her with the realisation, *I'm at eye level with human shit*. This was more than enough to send her into a blind panic. She tried to control her breathing. It wasn't a nice epiphany, although what else did she really think she'd find in a sewer?

The employee stepped to one side as they reached the crime scene, allowing Karen to wade through and stop just a few feet in front of the corpse. Karen wasn't too sure what turned her stomach more, the smells, the sight of shit lining the brick walls, or the victim in torn and tattered clothes, flesh wounds littering his skin.

Karen paused for a moment, taking in the sight before letting the scenes-of-crime officer navigate the sticky sewage that rippled around them. Flashes of bright brilliance lit up the darkened space as the SOCO began taking photographs from different angles, before zooming in on certain body parts. The female SOCO occasionally glanced back towards Karen, and Karen could see the horror and unsettling feeling in her eyes. It was so damp that her camera misted up and had to be wiped down every few shots.

Karen found something else disturbing. A small metal cage had been strapped to the victim's abdomen, and inside were two rats gorging themselves on the victim's innards. Karen shuddered as a bolt of electricity darted down her spine and sent shivers racing through her.

Due to the unrelenting humidity, thousands of worms, woodlice and spiders kept them company. Bugs crawled away in the light of their torches up and down the moist wall. The build-up of heat started to take its toll on Karen, as weariness set in, and light-headedness made her unsteady on her feet.

Seeing Karen sway, the Thames Water official signalled for them to return up to ground level, and Karen didn't need to be asked twice as she spun around and ploughed through the mess, swiftly followed by the SOCO who had seen enough as well.

Karen took some deep drags of oxygen that one of the paramedics provided for her. She sat on the side of the pavement, waiting for her head to stop spinning. Even though she had stripped off her layer of protective clothing, her skin felt damp, as beads of sweat erupted on her forehead and around her neck.

Steve and Mason Brophy, the crime scene manager, stood by her waiting for Karen to regain her composure.

"Was it that bad?" Mason asked.

Karen tipped her head back and stared up towards the grey skies. "I've seen a lot worse. I guess it was a combination of the heat, the smells, and this claustrophobic feeling that the walls were closing in, that got me. Just a few minutes more, and I would have passed out."

"What are we going to do about recovering the body?" Steve asked Mason.

Mason shrugged. "We can't get down there, so will have to arrange for a recovery team to bring the body to ground level, and then my team can get to work. The fire service has a specialist team to do that. I'll arrange for that to happen, if that's okay with you, Karen?"

Karen nodded and waved him away, "Yep, you crack on with it. I'll hang around so that we can examine the body in daylight."

A flash of embarrassment raced through Karen's mind. She had never reacted like this at any crime scene. With so many emergency service personnel around her, and all eyes trained on her when she had returned to the surface, she'd felt foolish for her reaction.

But it was more than that. Had the victim been eaten alive and died from his injuries, or had he been dead already and saved from such a painful and grotesque death?

19

Karen staggered to her feet and was hit with a bout of giddiness from standing up too quickly. The paramedics had offered to check her over but she didn't want any fuss. She walked in circles to get the blood flowing and take in her surroundings. Nothing stood out. A typical street found across the whole of London, a combination of shops nestled in amongst small terraced housing, with front gardens barely wide enough to hold a bin, let alone a car. On the opposite side of the road was a pavement with wire fencing, and beyond that, a steep grassy bank which shielded an overground railway line.

The sound of further emergency sirens caused her to look around to see a fire engine followed by another vehicle specialising in rope rescue and recovery, carving through the traffic being held back beyond the cordon.

It would be a complex process to recover the body to ground level, but Karen's concern was the preservation of forensic evidence. How they would do that, she wasn't sure. Karen saw Wainwright's car park up behind a police van, and she made her way over towards him.

Wainwright stepped out of his vehicle to meet her. "You're not looking your usual perky self, Karen. Are you okay? You look a little pale," he said, placing a concerned hand on her arm.

Karen offered the weakest of smiles, still not feeling herself. "I'm okay. I just felt a bit rough after coming out of the sewer. I'm not sure what it was. Maybe the heat or the smell," she said, waving away his concerns. "I'm fine now." Though she wasn't fine. The fact she had taken a slight turn bothered her. She hated showing any sign of weakness, and for the first time in ages, she felt like a fool in front of her colleagues.

Wainwright shrugged and nodded as he studied her through furrowed brows. "I don't think there's much I can do around here at the moment," he said, watching the fire service vehicles park up, and half a dozen men getting out and making their way towards the white tent. "It's going to be a while before me or forensics can examine the body. I don't know how this will fit in with your availability now, but I managed to get us an appointment with the forensic psychologist for this afternoon. If you can get away, let me know."

"I'm going to hang around for a bit, as the scene is quite fresh. But I'll get back to you within the next hour. My guess is they are going to have to figure out how to get down there, how to bring the body up to the surface, whilst also being careful of the noxious gases down there. I don't envy their job," Karen speculated.

"Indeed. They'll check the weather report to make sure there's no rain due. Those sewers can quickly fill up when we get a downpour."

Karen agreed to talk to Wainwright a little later as he headed back to the mortuary, and she made her way over to Don Barrett.

"How are your guys doing?" she asked.

Barrett shrugged. "I think they're pretty messed up to be honest. We see a lot of stuff down there, but the only living things we tend to see are rats and the occasional snake. I've heard of bodies being discovered in other parts of the country, but I've not heard of anything in the Thames region."

"Thankfully, it's rare."

"I remember seeing an article about a body being found in a fifteen-foot-deep sewer up in Worcester. It took a specialist line rescue service to recover the body. But that's the only one that springs to mind," he recalled. "It's just beyond belief how people end up in these places."

Karen crossed her arms and stared at the white tent. "How often are these sewers inspected?"

"It varies depending on the location. Some have a lot more flow than others. Some sewers are in better condition and don't need to be checked that often, others are in a poor state of repair, and need to be inspected regularly for signs of blockages. We tend to find that the ones in the older parts of London need more attention, purely down to the fact that there are more people per square mile, so more shit for us to deal with." Barrett threw his arms up in the air. "We also have a bigger density of restaurants, who chuck their oil and fat down the drains, so we get more instances of fatbergs, so that's why we're here today."

"And this drain?" Karen asked.

Barrett checked his paperwork. "It was checked three months ago."

"No one's been down there ever since?"

"If they had, I'd know about it."

"And how easy is it to get down there for a member of the public?"

Barrett laughed. "It depends. Some larger manhole covers like those in the street need two men to lift them, and they're bloody heavy."

"One person couldn't lift it?"

"Normally, I'd say no." Barrett shook his head. "Unless you were a powerlifter or a bodybuilder or something like that. And more importantly, you have to have access to specialist keys that hook into the surface of the plate to pull it out. But these smaller ones like the one here can be lifted out with a bit of effort."

Karen thought that over, as the revelations conjured up a multitude of theories in her mind.

They both made their way over towards the white tent to see the rescue team setting up their equipment and discussing their strategy before commencing the difficult task. With one ear on their conversation, Karen continued her discussion with Barrett.

"Are there any other entry points into that part of the sewer?"

Barrett opened his folder and pulled out a map that contained a grid of the sewer network that criss-crossed the London area. To Karen's eyes, it looked like a disjointed spider's web, as lines criss-crossed each other, many of them in different colours. There were red, green, and blue lines that merged at various points and crossed one another. The coloured lines represented the different depths of each part of the sewer network, and Barrett went to great lengths to describe which parts of the network they had inspected recently, and more importantly, where this particular entry point was in the network of drains.

In a childish way, Karen was in awe as she stared at the map. A Victorian sewer system built one hundred and fifty years ago to serve two million people now served nine million in London. She marvelled at how they could have managed this back then. They had no technology, mechanised equipment, laser tracking, or large boring equipment that's commonly used now, and yet they built something that had stood the test of time.

"This stretch of sewer has seven entry points within a mile taking into account both directions," Barrett added.

"And what's access like at those points?"

"If you're asking, could a member of the public gain access to that part of the sewer through any of those points, then the answer is it's possible," Barrett said, heaving a sigh.

"Mr Barrett, you've been incredibly helpful. I'll let you crack on, but I might need to come back to you if we need more information on the sewer system, okay?"

"Sure, your officers have my details already. I hope it goes well for you," Barrett offered as he made off towards his car to complete his paperwork.

Jade and Steve joined Karen and updated her on the enquiries already made by uniformed officers.

"What do you think?" Jade asked.

"Well as an informed guess and based on what I've seen, we have a body tied to a rope, the body was probably lowered down the shaft, and then dumped at the bottom with the rope still attached, But why?" Karen shrugged, as she tried to ignore the sinking sensation in her chest.

Karen updated her team on her discussion with Barrett.

Jade looked perplexed. "What I don't understand is that you said the victim looked older? What age would you put him at?"

Karen shrugged and tightened her lips into a thin line whilst she recalled what she had seen and shook her head with uncertainty. "I'm not sure to be honest. It was dark; it was dirty. I couldn't tell, but if I had to guess I would say fifty to sixty, maybe older. Who knows?"

The team had more questions than answers, which left Karen wondering how much evidence they'd be able to recover during the forensic and post-mortem examinations.

They'd already decided to place the body in a body bag, to preserve as much forensic evidence as possible, and from there the body would be taken straight to the mortuary where SOCO and Wainwright could conduct their examinations without the loss of vital clues. With Mason's team unable to examine the underground crime scene, they were solely reliant on the body.

"Jade, can you inform the PNC bureau, so an information marker gets created in the PNC, that we've discovered an unidentified body? Can you both stay here to oversee the scene? If there's anything urgent, call me, but Wainwright has set up a meeting for us to meet a forensic psychologist about our first victim and the issue of dismembering bodies."

20

"I think I'm in the wrong job," Karen said, as she sat in a deep burgundy leather sofa that swallowed her up. Wainwright sat alongside her in a plush Harley Street private office in London. A few magazines were laid out in an immaculate fan shape on the table in front of them, a few decorative art pieces lined the white walls, and her shoes sunk into the deep pile cream carpet.

They were welcomed by a secretary sat behind a wide desk. Everything about the room suggested money and respectability.

"I don't think they earn that much," Wainwright commented. "This will be rented," he added, casting his eye around the room.

Without being a moment overdue, an Asian lady who Karen estimated to be in her late thirties, breezed into the room with a warming smile, and her hand extended.

"Christopher Wainwright," Wainwright said, as he shook her hand and introduced Karen.

"I'm Dr Anita Rai. It's a pleasure to meet you. Do come through," she said, and organised coffee for them before heading to a first-floor office where she showed them to two expensive-looking seats to one side of her desk.

Karen glanced around the room, which carried the same large proportions as the waiting room downstairs. She was surprised to see that the office was larger than the living room of her apartment.

After a soft tap on the door, the receptionist entered with a tray of three cups, and a cafetière of fresh coffee, which she proceeded to pour before offering the pair sugar and milk.

Wainwright waited for her to leave before he spoke. "Thank you so much for taking the time to see us, Dr Rai. We could do with your help."

"Please, call me Anita," she replied, waving away the need for formality.

Wainwright cleared his throat, which made Karen smile, as she knew how much Wainwright relied on formality and professional correctness. As Karen sat there, there was a marked contrast between these two professionals. Wainwright had a stiff upper lip, dressed professionally, and preferred to address people in the correct way, and had precision in his words. Anita, on the other hand, appeared softer with her warm smile and more relaxed body language. She had a smooth complexion, and dark brown hair, and matching dark brown eyes with a classic Asian look about her, that highlighted her strong cheekbones, blemish-free skin that didn't appear to have aged in any way, and a smart but casual dress sense.

"Anita… my colleague here, Karen, is dealing with a particular case at the moment which has involved the discovery of a dismembered body, and… well, Karen…" Wainwright paused, prompting Karen to continue.

Karen took a sip of her coffee and welcomed the caffeine shot hitting her body. "As Wain… Christopher alluded to, we have a case where the dismembered body of an elderly white woman has been discovered in certain locations around London. We can't confirm if the locations have any significance to these discoveries. What I would really like to get to grips with is understanding the mindset behind someone who goes to such extreme lengths to dismember a body?"

Anita rested her elbows on the armrest of the chair, and formed a steeple with her fingers, listening intently, nodding in the right places, and widening her eyes with interest.

"The dismemberment of a victim appears to be on an entirely different level of hate. Dismemberment dates back to the twelve hundreds when beheading and torture were embraced as a sociological norm and even considered a festivity of the highest regard."

"Really?" Karen replied in surprise.

"Oh, yes. In fact, decapitation was perceived to be the most prestigious form of death during this period. Dismembering a victim illustrates an extreme notion of abhorrence towards the victim, psychologically dismissing their existence and disregarding them as being of any value whatsoever. And there's plenty of analysis and research to back that up," Anita replied with a degree of enthusiasm in her voice, which grew as she became more animated. "The perpetrator that elects to dismember their victim desires to end their existence, refusing to acknowledge them on a conscious level. Furthermore, taking their body apart is perceived to be gratifying sexually and psychologically necessary."

Glancing across to Wainwright, Karen added, "We believe our victim wasn't interfered with sexually, so we don't believe there was a sexual motive to this killing."

Wainwright nodded in approval and confirmed that to be the case.

"Okay, well there has to be a psychological component towards your crime which suggests far more malicious intent on the part of your perpetrator. Dismembering a body is a strenuous task that's almost always done to hide evidence in a way even most hardened criminals couldn't stomach."

"You're suggesting someone who goes the extra mile like that is either psychotic or plain evil?" Wainwright questioned.

"Quite possibly, and I mean really evil. There are very few people who would cut up a body, even amongst criminals. It's a very different mindset."

Anita stood up to retrieve the documents from one of her heavily stacked bookshelves before returning to her desk and flicking through to find an article. She glanced through it for a few minutes, nodding in certain places as her eyes tracked along each of the sentences. "Sorry, I just needed to be reminded of something. There are lots of different ways in which the active dismemberment sends a message. Especially if the body parts are sent to others." Anita paused for a moment to look for any form of agreement that it had happened in Karen's case. When Karen shook her head, Anita continued.

"Okay, so I won't go into that much detail but basically if that did happen in your case, then this would have been needing to get attention and sensation seeking, grandiosity and narcissism. It is likely that the killer had fantasised many times the reactions that opening the post would provoke."

"What emotional state would the killer be experiencing?" Karen asked, still scribbling away in her notepad.

"Characteristically, for this kind of killer, I'd expect your suspect to experience a lack of empathy and emotions. You can't presume that they would have felt anxiety, horror or guilt when performing these acts."

"Will this inability to feel anything be a recent change in their behaviour, or something more long-term?" Karen asked.

"Often far more deep-seated."

Karen listened as Anita recalled a case study in the US where an offender had eaten some of his victim's body parts. He told his interrogators that he ate them precisely because he was aiming to feel something. When he was asked, "so how did it feel?" he replied that, "he didn't know", because it felt no different to anything else in his life.

"What else could you tell us about their personality, relationship status, jobs, anything else that might give us the lead?" Karen probed.

Anita took a moment to reflect and gather her thoughts. "Their self-image is often disturbed and negative, although they may appear to show a degree of self-confidence. But that's very much a smokescreen. They would often find it very difficult to keep relationships, because ultimately the fantasies that they experience serve the purpose of feeling superior to others, so they would struggle in a relationship if they didn't feel at least an equal, or more dominant."

"Would they struggle to hold down a job if they were an employee because they would see their boss as the superior, and that wouldn't sit well with them?" Karen asked, tapping the back of her pen on her notepad as she attempted to make sense of what she had picked up.

Anita nodded in agreement.

Karen added that their female victim had been strangled, and Anita confirmed that death by strangulation was apparently quite common in this kind of homicide.

"Anita, I think that's all I need for the moment. This has been fascinating, and incredibly helpful. We really appreciate your time," Karen said, looking towards Wainwright who nodded his appreciation as well.

"It's my pleasure, and I'm glad it's been of use to you. It's also worth considering another key clue that I believe may help you in tracking down such killers in the future. Unlike other kinds of homicide, the offender is always known to the victim. In nearly half of the cases it's being a family member or a partner, and beyond that someone that they may have spent considerable time with."

21

Karen dropped into a chair and tipped her head back, resting it on the headrest. She stared towards the ceiling as her mind crunched through the dozens of thoughts that tumbled over one another. She questioned whether she was doing the right thing in pressurising Charlie to help her. This was her battle; she needed answers. The problem was everything she had tried had resulted in a dead end.

She glanced at her phone in hope. Barbara hadn't called back. Had she scared her away as well? Karen had tried Barbara's number several times, going through to voicemail each time. She had chosen on each occasion to not leave a message, but had her fingers and toes crossed that Barbara would eventually be brave enough to call back. How she would handle a call from the woman, she was unsure.

Do I need to be more forceful, or will that scare her away? Perhaps I need to be more sympathetic and understanding? Maybe I need to tell her about the mental and emotional torture that I've experienced for more than a year now, as the scene plays out in my mind. Maybe that's my way of getting through to her?

Karen's phone buzzed, causing her to jump out of her seat and snatch it from her desk. Her heart raced, willing it to be Barbara, only to groan when she saw the name of the caller. She was in two minds whether to answer, unsure if she could trust herself to stay calm. Karen let it ring for a few more seconds before answering.

"Wallace! What do you want? You've got a nerve calling me," Karen spat as she clenched her teeth, willing herself not to throw a load of obscenities down the line.

"Now what have I done? When are you gonna give me a break and stop being so defensive?" he said, raising his tone.

"A break? Did I hear you correctly, a break? You talk about cooperation and wanting to be the first to hear about something, and then you criticise me publicly and lay the blame at my doorstep! How do you expect me to react?"

"Finished?" Wallace chipped in. "I am literally chasing you all over the city trying to get a response from you. And every time you've palmed me off. What do you expect me to say when my job is to expose the truth, but I'm considered a pariah by you?"

"Wallace, what do you expect from me? There were things I said to you off the record, and you had the barefaced cheek to repeat that conversation in public. So if you're looking for trust, you need to look at yourself and question why I don't trust you, or do you want me to spell that out for you too, so that you can report that in your paper?!" Karen shouted.

"Detective Inspector, if you're looking to build a strong relationship with your colleagues in the media, I suggest you put yourself down for media training, because I find your tone very aggressive."

Rage exploded inside Karen, red mist fast clouding her thoughts, feelings, and her emotions. "Aggressive! Aggressive! You have no idea what I'm like when I'm aggressive, so button it. I will let you know through Sally Marchant the moment we have anything of interest. In the meantime, I suggest you give us the space to get on with our job." Karen hung up and slung the phone across the desk. "You first-class knob!"

"I try not to be…" Jade said as she appeared in Karen's doorway, holding two mugs of coffee.

Karen placed a hand over her mouth and stared at Jade wide-eyed. "Oh gosh, I'm so sorry. That wasn't aimed at you. You didn't hear all of that, did you?" Karen asked, narrowing her eyes.

Jade laughed as she placed the mugs on Karen's desk and dropped into a chair. "Um, I think the whole building heard that. Men trouble?" Jade winked.

"Kind of. Wallace. That's all I'll say."

Jade rolled her eyes. "Oh no, not him again."

"Yep. He had the cheek to suggest I took up media training to improve my relationship with the media," Karen said, slapping her hand on the table. "Me. Media training."

Jade wasn't sure whether Karen was more offended by her argument with Wallace, or that he had implied that she needed to brush up on her skills. "I wouldn't worry about it. He deserved it. I haven't heard a good word about him.

The sleazier and more grotesque the case, the more it appears to excite him. I think he likes the idea of sensationalising a story."

Karen agreed as she sipped her coffee. She welcomed the soothing sensation as it trickled down her throat and warmed her stomach. "What are you doing here, anyway? I told you lot to go home?"

"I know. I was finishing up and leaving when I heard you having a rant on the phone. I thought you could do with a coffee…" she said, offering a cheeky smile.

Karen checked her watch, it was nearly ten p.m. Her thoughts turned towards getting home as soon as she could. Her neighbour would have popped in and fed Manky, but she'd hardly been home to give him attention, and snuggle up on the sofa in her onesie with a glass of wine whilst catching up with her recorded programmes.

Karen ran a hand down her face. They were nearly five days into a major investigation, and desperately short of a breakthrough. She heard footsteps on the main floor, followed by a soft swoosh as the bottom of the door glided across the carpet. Another one of her officers heading home for the night.

"You know what worries me? Why would a woman in her sixties be hacked to death like that? I just don't understand what goes through the mind of a killer who attacks someone of that age," Jade commented, scrunching up her face whilst trying to comprehend the scenario.

"Me neither. But if Dr Rai is correct, and the killer knows the victim, then she was attacked because of something that went on historically between them. This wasn't a random killing, where an intruder broke in, attacked the frail old lady, and chopped her into pieces. This has been thought through and probably planned for a while."

Karen spent the next few minutes talking through the case with Jade, covering all the tasks undertaken so far as well as the detailed steps they had taken to investigate the murder. But with no suspects, and no motive, it would be easy for the team to lose the momentum that always came with a new case. As each day progressed, the frustration would grow, and the realisation would set in that they were in for the long haul.

"Do you think that these two bodies are connected in any way?"

Karen shook her head. "I don't know. One has been hacked to death and chopped into pieces, and the other victim was found in a sewer, in one piece. If you're dealing with a serial killer, their MO tends to be similar between all the victims. These two cases can't be more poles apart."

"Oh, that reminds me, there should be a report from forensics in your inbox. It's only just come through this evening. They've confirmed that all the body parts are forensically linked, it's a DNA match. In the fine analysis of each dismembered limb, they confirmed the same instrument was used. They suspect something like a large butcher's meat cleaver. Though they can't be a hundred per cent certain."

The information from Jade confirmed Karen's suspicions, but it was good to get an official confirmation.

Karen finished the last of the coffee, and logged off, before leaving the building with Jade and heading to the Tube station.

Karen made it back to her flat shortly before eleven thirty p.m. Often she would walk back from the station to give her time to clear her mind, but with the lateness of the evening, she grabbed one of the cabs that hung around outside.

She stepped into a darkened hallway and kicked off her shoes, before padding into the lounge and feeling the pile of the carpet between her toes. Manky was curled up in a small fluffy ball on the sofa and barely opened one eye when she approached and knelt down beside him. "I'm so sorry, little man. It can't be much fun for you waiting for me to come home. I promise I'll take a few days off after this case is over because I need some downtime, and you need your mummy around a bit more, don't you?"

Karen tutted when Manky didn't stir. "I'll take that as a yes," she said, stroking the back of his neck.

She grabbed the mail that lay in the hallway and flicked through the various envelopes, searching for anything of value before heading to her bedroom. What she needed more than anything was a long soak in the bath to ease her aching back and tight neck muscles, but time wasn't on her side. She stripped off and opted for a quick shower, before jumping into her onesie and diving under the duvet. She only had her heating on for an hour in the morning, and then an hour in the evening, just to take the chill off the apartment, but by the time she got back, all the heat had gone.

With the duvet tucked in under her chin, she stared into the darkness hoping that her mind would quieten, but her tiredness beat her to it, and within a matter of minutes, she'd succumbed to sleep.

22

Karen bolted when the phone beside her bed sprang into life and rattled across the top of her bedside cabinet. She blinked furiously as she made sense of the noise. *Surely, I've only been asleep for a few hours, if that?* She glanced over towards her window and saw nothing but darkness beyond. The incessant noise sounded like a pneumatic drill in her head, as she clumsily groped for the phone.

"Heath," she said, just managing to get the word out. Her mouth tasted gunky and bitter, and her throat felt parched. Karen licked her dry lips and tried to focus, even though she hadn't bothered to look at the screen of the phone.

"Boss, it's Jeff. Sorry to wake you up, but we've just had a breakthrough and wanted to call you straight away."

That was enough for Karen to swing her legs out of bed and on to the floor as she sat upright. She glanced across to her bedside clock, it had just gone five thirty a.m.

"Hot off the press, we've finally got the information

through from the National Joint Registry. The identification number on the joint belongs to Annette Buckley."

Karen rubbed her eyes and swallowed hard. "Do you know how old Annette Buckley was?"

"Seventy-nine years old."

Karen grabbed clothes out of a cupboard as Jeff filled her in on the other details. They finally had a name for the first victim, and the age range tied in. She asked Jeff to forward the address and to alert Jade to meet her there, whilst also asking for a patrol car to swing by.

UNIFORMED BACKUP HAD JUST ARRIVED at the location as Karen drew near to the property. The victim's address turned out to be a small bungalow close to Highbury Fields. Karen found a suitable place to park before stepping out of her car and looking up and down the road. It was a mixture of well-maintained properties, intermingled with a few that screamed for attention. Karen spotted Jade further up the street exiting her car and jogging towards the address. It was a crisp and cold morning, with little cloud in the sky. Jade had her hands tucked inside her coat whilst she blew out her cheeks.

"Have you been here long?" Karen asked as she rubbed her hands together.

"Only a few minutes. I needed to find somewhere to park and ended up right back there," Jade said, waving a hand over her shoulder. "It seems a pretty quiet place, to be honest."

Karen led the way through the garden, walking along the

crazy paving path that split the lawn in two. Weeds crept through the broken mortar in between the slabs, and the lawn looked like it hadn't been cut all summer.

Karen rang on the door and heard the bell chime in the hallway. Whilst waiting, Jade cupped her hands around her eyes and peered in through the nearest window. With the windows being dirty, and thick net curtains, Jade struggled to see past them and into the room. She couldn't be certain if she was looking into the bedroom or the lounge.

"Anything?" Karen asked.

Jade grimaced. "No. Windows are too dirty."

Karen rang again and knocked, before crouching down and peering through the letter box. She at once recoiled and scrunched her nose as she caught the slight whiff of a smell which escaped through the small opening and assaulted her nostrils. She took a step back, sensing the immediate danger.

Jade didn't need an explanation as she stepped away and retrieved her phone from her bag to call it in.

Karen tried the handle on the door to find that it was unlocked. Recovering a pair of nitrile gloves from her handbag, she threw another pair in Jade's direction before opening the door and stepping to one side alongside her uniformed colleagues. Karen bit her lip and waited for the first rush of foul air to escape before she placed one hand over her nose and mouth and peered through the opening and down the hallway. There was nothing that she could see out of the ordinary.

Jade followed Karen as they stepped through the carpeted hallway, watching where they placed their feet. The hallway was short and narrow, before it took a turn to the left. Karen tilted her head around the corner and froze. Flies buzzed in every direction as Karen batted a few away. She could see smears of blood across the floor and in one doorway ahead of her, with more of it creeping up the door frame and on the walls. That was all Karen needed to see before she took a step back. They retraced their steps until they were in the front garden keen to avoid further contamination of the scene.

Karen took a lungful of clean air and puffed out her cheeks. "It's a fucking bloodbath in there. I think we may have found where Annette Buckley was killed."

Jade was already on the phone, putting in a request for SOCO and extra uniformed resources as she walked back out to the pavement.

Karen followed not long after and then stared at the front of the property. Whatever had happened to Annette Buckley had started here and ended with her remains being dumped across London.

IT TOOK LESS than thirty minutes for the crime scene to be locked down with uniformed officers cordoning off the property. SOCO began their investigation as officers moved about the property kitted up in white protective Tyvek suits, face masks, nitrile gloves, and blue plastic booties.

Neighbours and residents from the street poured out on to the road, visibly shaken and concerned by the heightened police presence. Karen's uniformed colleagues did their best to move amongst them, offering reassurance, and saying nothing more than an incident had occurred at the property in question. Many of them knew Annette and asked if she was okay.

Karen paced up and down the pavement impatiently, desperate to get back inside the property. This was the first clear breakthrough in five days, which meant that the case was progressing. Jade had been busy relaying live footage from her bodycam back to the office whilst also collecting information on the deceased.

The cold that Karen first felt melted away, as adrenaline gripped her body, causing her to fidget. One minute she was crossing her arms and throwing her weight from one foot to another on the spot, the next, she was crossing from one side of the street to the other.

"Karen, we've got more information on Annette Buckley. She was seventy-nine years old, a widow, and married to Alfie Buckley, who died at the age of sixty-four. We have no information to suggest she had any immediate family or children."

"That figures why she wasn't reported missing, Jade."

Mason Brophy, the crime scene manager, appeared at the doorway of the property, before spotting Karen and making his way over to her. "It's not pretty in there. I'd certainly say that this was the location where your victim was dismembered. Most of the activity centres around the bathroom. Early indications suggest she was dismembered there."

"Can we get in there?" Karen asked.

"It's a bit early at the moment."

"Oh, come on, Mason. Just a quick look. We need to get

going on this. Once we've looked, we'll step away and let your lot get on with it."

Mason flicked his head towards the doorway. "Five minutes. Once we're done, you can have full access to the property."

Karen didn't need to be told again, as she and Jade shot past Mason, and grabbed a set of overalls, gloves and foot coverings from the box beside the scene guard. A female officer thrust the scene log in Karen's direction, where she quickly scribbled her name, before passing it to Jade, who did the same, before returning it.

Metal stepping plates placed in the hallway preserved the scene. Karen stepped on each one and retraced the route she had followed earlier, before turning and making her way towards the first door on her right. Smears of blood streaked the woodwork around the door. As Karen stepped into the bathroom, the white tiled walls were splattered with thick streaks of blood. Further blood smears lined the sink, and as she peered to her left, the bath was filled with crimson red water.

Whichever direction Karen looked her widened eyes met carnage. She noticed several footprints in the blood on the floor, and what looked like partial handprints on the wall. The scene was horrifying, and Karen only imagined the barbaric and grotesque act that took place here. Karen stepped to one side and back into the hallway before letting Jade take a look. Jade remained silent as her eyes scanned the room. The once white tiled walls were nothing more than witnesses to a killer's violent and savage attack. Sprays of blood crept up the walls above the bath in much the same way that an artist would flip a paintbrush and leave a spatter trail of paint on a canvas.

Karen watched as the scenes-of-crime officer examined several footprints left in the blood. Whilst Jade remained by the doorway of the bathroom, Karen took a brief opportunity to look around the property before Mason threw them out. There appeared to be no forced entry, nor any signs of a robbery gone wrong. She peered through the doorways of the lounge and the main bedroom, pushing the doors with her elbow, avoiding the need to touch handles, door frames and the doors themselves. Karen noticed that drawers and cupboard doors were untouched, their contents not scattered across the floor as would have been the case in a burglary, but they would still need to be dusted and photographed by SOCO.

The property felt old, with dated furniture, sofas that had seen better times, floral bedspreads that Annette's generation fondly loved, and a distinct lack of modern kitchen appliances. An old Kenwood Chef sat on one of the kitchen surfaces, along with an unopened pack of flour, a closed egg carton, and a tub of butter partially devoured by flies.

Karen desperately wanted to spend her time searching for clues within the property, but knew it was best to retreat and leave SOCO to do their work. She'd head back to her office for now and return with Jade once they had been given the all-clear.

23

Karen scribbled information on the incident board as her team gathered around her. She circled pictures of all the body parts and then added the words Annette Buckley beside the grouping.

"Okay, team. We've just returned from Annette Buckley's home, and you should have all seen Jade's footage."

A sea of nodding faces surrounded Karen, as well as a few shaking their heads and exchanging glances of disbelief as their conversations grew quieter.

"There are some twisted and warped people out there," said an officer.

"I agree," Karen replied. "From what we can gather, Annette was attacked, and more than likely murdered in her bathroom, and hopefully SOCO will confirm that for us. If her body was dismembered at the scene, then we'll need to figure out how her individual parts were removed. As you saw from the footage, it's a very messy scene, so I imagine it wouldn't have been easy for them to move them without leaving more evidence."

"I saw the impressions in the bathroom, anything on them?" Brad asked.

"Nothing at the moment, Brad. But you may have noticed the footprints. The good thing is that Mason suggested that they can get a lot of evidence from analysing each footprint. He said it can show a person's unique walking style. For example, those with high arches or those whose feet roll inwards will have a unique wearing pattern on the soles of their shoes. I'm curious to see what Mason's team comes up with."

Karen knew the importance of footwear analysis. It was the second most common type of evidence left at crime scenes. And through forensic footprint analysis, experts could obtain vital information that included the identification of the type of shoe, the manufacturer, and shoe size. How they did it, she wasn't sure, but Mason had assured her that they could identify the approximate height and activity that the person was performing when the shoe print was made.

"Any witnesses or did anyone notice anything suspicious?" asked Jeff. He had been on all night, and the one to break the news to Karen. With a yawn, he stretched back in a chair and checked his watch, knowing he'd be going home after the briefing.

"Nothing that we are aware of at the moment. Of course, we've got uniform doing door to door, but we need to do our own enquiries. Jade, can I leave you to organise that?" Karen asked.

Jade gave the thumbs up and added that to her to-do list.

"There were no weapons found, but clearly there were signs of a struggle, and the attack. We need to find out…" Karen turned towards the whiteboard positioned alongside the map of the area and started to write down her questions. "Was the assailant known to Annette Buckley? Did the killer want the victim to suffer? If so, we need to find out what was driving such a deep rage. And why were the body parts and torso dumped elsewhere?"

Karen turned to face her team again, many were busy writing notes. "Any questions before we start looking at tasking?"

Brad stopped chewing the top of his pen and waved it in front of him. "Considering there's no forced signs of entry, Dr Rai's suggestion that the assailant was known to the victim appears to be true. That should narrow it down for us."

Karen nodded in agreement. "There's lots for us to get working on straightaway. Whilst we have officers at the scene conducting door-to-door enquiries, make sure you are looking for properties that have CCTV footage. Generally speaking, if it's a street full of bungalows, the majority of residents tend to be elderly, or downsizers. They're often more wary of their safety and install extra security features like strong door locks, and CCTV."

"We'll also check hospital admissions, in case the assailant hurt himself."

"Good call, Jade. And whilst you're at it, look into her background. I spoke to one of her neighbours, and he said she led a quiet life after retirement from owning a children's care home but didn't talk to many people. A bit of a recluse by all accounts. She'd say "Morning" or offer a small smile if she was in the garden and a neighbour walked by but didn't venture out much or chat over the garden wall. Find out if there was anything else going on in her life."

"Will do, boss."

Karen turned towards Steve. "Could you do the usual, bank details, mobile phone records, pensions, bills, medical records… that kind of stuff?" Karen knew she could rely on Steve to do that. He had an eye for detail which would often lead him to adopt different lines of enquiry that some officers often overlooked.

"Let's get moving on this. We need to find the motive. That has to be key now. We need to find out why someone would want to kill Annette Buckley."

KAREN MADE herself a coffee in the kitchen before returning to her office. She had brought a croissant from home and could finally have breakfast whilst she logged into the database. Checking her emails and scoffing her croissant in a few bites, she hadn't realised how hungry she was. She cursed for not bringing two as her stomach rumbled in protest.

The footage from Jade's bodycam had been uploaded into the HOLMES2 database, so Karen pressed play to review the footage again. There were things that she had missed during her first visit. The wilted flowers that sat in a vase on a small table in the hallway. The ruffled rug just beyond the bathroom. The six by four picture frames pinned close to the doorway in a vertical line.

Karen only spent a few minutes in the property, her awareness searching for signs of life or danger. Simple features that many households had up and down the country had faded into the background whilst her eyes searched out trouble. She reviewed the footage twice, before sitting back in her chair and staring at the frozen screen which held the entrance to the bathroom. Checking her watch, Karen logged off her PC and grabbed her handbag. Not only did she need to revisit the crime scene again and conduct a more thorough search, but instinct told her that the answer to Annette's death lay within the four walls of that property.

24

The street was busy as Karen stepped out of her pool car within the outer cordon and made her way towards the bungalow. The scientific services vans were still there, along with several police cars. Local residents huddled together in front gardens, hushed conversations taking place, concern and worry etched on their features, with occasional glances thrown in the direction of the crime scene.

Karen noticed a few of her team work their way from one end of the street to the other. The presence of reporters and photographers beyond the outer cordon added to residents' fears. Karen scanned the faces of the gathered press but didn't spot Wallace amongst the crowd.

Grabbing a protective suit, mask, nitrile gloves, and foot coverings, Karen signed in the scene log again, and gave a cursory nod to the officer who stood in the front garden as the scene guard. "Any new developments?" Karen asked.

"Nothing that I'm aware of, ma'am," a female officer replied with a shake of her head.

With Mason giving her the green light to enter the property, Karen worked her way through the hallway, taking her time to take in her surroundings. Unopened letters and circulars sat on the small table in the hallway. Karen leafed through them to see if there was anything of interest before putting them back down. She turned the corner and the horrors that had taken place here flooded back to her in a rush of discomfort. SOCO milled about the corridor, moving in and out of rooms, their work mainly done. Flashes of brilliant white lit up the darkened hallway as SOCO took photos in rooms either side of the hallway.

Door handles, architraves and the kitchen worktops bore leftover black carbon residue where SOCO had dusted for any prints. There was evidence of their work in the other rooms, as drawers, window catches, and windowsills appeared to have been given the once-over by Mason's team as well.

Annette's bedroom was clean and functional. The bed had been made, with the floral bedspread stretched out over the pillows to form smooth lines. Several hairbrushes, talcum powder, a tub of Nivea cream, and a bottle of TCP sat on top of an old dressing table. It was a table from a bygone era, with three mirrors set in an arc, a glass covering over the wooden top, and three narrow drawers on either side. Black residue remained on the glass, evidence that SOCO had dusted for prints. Karen pulled open each of the drawers, to find nothing more than trinkets, small items of inexpensive jewellery, and hair accessories like bows, clips, and combs.

She moved through the rest of the bedroom, looking

through cupboards, under the bed and through shoeboxes. From experience and time in the burglary squad, she knew that many elderly people kept personal possessions and mementos in shoeboxes either at the bottom of cupboards, or under their beds. When she found nothing of interest, she continued her search through the rest of the property. The bungalow had a lounge, two double bedrooms, kitchen, bathroom, and a storage cupboard.

Karen came to the second bedroom where the curtains remained drawn, but a small arc light had been set up in one corner by the crime scenes team. The room was filled with black bin liners clumsily thrown wherever there was space. Karen counted at least twenty-seven boxes of varying sizes stacked precariously. Several had already been opened and examined by the search team and SOCO prior to her arrival.

The first few boxes contained clothes that Annette had stored away many years ago. The designs were outdated, and the fabrics faded with the distinct whiff of mustiness as she rummaged deeper. The next few boxes were larger and heavier, with dozens of items of cutlery, dishcloths, and towels. The more she looked, the more curious she became. She uncovered large pots and pans, more suited to an industrial kitchen than a domestic house. She wondered whether they had come from the children's home.

Karen grimaced and pulled a face as she disturbed the dust and grime from boxes that had probably sat there for years. Having pulled her mask off earlier, she coughed and sneezed as her nose itched. Her protective suit had captured floating dust particles.

"Gross!" she muttered, waving the floating specks away from her face.

Determined to carry on, she continued to work her way through the boxes and felt the first feelings of excitement when she opened a box to discover framed awards and pictures inside. Karen began to lay out a few photographs. She picked up one photo frame and studied a faded colour picture. It showed a woman, probably in her forties or fifties, standing alongside a man of a similar age, with a row of younger children lined up in front of them. There were nine children that appeared to be of varying ages. Karen turned the photograph over to see a sticker on the back which had Annette and Alfie Buckley scribbled on it. She turned it over again. Karen finally had a picture of the victim. Even though it wasn't a recent one, it was the first time she had seen Annette Buckley's face.

Curiosity pushed Karen on despite disturbing the grime and dust. It was a further few minutes before this woman piqued Karen's curiosity even further. Karen discovered another box which contained lots of tunics, the kind that dinner ladies used to wear in schools. But she found it odd as to why Annette would hang on to all those things. The more Karen delved into this woman's background, unearthing her life from within these boxes, the more questions it threw up.

Her interest intensified as Karen found more framed photographs showing kids. The photographs appeared to have been taken in different rooms. Karen gently pulled out a photo from the bottom of one of the boxes that surrounded her. It showed the outside of a large building, with Annette standing proudly at the bottom of the steps, with her chin up, arms folded defiantly across her chest, and a stoical look on her face.

Karen grabbed her phone and put a call into Brad asking

him to uncover Annette's employment details as far back as they were able to, before stuffing it in her pocket through an opening in her suit.

Karen sat back on her heels and stared at the photograph for a few minutes, before glancing around at the bags and boxes that remained unopened. Annette's whole life was contained within this room, captured through the images, her clothes and objects that Karen had uncovered.

Her phone buzzed again, and Karen tutted, assuming Brad had another question. She leant to one side to retrieve it from inside her suit. Her eyes widened and her jaw dropped as she noticed the number on her screen.

"Barbara! Barbara, is that you?" There was silence on the other end. Karen bit her lip, desperate not to frighten the woman away by saying too much or sounding too forceful. She softened her tone, tempering her excitement. "Barbara. I know you're scared. I want to help. Please."

Karen waited… for what felt like minutes.

A soft and timid voice broke the silence. "I'm scared. And frightened. I need help. But… I don't know what to do…"

Barbara didn't finish her sentence as she began to cry.

Karen ran a hand through her hair, and then silently cursed as she stared at her dusty gloves.

"I know you're scared. And trust me, I really do want to help. Please let's just meet. I'll meet you anywhere, anytime. You call the shots." Karen bit her lip when she realised what she had just said. It was such a common phrase, and it tripped off her tongue without her realising. "Anywhere, anytime."

Karen's stomach performed cartwheels as her mind raced through dozens of scenarios. Snippets of the hijack flooded her thoughts, her mind frantically trying to join the pieces together. *Can this be the breakthrough I've been dreaming of?*

"Okay. I'll meet you."

25

Karen found a place to park within the grounds of Clayhall Park in Ilford. It wasn't an area she was familiar with, and with traffic being heavy along the A406, every minute had felt like an hour. Karen's instructions were to make her way over to the park and wait by the children's activity area.

With it not being a big park, Karen made a mental note of the boundary in every direction. To her left were several tennis courts, and an outdoor gym. Two people were going through their daily exercise regime, moving from one piece of apparatus to another. Several mums with small children in tow were within the gated children's play area, which had swings, slides, and a rope zip line. The sound of kids squealing with delight echoed around her. Further to her right, she noticed five people standing in the middle of what she assumed was the cricket pitch, the dogs running, chasing and play fighting, whilst their owners huddled in a small circle chatting. *It's hardly what I'd consider taking a dog for a walk.*

In whichever direction she looked, Barbara was nowhere to be seen. Karen wondered if Barbara would turn up. Had she chickened out at the last minute? Karen paced up and down the footpath by the children's play area, glancing around for any signs of Barbara hiding, or lurking behind the trees that filled the park. She checked her watch. Fifteen minutes had passed since they were due to meet, but Karen decided to wait for as long as it took.

Karen checked her phone in case Barbara had left a text message or further instructions. Nothing. It was then that she noticed a solitary figure appear from a side gate and walked towards her in a hurry. Barbara's movements were jittery, her arms crossed over her chest, her face shrouded beneath a baseball cap, and a thick parka coat to keep warm. She was furtively checking over her shoulder, her eyes scanning in all directions for any sign that they were being watched.

The first thing that struck Karen was Barbara's features. Her eyes were sunken, with dark circles around them. She appeared gaunt, her cheekbones more pronounced, and her hair, predominantly grey now.

"Thanks for meeting me, Barbara. Are you happy to talk here, or would you prefer to sit in my car?"

Barbara shook her head and chewed on her fingernails. "Here is fine."

Karen noticed the woman shivering and couldn't decide if it was through fear or the fact that there was a cold chill in the air. "I want to help you. You need to tell me what's going on. If you're in trouble, I can help."

Barbara gulped air as if struggling to breathe. She licked her lips. "I did witness what happened to you and your colleagues. I saw it all. But three men visited me. They threatened to kill me if I continued to talk to the police. That's why I told you that I hadn't seen much."

"Who threatened you?"

"I don't know. They told me if I carried on helping you with your enquiries, they would kill me, and they said they knew I had a granddaughter, and said I would never see her again."

Barbara's eyes misted over, and the first tears began to escape from the corner of her eyes.

Karen decided to stay silent to give the woman space to talk.

"They gave me five grand to disappear, so I went to stay with a cousin in Aberporth because it's so remote. I hoped they wouldn't find me there."

"So why did you get in touch?"

Barbara wiped the tears away with the back of her hand. "Because I couldn't hide forever. The guilt was killing me, and I was looking over my shoulder wondering if I was being watched. Each new person I came into contact with, every person who looked at me, every time the door knocked, I wondered if they were here to…"

"Would you recognise the men if you saw them again?"

Barbara nodded. "I think so. But to be honest, I never want to see their faces again. How can I fucking live like this? I'm a bag of fucking nerves. I'm not sleeping well and not eating properly. My stomach's in turmoil; I'm scared shitless. How can this be the rest of my life?" she pleaded, searching Karen's eyes for an answer.

Karen saw the torture in Barbara's eyes and felt her pain. She too had been trapped in this living nightmare and understood what Barbara was experiencing.

"I've read the books. I've seen the films. I'm always going to be a loose thread. I'm always going to be a danger to them." Barbara shook her head in disbelief and stared at the floor. "You know, I want to be there when my granddaughter is eighteen, twenty-one, or even gets married. With the way things are now, I don't even know if I'll be here next year."

"I can help Barbara. I want to help. Let's take a walk. Tell me what you saw."

They followed the path around the park, only silencing their conversation when passing a dog walker or jogger.

"I remember walking along the road, and I heard the screeching of tyres and loads of shouting. I turned to look over my shoulder and saw a dark car heading straight for me. I jumped out of the way, tripped and fell to my knees. No one helped me. I think everyone was shocked. When I got up, the same car was ahead of me, perhaps twenty or thirty yards, and it was all going off."

Karen desperately wanted to make notes but didn't want to do anything that would jeopardise the situation. As Barbara recalled the scene, Karen's mind dragged her back to that eventful day as the tragedy unfolded.

"There were a lot of cars stopped at different angles. The men got out of one car and began waving baseball bats. At first, I thought it was two rival gangs kicking off. It happens all across London these days, doesn't it? And then I saw it. One of them was waving a gun. He fired it up in the air, and everyone slammed to the floor." Barbara slowed, her mind replaying the memory. "I wanted to run. I think we all did. Everyone looked at each other, absolutely petrified. I watched one of your officers run towards the man with a gun. But he didn't get there in time… Next thing, I heard a load of screams as an officer clutched his chest and fell to the ground."

"Did you hear any names being mentioned?" Karen asked.

Barbara shook her head and narrowed her eyes. "I don't think so. Maybe. I don't know. It felt like it happened so quickly. I saw that poor woman being pulled from the car by her hair. She was dragged along the ground on her hands and knees to another car. I remember her screams. They were blood-curdling screams. Just thinking about it sends chills through me."

Karen listened intently. The recollections were similar, but Barbara's sequence of events sketchier than Karen's.

"Some men were fighting. I wasn't too sure who was who. And I heard another gunshot, like a really loud pop that hurts your ears, and one of the group fell to the floor. It was only later that I realised it was another police officer. At the time, a second shot had everyone in the street running in every direction. It was chaos, blind panic." Barbara inhaled deeply, puffed out her cheeks and exhaled slowly, as her eyes fixed on some inanimate object in the distance. "I remember hearing cars pull away, tyres screeching… and then something really weird."

"What was it?"

"Silence. It went quiet. First, I thought I'd lost my hearing. Then I heard people crying, shouting, and all the sounds returning to normal."

"This is helpful, Barbara. You're doing really well."

Barbara wagged her finger in the air as she dragged something else from the deepest part of her subconscious mind. "Tel, or Terry. Maybe both. I heard that name being shouted. Someone was telling him to grab the woman. Tel or Terry was quite a chunky bloke, carrying a bit of weight. I remember him going ballistic because his name had been mentioned."

"Did you see his face?"

"No. They all had balaclavas on, except one. I remember when the car swerved towards me, and I glanced over my shoulder. The driver was pulling the balaclava down over his face. I think that's why his car swerved."

"What did he look like?"

"Hard to say. There was a slight glare of the windscreen." Barbara closed her eyes to picture the man's face. "A round flat face, thin nose, and his eyes seemed blank. There was no expression. He just looked cold. Scary almost."

The information gave Karen the breakthrough she needed. For the first time in over a year, she was getting on top of this living nightmare and finally getting to the bottom of this. Karen made a few phone calls to organise a safe place where Barbara could stay, deeming it unsafe for her to return to her apartment. She would take Barbara there herself. Wanting to know more, Karen opened the gallery of photographs on her phone and handed it to Barbara as they set off.

"Can you have a flick through these and tell me if you recognise any faces?"

Barbara cradled the phone in her hands, reluctantly swiping

through the photographs, scared of what she might see. A few minutes later she paused, causing Karen to pull over in Barkingside High Street. "That's one of the men who threatened me in my apartment. He was the one who threw the five grand on the table."

Karen studied the image and felt the first jolt of electricity race down her spine, causing her skin to tingle. She told Barbara to carry on flicking through the images whilst they remained stationary.

Barbara froze, her hands trembling, as if holding the most delicate piece of china and feeling scared about dropping it.

"What is it, Barbara?" Karen asked, her eyes tracking between Barbara's face and the phone.

Barbara's eyes widened with fear as her bottom lip quivered. "I think… I think that was the driver."

Karen tipped her head back in the seat. Her mind wanted to scream as she thumped the steering wheel in a mixture of anger and frustration. She knew both men that Barbara had picked out, and who had orchestrated the hijacking.

26

Anger boiled deep in her system, as hot as lava, as she tossed her bag on the table and sat down in her chair. Karen felt so agitated. She didn't know what to say, or where to turn after meeting Barbara. Part of her wanted to cry, and the other part wanted to run down the middle of the street screaming so hard her lungs burnt. Yes, she was irate; it churned within, hungry for destruction, and she knew it was too much for her to handle.

Armed with this information, she worried about saying things she didn't mean, or expressing thoughts suppressed for months.

She chewed on her bottom lip logically trying to fit the pieces of this puzzle that had rattled around in her mind for over a year. *Is Barbara mistaken?* Barbara had experienced highly pressurised situations, and the mind had an uncanny habit of playing tricks. She had perhaps only seen the driver for a split second, or a few seconds at the most. If it ever went to court, prosecution lawyers would tear her to shreds, and throw it out on the grounds of credibility. *Can*

Barbara face that? Can she face such intense scrutiny under questioning? And more to the point, can I put Barbara through that?

The man Barbara had identified as being one of the three who had visited her, was a known enforcer for the Connells. For the first time, a direct link had been made between the Connells and the hijacking. The Connells often outsourced the "heavy work" to smaller firms. The head of the clan, Sally Connell, had a well-organised crime syndicate where she put several layers between herself and the coalface of the business. That's why it had been hard to find any direct links between the Connells and the raft of unsolved murders, beatings, protection rackets, and drug smuggling operations. Many officers before her had tried and failed. Rumours had been rife for many years that with police officers and bent criminal lawyers on her payroll, Sally Connell was untouchable.

Karen rubbed her eyes as tiredness spread through her like a wave. There was plenty for her to do, and several of her officers stayed late, opting to sacrifice their evening to follow up leads and update reports.

Though she didn't want to for fear of leaving another electronic breadcrumb trail, Karen logged into the database and pulled up details relating to the hijacking. It was starting to make sense. The disappearance or lack of cooperation from witnesses had all been about removing any links to the Connells. Marvin Harris, the taxi driver, had disappeared, his taxi found burnt out. Then there was Omar Rashid, the shopkeeper who'd suddenly developed amnesia when Karen visited him. She'd noticed the fear in his eyes at the time.

Karen didn't know where to start. One thing was certain, if

she continued, there would be no going back. She was about to open a can of worms which could engulf her and impact her career or possibly her life.

The cursor on her mouse hovered over the file linked to Sally Connell. She was just about to click it when Charlie Whitworth appeared in her doorway. Karen's heart skipped a beat. And all for the wrong reasons. She was scared to ask, afraid of what she might hear.

"I thought I might catch you. Have you got a minute?" he asked.

Karen noticed that his voice was flat and monotone, and not the chirpy soul she had grown used to. "Um… yeah… come in. Is this a social or work call?" she probed as her palms began to sweat and her mouth dried.

Charlie turned to look over his shoulder and glanced up and down the corridor before stepping into her office, closing the door behind him.

His visit felt clandestine and secretive as Karen shuffled in her chair and offered him a seat opposite her.

"I really don't know why I'm doing this, but I thought about what you said. I've got this for you," Charlie said, thrusting a printout across the desk. "It makes interesting reading. I don't know if it's what you're looking for…?"

Karen's eyes danced between Charlie and the papers on her desk. A part of her wanted to grab them and devour their contents, the other part of her was too scared to find out. She extended her arm across her desk and dragged the papers towards her before glancing down at them. Some of it was computer jargon Karen wasn't familiar with, but her eyes were drawn to the section labelled "IP address access". It detailed the reference numbers relating to the hijacking files, as well as the IP addresses of the computers that accessed the records. Beside them, Charlie had written the usernames.

It took a few moments for Karen to register the information, her eyes tracking back and forth between the three lines of data in front of her. Three workstations had accessed the records repeatedly. Karen's name appeared alongside one entry. She paused for a second, her eyes blinking rapidly as her body trembled. Skelton was one of the usernames accessing the files on a weekly basis. But a third username popped up, linked to an IP address in a different part of the building.

Karen looked up to study Charlie's face, who shrugged a shoulder to imply, "you asked for it."

"User access details are hidden behind layers of coding. Only second or third line support can access user details. I had to get those details by using a workaround that wouldn't leave my digital print. But someone within IT with that username has been accessing, manipulating and deleting details from the case file." Charlie paused for a moment, waiting for Karen to understand the ramifications of that before he continued. "I also found a piece of coding used to delete or shield another user ID. I tried to see who it was, but the records relating to the times and dates had been wiped. There are just blank entries, and it's those blank entries that tell me someone else accessed the system."

Karen looked confused. Much of what Charlie was saying sounded like double Dutch. She rubbed her temples and closed her eyes whilst she processed her thoughts. "So basically, you're saying that someone who is very computer savvy, or has access to someone who is very computer savvy, also reviewed details on this case?"

Charlie nodded. "Make of it what you wish, but that's on a different level of technical ability. That's in the realms of super programmers, and hackers who cover their backsides really well. That's why if computer systems are breached or hacked, it can take ages to discover it, and even longer to discover who was responsible. Sometimes we never find out." Charlie shrugged as he exhaled loudly and stood.

"I can't thank you enough, Charlie. I was hoping this would give me clarity, but it's left me with more questions," Karen replied, staring at the ceiling in disbelief.

"I know. Listen, you didn't get this from me. If anyone comes and asks me, I'll deny all responsibility. Understood?"

"Understood," Karen replied, as she watched Charlie leave.

27

Karen pulled up her duvet and rolled towards the darker side of the room. The blinds shut out most of the glow from the street lights outside her window, but rectangular boxes of light projected from the gaps on to the opposite wall. She watched the artificial yellow glow of the street lamp. She tossed from one side to the other, heavily sighing each time, her bed now a tangle of covers that snaked around her legs.

For spells she had closed her eyes and been conscious of breathing slowly, rhythmically, having watched YouTube videos on better sleeping practices. She had considered herbal sleeping pills from the chemist. They worked well, but left her mouth tasting of metal. The night had worn on. Thoughts tumbled through her mind in rapid succession. Problems resurfaced for another evaluation. Things she mustn't forget for the next day nagged at her all night. After a tortured eternity and resignation, she threw back the covers and stumbled out. Sleepless.

Last night's conversation with Charlie sat heavily with her, as she padded into the kitchen, and winced as the cold floor tiles sent a chill racing through her bare feet. She flicked the switch on the kettle and made herself a strong cup of coffee before heading into her darkened lounge and sinking into a sofa. Her mind and thoughts felt tattered. She felt lost, unable to decide on her best course of action. Karen wanted to text Barbara to make sure she was okay but thought better of it. It was too early in the morning still, and Karen knew that Barbara was safe. But there was more to it. It felt like she had a million questions she wanted to ask Barbara, certain the woman wouldn't know the answers, but curiosity and a burning desire for truth gnawed away inside her.

She had entertained the thought of tracking down Sally Connell to put the frighteners on her but doubted it would have any impact. If anything, she decided that it would cause more harm than good, not to mention the risk to her own life. No, she needed to think this through, and have a strategy. The chances of getting Sally Connell were slim to none, and they would always have junior members willing to be hung out to dry to preserve the integrity of the firm.

If she went to Hinchcliff, what would he say? Senior ranks always closed in. They would say that she had gone mad. They would question why she was looking at the case in the first place and would explain it away as a simple IT bug. Hinchcliff would point out it was a matter for the Directorate of Professional Standards, and not to worry. Not knowing who else was involved with the tampering of evidence meant she needed to be wary. Karen knew she needed to start with the weakest link, and that happened to be the person in IT. She only had a name, Karim Malik, but was determined to track him down today.

Karen put her coffee down and turned towards Manky who lay in a tight ball beside her. She ran her hand down his back. Manky responded to the welcomed attention with a purr. And the more Karen did it, the louder the purring became. "I'm sorry, mate. I keep letting you down. You enjoy these little moments, don't you? Well, I'll let you into a little secret, just between you and me. I enjoy them too!" she whispered with a smile.

With a seven-day case review on Annette Buckley's death just twenty-four hours away, the sense of urgency wasn't lost on Karen. This would be the first of many reviews, depending on how long the investigation took. A review of any case would take place after seven days, then twenty-eight days. If the case continued longer than that, further reviews would take place at three and six months, and then a year. For Karen, it helped her and the team to refocus, and reassess priorities, resources, and any oversights.

Karen checked the time. It was still way too early, and if she sat there any longer, she'd fall asleep. She peeled herself away from Manky, kissing the top of his forehead as she went back to her bedroom and stripped off before jumping into the shower. She needed to wake up and shake off the sleepiness. Karen turned the dial on her shower, the water cascading from the showerhead, so cold at first, she almost screamed. The stream thickened. She felt the waves of warm steam rising to massage her face. Though the shower would bring her pleasure, it was just another part of her regimented day, before she could return, and tumble into bed to fall asleep until her next shift.

28

The investigation had fresh impetus following the discovery of the first victim's identity and then, her possessions. For Karen's team, it meant they could begin to piece together Annette Buckley's last known movements. With so much to do, Karen rallied her troops and gathered them in a large sweeping arc around her. The work she had tasked Brad with had revealed startling insights, and the sheer volume of data had led to Brad pulling in a few junior officers and support staff to follow up active lines of enquiry, search the database, and document it for the benefit of the team.

Karen stared at the photographs of Annette Buckley. She averted her gaze from the dismembered limbs and chose instead to stare at several photographs retrieved from the woman's house whilst searching through her possessions. In her mind, the case now felt real. With the name and face, Karen felt like she was dealing with the death of a real person.

"Okay, team, we have a lot of digging to do now. Time isn't

on our side, but we certainly have a lot more information than we did twenty-four hours ago." Turning to Brad, she signalled for him to feedback on what he had discovered.

Brad's bulging eyes widened, and several gulps of air saw his Adam's apple bounce up and down like a bobbing apple in water. "Enquiries into Annette's background showed she was the owner of Lighthouse Children's Home in Hackney. She ran it for fourteen years. It was closed by Annette in 2002 after it failed several local authority inspections."

"Why was that?" one of the officers asked.

"Not one reason. I believe it was a catalogue of issues that ultimately worked against the viability of the home. Questions were raised about the welfare of the children under Annette's supervision. The authorities also identified that the kitchen and bathroom facilities fell way short of minimum standards."

Another officer sitting beside Brad chipped in. "The council opened a new care home not far from the existing site, and a few of the *problem* kids were transferred out."

Karen picked up on the accentuated tone. "Problem kids?"

Brad continued after shooting the other officer a glare, annoyed at her stealing his thunder. "Yes. There were complaints from local residents about unruly kids. Things like a rise in petty crime, stealing from shops, smoking, and underage drinking. Apparently, the off-licences were forever turning away kids from the home."

Karen's mind drifted back to all the photos featuring Annette with various children. "And what did Annette do about it?"

Brad shrugged. "Apparently nothing, boss. Some residents

hurled abuse at the kids and took it up directly with Annette about making their lives a misery. It hit the local press a few times, with disputes between the council, the care home and residents."

A member of the civilian team distributed printouts of the press articles.

Karen skimmed the details, studying pictures of residents standing on the same doorsteps that Karen had seen in the photographs she had unearthed. The photographs in the newspaper painted a different picture altogether. Half a dozen residents held up home-made banners calling on the council to shut the care home down. She rolled her eyes towards the end of one article. When contacted by the newspaper, the council had been unavailable for comment.

Karen moved on saying, "Steve, can I ask you to organise a follow-up on the door-to-door enquiries that were done by uniform? It's not that I don't trust them, but we need to be certain of anything suspicious, or out of the ordinary involving Annette in the days and perhaps weeks preceding her death. Can I leave it with you?"

Steve nodded.

"Where is Jeff?" Karen asked, scanning the sea of heads around her.

Jeff raised a hand from the back of the crowd and wiggled his fingers.

"Ah good, there you are. Any updates on CCTV so far?"

"We are still looking, boss. But we have managed to retrieve a short piece of footage from a few hundred yards away, and there's just a fleeting appearance of a grey BMW. No other visuals apart from that, but the model appears to be an E30, or something remarkably similar. It may or may not be something," he offered with a heavy and exaggerated shrug as he tipped his head to one side.

Karen instructed him to continue looking, and if necessary, extending the search zone.

"I think we all need to examine Annette's background in greater detail. Neighbours said she led a quiet life, and was retired, though didn't talk to many people. Who did she talk to? Check her work record, review her contacts, who else did she know? And whilst you're at it, do all the usual checks."

Brad flicked through his notes before commenting. "We've already started that process. So far, she didn't appear to have a mobile phone. We drew a blank there. She did have a pension, and that was paid into her bank. We are still waiting on her banking records. I'll let you know as soon as we have more…"

"What are you thinking?" Karen asked.

"Do you think her death is connected, or could this have been a random attack by a complete psycho who operated under the radar for however long?" Brad asked.

"At the moment we need to keep an open mind. Dr Rai did say that there was a high probability that Annette Buckley knew her killer. That's why we need to investigate her background as thoroughly as possible. Do a quick search and see if she had been the victim of any crimes. There are so many things that we don't understand about her as a person. What was she doing before managing the care home? Did she have any run-ins in any of her previous roles?"

"What about the husband?" an officer asked.

"Well, we know that he passed away, so unless his spirit came back as an aggrieved and downtrodden husband, I think we can safely rule him out!" Karen winked.

Karen's comment was met with a brief ripple of laughter that lightened the mood.

"No, I mean what if her death was connected to him? We don't know enough about his background, and whether he had put Annette in danger?" the officer clarified.

"Check it out… follow your hunch. I don't need to spoon-feed you, do I? How long have you been in the job…? About four years, right?"

The officer smiled, taking the hint.

Karen glanced at her team as she wrapped up the briefing. "Find out more about the Lighthouse Children's Home. We need a list of employees and kids who attended, plus any complaints, any further press articles, dig up anything you can. I want the names of anyone connected to Annette, in any shape or form. Her dentist, if she had one, her doctor, the postman, even the local newsagent. We need to look for anything or anyone who may be able to shed some light on Annette Buckley and why someone wanted her dead."

29

Karen hovered by the incident board as her team scattered in all directions, a sense of urgency in their movements. The longer the case dragged on, the harder it would be to find the killer. She stared at the images of the two victims and the crime scenes. Both victims had differing MOs in the manner of death, and for the time being, the team needed to work on the Annette Buckley case until they discovered further information relating to the deceased male in the sewers.

Other than pictures of the victims and the locations, the incident board still looked sparse. Information had been added relating to the Lighthouse Children's Home, and Karen was sure further details would soon fill the gaps. The press office had already been inundated with requests from reporters relating to the second gruesome discovery just two days ago. Karen knew it wouldn't be long before the reporters, including her favourite, Wallace, concocted their own stories and spread unhelpful rumours.

Wallace had tried her number twice this morning, but she

had chosen to ignore him. Though the second victim had attracted plenty of attention, there had been little for onlookers to see other than the comings and goings of the emergency services.

Karen checked her phone. She would need to leave for the post-mortem on their second victim, but something niggled her about the dismemberment. Dr Rai had talked about the perpetrator being highly disturbed, lacking in emotion, and experiencing a deep desire to feel superior to others. She laughed inwardly, as that described Skelton in a nutshell. Karen wondered if the person they were looking for was in a relationship. Did his partner know that he lived a double life? She wondered what he did for a job. If he had a need to feel superior to others, did he hold a supervisory or managerial position? Did it satisfy his need for domination in the normal world?

A barrage of questions swam around Karen's mind. With two cases at different stages, it became a fine balancing act between where to apportion resources, and which one took precedence.

"Are you ready to go, boss?" Jade asked, as she came alongside Karen and nudged her in the ribs.

"Yes. Sorry. I was in another world. I keep looking at this board, thinking that at some point it's going to make sense. Let me grab my handbag and I'll meet you downstairs by the back door?"

"Sounds good to me. I'll just go to the loo first," Jade replied before heading back to her desk.

Karen whipped out her phone from her back pocket and tapped out a quick message to Barbara.

"Hope you're okay. Let me know if there's anything you need? I'll check in with you later. Karen."

JADE AND KAREN put on protective gowns as soon as they arrived at the mortuary. One of Karen's officers viewing the beginning of the post-mortem breathed a sigh of relief when the cavalry arrived in the form of Karen and Jade, who breezed through the double doors into the examination room.

"Ah, Karen, Jade. Good to see you. I'm glad you could both attend. We've had a ball uncovering the nastiness inflicted on this poor soul," Wainwright said, placing his hands on his hips and taking a step back to view the cadaver.

Karen and Jade positioned themselves around the other side of the table and took a moment to examine the victim. Karen noticed the full extent of the man's injuries, which hadn't been clear when she had seen him in the dark and gloom of the sewers.

"You were a bit delayed with this one? What have we got?" Karen asked with a sigh.

"Unfortunately, I was. I needed to conduct a post-mortem on two bodies found in a car, with no evidence of foul play. Okay, to your victim. Male, aged somewhere between sixty and seventy would be my guess. He has an inflamed liver, with heavy scarring. Commonly associated with cirrhosis, which would suggest that our individual liked a drink or two. I would say that there is evidence of at least ten to fifteen years of decline in the quality of his liver."

"Any other basic background details on our vic?" Karen asked, as her eyes travelled up and down the victim.

"There are no surgical implants for identification, so we'll take DNA samples for NDNAD and MPDD, as well as fingerprints. Forensics can relay back to you, if that's okay, Karen."

Karen agreed that that would be the best way forward.

"Both tibiae are broken."

"Both?" Karen asked in surprise.

"Oh, yes. Both. Recent breaks as well. There is extensive bruising to both of his shins. I would speculate that he was beaten around the lower legs. I need to not only assess the mechanism of production of the bruising, consider the impacting surface and the magnitude of force used, but also estimate when the injury was caused."

Wainwright grabbed a metal probe and pointed towards the dark discolouration on both shins. "Although not producing a 'mirror image' of the offending agent, the bruising has produced characteristics that are typical of the impacting agent. For example, round or discoid small bruises can be caused by fingertips, and tramline bruising can be caused by objects that have a longitudinal cylindrical surface such as a rod or baseball bat."

Karen noticed the dark discolouration in stripes across the surface area, suggesting that the injuries had been inflicted with something like a metal pole or, as Wainwright suggested, a baseball bat. She winced, imagining the damage and the subsequent pain.

"When I initially examined the victim after they were bought in, the bruising was fresh enough for me to assume they had been carried out no earlier than twenty-four hours before the discovery of the body. The bruising was fresh."

"How can you tell?" Karen probed.

"Well, for example, a deep bruise in the thigh muscle might not appear for a day or two after its infliction and might have a fresh appearance, whereas a bruise over a bony prominence and where tissue is loose – for example, the eyebrow or in this case the shin, would appear very quickly and with accompanying swelling."

Jade made notes whilst Karen watched Wainwright's technician taking further photographic evidence.

"Have you found out anything about this victim?" Wainwright asked.

Karen shook her head. "Not yet. I was hoping we'd have something to go on after today."

"Yes, you should be able to. His teeth are intact, so we have taken dental impressions, and will check dental records for any likely matches."

"What else can you tell us about his injuries? I remember seeing that horrific image of a metal cage with rats inside it strapped to the man's belly. Why? Why would someone do that?" Karen shook her head in disbelief.

"Indeed. That was particularly nasty. We discovered extensive internal damage beneath where the cage was strapped to the deceased's body. And we also found a wound to the left side of the abdomen," Wainwright said, pointing to a large disturbance of flesh to an area just beneath the ribcage.

"Inflicted by a knife or something?"

"I don't think so, Karen. It's too large, and the surrounding tissue structure is extensively damaged. There doesn't appear to be any clean lines that would suggest that a knife was used."

"What then?" Karen asked as she came round and leant forward for a closer look.

Wainwright shrugged. "I'm not certain at the moment. We'll take skin and tissue samples for forensic analysis. Hopefully, that will throw up something for you."

"What about his cause of death?" Karen asked, just before leaving.

"Blood loss foremost. He had multiple lacerations to his chest and thighs. There is substantial evidence of small flesh bites. I think he provided a hearty meal for the rats. The loss of blood probably attracted more of the little buggers."

KAREN HAD NOT BEEN LONG in the office when she received a reply from Barbara stating that she was well but scared shitless. The woman felt like a sitting duck cooped up in the hotel room. Karen replied, offering reassurance, and said she would try to call Barbara later. There wasn't much Karen could do for the time being. If she was honest with herself, she hadn't even thought about what to do next. Karen had been so focused on dealing with two ongoing cases, that of the last few hours, Barbara only flashed through her thoughts occasionally. But it was enough to start doing something about it as she left her office and made her way through the building.

Hovering outside in the corridor, Karen tried to get things straight in her own mind. She needed to be in and out quickly without attracting too much attention. On the odd occasion she needed to come to this department, the floor remained silent, as team members sat hunched over their keyboards, tapping away furiously, and staring at their screens.

Before opening the door to the IT department, Karen took a deep breath and blew out her cheeks. She had a rough idea who she was looking for, and what he looked like based on Charlie's description. Her eyes scanned the various team members. Several of the desks were empty, which made her search easier. Or so she thought. *I can't see him, where the fuck is he?* Her eyes moved from one face to another. *Bollocks, he's not here.*

She checked every face as she scanned the room for a second time. Karen was just about to give up when she clocked him. The person she was looking for was sitting at a different desk to where he should have been. Her breath caught in her throat, and her skin tingled as her heart raced. So much of her wanted to charge over, drag him to the ground, and beat a confession out of him. Karen felt herself getting edgy as her eyes bore into his face before jolting herself out of her trance and leaving.

She was now one step closer to resolution.

30

Karen made her way through the desks in the incident room, stopping with various officers to find out what they were working on, and to offer any advice to speed up the process. One of her team confirmed that Annette Buckley had been the victim of an attempted break-in three years ago that had been disturbed when Annette heard the back door being forced.

Other than that, there were no other reports on the system of Annette Buckley being a victim of any other crimes, and for the time being Karen would keep an open mind as to whether that was connected to her death. On the face of it, it appeared to be nothing more than an opportunist burglary, the likes of which happened up and down the country every day.

"How are we getting on, Jade?" Karen asked as she shunted aside stray paperwork on Jade's desk and sat in the empty space. She knew the team worked tirelessly to chase down every lead and snippet of information. Glancing around, many officers appeared to be glued to their phones, and the rest stared at their computer screens.

"We've got seven officers out and about doing door to door and following up lines of enquiry. But we have already gathered information on the children's home. Annette Buckley was in charge. She had a manager reporting into her, and there were between two and three assistants present at all times."

"And how many children?" Karen asked, jotting down the salient points in her notebook.

"No more than twelve at a time. In total they housed sixty-four children over the time that they were open."

Karen grimaced. She knew every one of them could offer a potential insight into Annette's life and may have witnessed something that eventually led to her death.

As if reading Karen's mind, Jade continued. "We've traced most of them. Unfortunately, five are deceased, sixteen are overseas, thirty-one moved to other parts of the country, and only four remain in London. We have eight that are unaccounted for, but we are trying to find them."

Karen pursed her lips into a thin line and nodded slowly as she crunched through the numbers.

"Let's start with the London names first, and then have others in the team trace and contact the thirty-one that moved to other parts of the UK. We can focus on the overseas search later. It's a bloody big job. Let me know if we get stretched, and I can ask the DCI for a few more bodies to help us."

"Do you think it will help?" Jade asked. "After all, many of them only had contact with Annette whilst they were kids.

For all we know, Annette may have preferred the hands-off approach?"

Karen agreed with Jade's theory. It was often the staff who had day-to-day contact with the children, so it would be key to track down Annette's staff. "Have we uncovered anything else to help us build a picture of Annette's life?"

"We are working on it. I've got someone looking at her husband. He had a colourful background. Arrested in his forties for violent disorder, after attacking someone in a pub. The case was dropped when the victim decided not to press charges. Before that, Alfie served eighteen years in the army. Royal Anglian Regiment, with several tours of NI. We'll contact the regiment to see if we can get a copy of his conduct record, but knowing them, they'll refer us back to the MOD."

The feedback piqued Karen's interest. She had heard of cases where soldiers and their families were targeted following "the troubles". Even though Alfie Buckley had died of cancer, she wondered if he had been involved in something that put Annette Buckley in danger. She asked Jade to keep her in the loop if anything surfaced. Back in the seventies and eighties, there had been claims and counterclaims of brutality, torture, and unauthorised killings on both sides. The Provisional IRA had been a formidable force, and the tentacles of their organisation stretched far and wide across the political and social landscape both in Northern Ireland and in the UK.

"Who are the four that we have still in London?" Karen asked.

"Alan Clark, Jack Dobson, Amy Burchill, and Kelly Roberts."

"Are they all clean?"

Jade shook her head. "Jack Dobson is the only one who gets flagged up on our system. He was cautioned for violent behaviour…"

Jade was cut off in mid-sentence as Brad rushed over towards her desk.

"We've got a name for the manager of the children's home. Martin Shields, aged sixty-six."

"Great job, Brad. Let's track him down so that we can have a conversation with him," Karen instructed.

Brad raised a brow. "We already have. He's the corpse from the sewer."

Karen's eyes grew wider. "Seriously?"

"Yep. A misper report was filed two days ago when Martin Shields didn't turn up for his AA meeting. All attempts to contact him failed. The AA organiser even went round to his place. There was no answer. The picture on the misper report resembles our victim."

Karen and Jade jumped up and headed for the incident board, with Brad a few steps behind. The three stood in line as Brad pinned a photo of Martin Shields alongside photographs taken from the crime scene and the post-mortem. Though the pictures of Shields carried bruising, the similarities were undeniable.

For the first time in a week, the reality dawned on Karen. The two cases she was investigating were now connected. The manager and the owner of Lighthouse Children's Home had both been murdered. One question hovered in her mind. Were they committed by the same person?

31

Karen spun on her heels. "Listen up, everyone. We have a new focus to our investigation!" she shouted, to make sure those towards the back of the incident room heard her.

Officers who weren't on urgent calls hung up and swivelled their chairs around in Karen's direction. Others, including many of the support staff, grabbed their notebooks and made their way towards Karen, grabbing any available space to listen to their new instructions.

"We've had it confirmed that both deaths are connected. Annette Buckley was the owner of the Lighthouse Children's Home. Early indications suggest the body discovered in the sewer was Martin Shields, the manager of the home."

The revelation was enough to stir up interest amongst the officers gathered, as they exchanged looks of surprise.

"We are still waiting on a formal identification of Martin Shields either through his dental records, or by a positive ID from the facilitator who ran the AA meetings that

Martin attended. Either way, I'm hoping to get his ID confirmed today. For the time being, we go on the assumption it's him."

"Where do you want us to start?" Steve asked, pen in hand, ready to jot down his instructions.

Karen studied the faces of her assembled officers, each one of them ready to step up their efforts. "It's vital that we plough all of our resources into tracking down all the staff, the ex-residents that were in their care, and everyone connected to the home. And by that, I mean the council, whoever did their maintenance, the catering, the postman, the milkman, the whole bloody lot. If anyone had contact with the home, or any of their staff, then we need to know about it."

"Do you think it was done by the same person?" DC Craig Martin asked.

Karen crossed her arms and looked over her shoulder at the various photographs pinned to the incident board. "I'm not sure. That's what we need to find out. We have two murders, with two differing MOs."

"What are the chances that it was committed by someone connected to the children's home?" another officer asked.

"That's an avenue we need to explore. We need to understand the full spectrum of people connected to the children's home. We might be looking at an ex-resident, or someone who came there on a regular basis," Karen speculated.

Craig chipped in again, to offer a different perspective. "Could have been a parent who gave up a child or had a child taken away from them? They might have heard all the complaints, and the local protests, and felt a huge sense of injustice?"

"Look into that possibility for me, will you, Craig?"

Craig nodded.

Karen looked at the time on her phone. It was getting late. "Right, those of you who are staying this evening, get cracking. The rest of you, get yourselves home and have an early night. We're in for a couple of busy days. Jade and I will visit the names on the list, starting with Alan Clark first thing tomorrow morning. Good luck, team."

32

"Delete, delete, delete," Karen muttered as she zipped through her inbox, pausing every so often to open an email if it looked interesting, or was flagged as being important. Several of her officers were scheduled to attend OST in the coming days, but Karen couldn't afford to have any of her team away whilst they were making progress with the investigation. Officer safety training was an integral element that every officer needed to undertake to make sure they were able to handle themselves in difficult and often physical situations. Karen made a mental note to have a word with the officers in question to check they were happy to have their OST deferred by a few weeks.

Karen had agreed to meet Jade at the office before they headed out to track down the names on their London list. And whilst she waited for Jade to arrive, it gave her time to catch up on emails that she'd ignored for the past few days and update Skelton. The meeting with Skelton had been frosty and awkward, like most of their meetings. She had struggled to look at Skelton in the eye after what Charlie had told her. It riled her that Skelton's name was one of the usernames that had accessed files on a weekly basis. During the meeting, Karen noticed that Skelton avoided making eye contact as well, more so than usual. To her, he appeared jittery, but then he was always jittery. His eyes darted away every time their eyes connected.

Nevertheless, Karen had updated him on their recent developments, confirming that they had names for both victims, with confirmation coming in during the night that Martin Shields had been identified through dental records.

She grabbed the mug from beside her mouse mat, took a swig and then promptly put the coffee down with tight pursed lips. She had been expecting enough heat to bring her out of her winter tiredness, but instead it was tepid like old bathwater.

"Are you ready to go, Karen?" Jade asked as she appeared in Karen's doorway. Dressed up for the cold, it looked as if Jade had come straight from the car park and hadn't bothered to take off her coat and scarf, the latter swaddling her neck.

Pushing back her chair, Karen straightened her suit jacket. "Yep, I'm ready to go. Have you got the address details that we need?"

"Yes, I pulled them off last night just in case I couldn't get into the office and needed to meet you at the first one."

"God, you think of everything, don't you? Always prepared. I bet you were in the Guides…" Karen teased.

"Actually, I was. And I even remember the promise. "I promise that I will do my best, to be true to myself and develop my beliefs, to serve the Queen and my community, to help other people and to keep the Guide Law"," Jade fired back.

"All right, smarty-pants. You've bloody got an answer for everything!" Karen said with a smile.

"There is no upper age limit to being a member, so you can still join. It's not too late."

"Jade, will you stop it! You're turning into an anorak."

"You can come round to mine one evening. We can get pizza in, and I can talk you through all the badges that I've sewn on to my camp blanket."

"Jade, enough! You're fast going down in my list of favourite people."

Jade threw her head back and laughed as they shared a bit of banter. This was why Karen got on so well with her. Jade had a natural knack of bringing light-hearted humour to every situation, and just when Karen needed it. She jostled Jade out of the door to her office, and they made their way down to the car park, with Jade giving her a running commentary about the history of the Girl Guide movement.

THE FIRST ADDRESS they visited was for Alan Clark. He lived in a first-floor apartment in a small residential block. After five minutes of knocking, they were about to move on to the next address, when a neighbour from an adjoining apartment poked their head around the corner.

"Can I help you?" the man asked.

Karen turned towards him. She estimated the man was in

his fifties, with an unshaven grey stubbly look, and untidy hair. He was still dressed in his blue chequered pyjamas, with a burgundy dressing gown thrown over the top. Blue woolly socks finished off the fetching look.

Karen opened her warrant card and flashed it in the man's direction. "We are looking for Alan Clark. Does he still live here?" Karen asked, jabbing her finger in the direction of the door they were stood at.

"Oh yes, he does. Is he in trouble or something?"

"No. Nothing like that. We wanted to ask him a few questions about a matter that we are dealing with at the moment," she said reassuringly.

"He's at work. The garage on New North Street. Do you know the one?"

Karen shook her head, being unfamiliar with the location. "No, but I'm sure we'll find it. Thanks for your time."

"Not a problem. I know Alan well; he tells me everything. Whatever, you can ask me. I'm sure I can help. You sure you don't want a cuppa or something? It's a bit chilly out this morning, isn't it?" the man suggested.

Karen turned down the invitation and thanked him as she left by the stairwell.

"Nosey busybody," Jade whispered as she followed behind Karen.

THE SMELL of grease and oil crept up Karen's nostrils as they found the only garage on New North Street. A radio blasted out music, and halogen strip lights cast a bright artificial glare that made Karen squint.

A mechanic climbed out of the inspection pit beneath a white Audi and wiped his dirty and greasy hands on an equally dirty and greasy cloth. "Yes, ladies. How can I help?" he asked in a chirpy, cockney accent.

"Alan Clark?"

The man shook his head. "No, I'm Brett Ward, the owner."

"We are looking for Alan Clark. We need to ask him a few questions," Karen said, holding up her warrant card.

The man's cheery disposition soon melted, and his face took on a more sombre and serious expression. It was a look that Karen had seen hundreds of times as soon as she announced herself as a police officer. Ward studied her with suspicion, his bright cheerful face long gone.

"I'm afraid Alan isn't here. He is out dropping a customer's car off. Is he in a bit of bother?"

Karen assured Ward that that wasn't the case, and they merely wanted to ask him questions about an ongoing enquiry.

"What's Alan like as an employee?"

Ward shrugged and continued to wipe his hands on the greasy cloth. "He's quiet, hard-working. I've never had a problem with his timekeeping. Most of the time he's outside before I've arrived. Officially our hours are eight thirty to five thirty. But he's here about eight fifteen, and he'll stay until he's got his job done. I've never seen him leave before six. He's a grafter, so what can I say."

Jade stood in the background taking notes, whilst glancing

around the workshop. Loose tools littered the workbenches, spanners hung off the wall to her left, all arranged in size order and compressed air lines snaked across the blackened floor. A small plastic box with sandwiches and an apple sat beside the radio, alongside a mug of tea, which had gone cold as she noticed the darkened scum on the surface.

"He should be back in an hour or so, if you want to pop back?" Ward suggested.

"We've got a few other places to go to, but we'll pop back for a quick word with him if that's okay?"

"Yeah, fine by me. He's normally quite prompt when he drops off a customer's vehicle. Even if it takes ages, I don't shout at him, he doesn't like it."

"I think most employees don't like being shouted at, do they?" Karen added sarcastically as she turned and retraced her steps out of the garage, avoiding the odd pool of engine oil that had collected in the uneven surfaces of the concrete floor.

Ward shook his head. "No, not like that. I mean, if I shout at him, he shrinks back and skulks off, and goes all quiet for ages like a little schoolkid. Anyone would think he's ten years old."

33

Whilst Jade hovered outside, Karen ran into the nearest coffee shop and picked up two cappuccinos before dashing back to the warmth of the car. The temperature had dropped a few degrees in the last few days. The cold that had seemed mild at first now numbed her face and extremities. What residual heat she had absorbed in the café was gone. It had been her buffer, but unwittingly she had squandered it believing her thin winter jacket was equal to the task of preserving her body heat. As she marched across the pavement towards the car, with each breath more heat rose in puffs of white vapour.

“Jesus, I hate the fucking cold. I swear I must have been a lizard in a former life. My joints ache, my back aches, everything feels so stiff,” Karen fumed as she handed Jade both cups, and jumped in, shaking off the shiver that raced through her.

“It’s not that cold. It’s all in the mind.”

"Says the woman who has a scarf long enough to wrap around her neck three times, and still have enough to do a loose knot," Karen said, looking across to Jade, who had buried the lower part of her face into the warmth of her scarf.

Pirouettes of steam rose from Karen's cup as she took a sip, enjoying the warmth as it trickled down her throat and warmed her stomach.

They spent the next ten minutes talking about Alan Clark, whilst checking their schedule and deciding when they'd be able to return to the garage. They both had theories about what Ward had said, which led them to speculate further on what might have happened to Clark during his childhood.

Jade turned the key in the ignition and pulled off, making her way to the next location. The satnav on her phone barked instructions as it guided them towards Golders Green, an area that neither of them were familiar with. Karen stared out of her window, watching suburbia pass by. Hendon and Golders Green had a strong Jewish population, and as they made their way along Finchley Road, Karen could see the influence that the Jewish community had had on the local area with salt beef bars, Jewish bakers, kosher delicatessens, and even a shop offering kosher wines and spirits. Orthodox Jews milled up and down the street, the men in their distinctive black suits, wide brim Fedora hats and side curl ringlets, the women dressed in dated modest clothing, and wigs.

Karen marvelled at the diversity that London had to offer, and the melting pot of different nationalities, communities, and lifestyles.

"Here it is," Jade said, pulling up in an available parking space and switching off the engine.

They had stopped in a residential street. It had an affluent feel, with lots of mature trees, several cars parked on each brick paved driveway and large houses.

The house they were visiting was one of the few houses that had been converted into two flats, and Jack Dobson lived on the ground floor of the property. It wasn't as well-maintained as its neighbours. Weeds grew up through the block paving in the driveway, the windows needed a clean, and paint blistered on the front door.

Karen rang the doorbell and waited for a few moments. She heard keys jangling behind the door, and bolts being unlocked, before the door opened just a few inches, and a man's face appeared in the gap. "Jack Dobson?"

The man's eyes drifted between Karen and Jade, before he looked beyond them towards the street. "Who wants to know?" he asked in a soft voice.

Karen and Jade held up their warrant cards. "Can we come in? We'd like to ask you a few questions about an ongoing enquiry. We won't take up much of your time."

"What questions? What enquiry?" he asked, a hint of suspicion in his voice.

Karen took a step closer towards the door. "I'd prefer to ask you these questions in private if that's okay. But equally, I'm quite happy to discuss this on the doorstep, especially if you're okay about your neighbours hearing our conversation..." Karen let the thought sink in.

Dobson hesitated for a moment, as he bit his bottom lip, before stepping backwards and allowing the door to open.

He led Karen and Jade through the hallway into the lounge and offered them a seat. He took a seat opposite them, and tucked his hands into his lap, as he teetered on the edge of the armchair, his shoulders pulled forward protectively.

Karen glanced around the room. It wasn't what she had expected as she shot Jade a look who widened her eyes in response whilst retrieving her notebook and pen from her handbag. The room was sparsely decorated. The sofas didn't match the armchair, a few dated floral photo frames hung on the walls, and a box of kids' toys sat in one corner. "Do you live here alone?"

Dobson shook his head. "No, me and my wife live here." He saw Karen glancing at the toy box. "We have a two-year-old daughter, Annie."

"Ah, that's lovely. Have you lived here long? It seems a nice area," Karen commented, trying to make small talk. She could tell that Dobson was uneasy and cautious.

"A little while."

"Are your wife and daughter here?"

"No. They're out."

Karen sighed inwardly. This was going to be harder than she imagined. Karen sensed Dobson was introverted and struggled to engage in simple conversation. "Thank you for taking the time to see us, Jack. We are involved in an active investigation and contacting people who we believe might be able to help us."

Dobson shrugged and averted his gaze towards the floor, before swallowing hard.

"This is a confidential conversation. I want to assure you

that anything you say will be treated in the strictest of confidence. We are dealing with the suspicious deaths of Annette Buckley and Martin Shields. We are trying to build a better picture of their lives, so we are reaching out to everyone who knew them. We believe from our records that you spent time in the children's home that they ran, is that correct?"

Dobson looked up, his jaw tightening. He offered nothing more than the slightest of nods.

Karen was about to continue when her phone buzzed in her handbag. She let it ring off, not wanting to interrupt the visit. "Do you have any contact with any of the others who spent time there?"

"No."

"Okay…" Karen thought this was harder than pulling teeth. She knew she would have to tread carefully and give him space and not pressurise him. "When were you at the care home?"

Dobson's voice had petered out to nothing more than a whisper. "I was there ninety-seven to 2002. I went in there at the age of twelve and left when I was seventeen."

"What was it like there?" Karen probed. By now she was leaning forward on the sofa, with her elbows resting on her thighs, her hands locked together, and her fingers intertwined. Her phone buzzed again to alert her of an incoming text, but she ignored it. Whoever it was could wait.

It took a few moments before Dobson began to shake his head. "Not a nice place. It was horrible."

Karen furrowed her brow. She noticed a tightening in Dobson's features. His whole body looked tense. "Horrible? I know it might be difficult for you, but why don't you tell me what it was like, so that I can better understand?"

Dobson wrung his hands in his lap and then looked up and stared Karen dead in the eyes. "The place was brutal. They were really strong on discipline and punishment. Lots of kids got into trouble. There was nothing for us to do. We were bored. We used to sneak out and nick sweets from the sweet shop and fruit from the food shops."

Karen found his response peculiar. "Fruit?"

"Yeah. It was a treat to get a bit of fruit. We never had any. It was a luxury. That's why we used to nick apples, bananas and pears. Some of the others used to nick fags or beer from the off-licence."

Jade busily scribbled notes. Karen looked over Jade's shoulder to see that she had circled "brutal" several times.

"You said brutal. And punishment. What do you mean?"

Dobson remained silent, refusing to answer Karen's question.

"Did you see anything? Or did anything happen to you?"

"No. That's all I know. I didn't see anything. It's just what I heard from the other kids. I just kept my mouth shut and did as I was told."

Karen's phone vibrated in her bag again and continued to do so. She stiffened, annoyed at the repeated interruptions as she fished it out of her bag. Glancing at the screen, she'd had two missed calls and one text from Barbara. Karen felt her heart sink and fear gripped her insides. *What's so urgent?* She opened the text and scanned the message quickly.

"I'm scared. I can't live like this. It was all a mistake. How can I carry on being scared of my own shadow??????"

Karen felt shudders race down her back as her mind somersaulted with worry. She needed to focus and get through this meeting quickly so she could call Barbara back. Having come so far, she couldn't afford to lose her.

"Okay. Okay. Did you ever see anyone turn up at the children's home who threatened Annette or Martin?" Karen asked, attempting to refocus on their visit.

Dobson grimaced. "I can't remember. Listen, my wife and kid will be home soon. I don't really want you to be here when they come back. Do you mind leaving? I don't know any more. I can't help," he said, shrugging his shoulders.

"Of course," Karen replied, standing up and waiting for Jade to pack away her notepad and pen.

Dobson led them into the hallway and opened the door. Karen stopped beside him and handed Dobson her business card.

"If you think of anything else, my number is on that card. Don't hesitate to give me a call."

Dobson fiddled with the card between his fingers, and opened his mouth, as if to say something, and then stopped.

Karen picked up on his hesitation but didn't push it. For the time being she'd have to be patient as she and Jade walked back up the front drive.

34

"What did you make of that?" Jade asked as she started the car and remained stationary.

"There was more going on at the children's home than we were led to believe. It sounds like nothing was going right, with complaints from locals, and problems with the kids."

"Mismanagement?"

"I think it's more than mismanagement, Jade. We are just touching the surface. The way that Ward spoke about Alan Clark, and seeing Jack Dobson's reactions back there, you have to question what really happened."

"It puts a whole new angle on the two murders, doesn't it?"

Karen stared out of her passenger window and murmured in agreement. "Listen, can you do me a favour? We need to take a bit of a detour to Barking. I need to see someone."

Jade turned in her seat and narrowed her eyes in confusion. "Barking? None of the people on our list are in Barking?"

"I know. It's that… um… I've got a friend who is in a pretty bad way, and she's staying at the Ibis in Barking. Domestic problems. She didn't sound too good this morning, and I want to pop in for ten minutes to make sure she's all right. I thought I'd be able to see her tonight, but I don't think I'll have time. Do you mind?" Karen asked, doing her best to cobble together a reason, even though it sounded lame.

Jade shrugged her shoulders. "Fine with me. You're the boss." Jade grabbed her phone and pulled up the details of the Ibis before dropping the postcode into her satnav and heading off.

Karen continued to stare out of her window. She felt shit for lying to Jade, but what could she say? She desperately wanted to tell her, but without knowing the full scale of the problem she was dealing with, she didn't want to put Jade in jeopardy. She was already worried about Barbara and her sanity. That was enough to stress Karen out. And even though she could trust Jade, she didn't want to put her in a position where Jade's trust conflicted with her professional duty. Karen knew the sensible course of action would have been to place Barbara in a protective safe house, but that would have meant telling Skelton, and God knows who else, that she had been actively investigating a case that had nothing to do with her.

If she exposed all of that, everything else would be out of her hands. Karen would have feared for Barbara's safety, and probably would have faced a disciplinary and possible suspension.

It took Jade forty-five minutes to travel along the North Circular to Barking as traffic and a stop at a newsagent slowed their journey, which only added further guilt to the feelings she already had. Jade pulled up into a parking bay and switched off the engine.

"You want me to come in with you?" Jade asked.

Karen smiled and shook her head. "No, it's fine. I don't want her to feel more embarrassed than she already is. I'll only be a few minutes. Back in a sec," Karen replied, opening her door and dashing off.

The rumble of heavy traffic along the A406 just metres away from the hotel faded into silence as Karen swept through the revolving doors and weaved her way through the corridors until she found room one two seven. She knocked three times, as they had agreed. The muffled sound of footsteps padded across the carpet and stopped. Karen imagined that Barbara was peering through the spyhole before she heard the door being unlocked and opened.

Barbara peered from around the gap, before opening the door to allow Karen to come in.

"Are you okay?" Karen asked, even though she knew that it was a stupid question.

Barbara paced around the small room, moving between the bed and the table. Her arms were folded tight across her chest, and her hands gripped the sides of her T-shirt. "I don't think I can do this. This place feels horrible and so claustrophobic."

Karen reached into her handbag and pulled two magazines, a sudoku puzzle book and a bar of chocolate. "These are for you," Karen offered, placing the items on the bed.

"Thanks," Barbara offered in return without a smile.

Karen rubbed her temples and looked around the room. She didn't blame Barbara for feeling like this, as the room offered nothing in the form of creature comforts. The magnolia walls and red carpet wouldn't win any house design awards. A double bed sat to one side, a small table with one chair beside it, and a small dressing table upon which sat the TV. Other than basic tea-making facilities, a pokey en suite bathroom and the travel bag with her clothing and toiletries, Barbara had nothing, and she had been under strict instructions from Karen to not leave the room.

Though she felt sorry for Barbara, this was something Karen didn't need at the moment. Yes, she needed Barbara, but babysitting her was putting a drain on her mental energy. "I know. But it's the safest place I can think of. Until I figure out who is involved, I need to protect you. No one, and I mean no one, knows that you're here. And it has to be like that."

"What happens if they find me? You won't be able to protect me!" Barbara shouted as tears welled in her eyes. "I was trying to help, and now my life has been turned upside down. I can't cope any more… I can't cope."

Karen strode over to Barbara and grabbed her by both shoulders and sat her down on the edge of the bed, before sitting beside her, and holding the woman's hand. "I know it's hard. But I'm determined to get to the bottom of this. Witness statements and information relating to the hijacking were being deleted off the system. Someone was trying to manipulate and remove the evidence."

Barbara's eyes widened as she placed a hand over her mouth.

"I found someone who had access to the system in our IT department and they were removing the data."

Barbara trembled. "Oh my God, oh my God. If someone in the police is doing this, what chance have I got of being safe? I can't trust anyone."

Karen gripped Barbara's arm tight as the woman tried to get up. She could see the panic etched in her red and swollen eyes. "Listen, now that I know someone has been deleting the information. I need to deal with them. They will lead me to the person behind all of this."

"And then what? We both die!" Barbara screamed.

"No. And then we get justice."

"I don't want to die. I want to put all this shit behind me and live my life how I used to."

"And you will. Let me deal with this… okay? We trust no one, and that's why I'm asking you to stay here. Please?"

Barbara buried her face in her hands and after a few moments nodded.

Karen breathed a sigh of relief, although in her heart, she knew she couldn't promise anything.

"EVERYTHING OKAY?" Jade asked, as Karen opened the car door and dropped back into her seat.

Karen blew out her cheeks. "Yes. You know what domestics are like. They can be challenging at the best of times. It's even harder when it's your friend."

Jade started the car and moved out of the car park. “It hasn’t turned physical between them has it?”

“Oh God, no. They are both very headstrong and stubborn. And it’s constant slanging matches between them. There’s never been any violence. And to be honest, she’s a bit of a drama queen. This time she’s stormed off, which isn’t a bad thing. It gives them plenty of time to think.”

“Oh well, I guess that’s a good thing. But you managed to calm her down?”

“Yes. At least for the moment. I said I’d give her a buzz later.” Karen curled her bottom lip up over her top lip as she looked out of her window. She felt guilty for not only lying to Jade but also promising Barbara something that was out of her power.

35

The next person they needed to see was Amy Burchill, another former child resident of the home who lived about thirty minutes away in Woolwich and would mean grabbing the Woolwich Ferry to South London. Thankfully, they were already on the right side of London to make their way along the A13. With them both feeling hungry and in need of a strong cup of coffee, Jade grabbed a McDonald's drive-through in Beckton, and they tucked into their food as Jade continued the journey.

"I can't tell you the last time I had French fries," Karen oozed as she savoured the salty fries in her mouth. "I know they're dreadful for your waistline, but oh my God, they are insane."

Jade laughed as she picked at her fries, which nestled in her lap.

They had both opted for chicken sandwich meals, with large diet Cokes, and black coffees to finish.

"Do you know, when I was at school, there was a guy in my year who held the record for eating the most amount of McDonald's in one sitting. He was only sixteen, but quite large," Karen said.

"You're kidding?"

"No. I'm deadly serious. I remember a load of us went to McDonald's with him. And he ordered… check this out… four Big Macs, four large fries, and a large strawberry milkshake."

Jade shot Karen a look of consternation, not believing a word.

Karen nodded furiously. "I'm serious. He polished off everything. We were pissing ourselves laughing. I've never seen anything so hideous in my life." She laughed.

Karen was just about to take a bite from her chicken sandwich when her phone rang. She fished it out from the pocket in her door to see that it was Brad before pressing the green button and putting him on loudspeaker. "Hi, Brad, what's up?"

"Boss, whereabouts are you?"

"We've just left Beckton and are heading towards Woolwich on our way to see Amy Burchill. Why? Is there a problem?"

"No. No problem. We've tracked down an employee from the Lighthouse Children's Home. Lesley Skinner, aged sixty-nine. You're on the right side of London, to be honest. She's in the hospital." There was a pause whilst Brad checked his notes. "She's at Queen's Hospital in Romford."

Karen felt the first hint of concern squeeze her chest. "Don't tell me…"

"No, nothing like that. Thankfully, not another victim. She's in there with emphysema. It might be worth you paying her a visit?"

Karen checked the time on the dashboard, and looked at Jade, who shrugged and nodded to suggest it wasn't a problem.

"Yep, will do that. Jade can turn around and we'll make our way there."

"Oh, by the way, boss, the team has been going through the boxes recovered from Annette's house. Most of the property belonged to the children's home. The files, equipment, cutlery, pots, aprons, the whole lot. It belonged to the council but was never taken away. It looks like rather than leave it there, she boxed it up and took it home."

"That would make sense."

"There was another thing, boss. A bit weird, but we discovered an old tobacco tin. It had seventeen teeth in there. But they were quite small."

"Okay, Brad, thanks for letting us know. I'll touch base with you once we've been to the hospital," Karen said before hanging up.

"I don't get it. Why take everything home? She clearly didn't use any of it." Jade questioned.

"Maybe it was a big part of her life," Karen replied, though she wasn't sure why Annette would keep all those items.

Though the hospital car park was a sprawling space, Jade had to crawl up and down the aisles along with several other cars waiting for spaces to become available. There didn't appear to be any orderly patience whilst waiting, as cars jostled and fought for the random spaces that appeared. A frustrating fifteen minutes passed until a space became available down one of the rows, and Jade shot forward to grab the spot just as another car approached from the opposite direction with the same intention.

Karen screamed at Jade to get there first, as both cars arrived at the spot at the same time. There appeared to be an uncomfortable stand-off, with the driver of the other car refusing to budge and gesticulated that she was there first.

"Fucked if they're going to get this spot," Karen said, whipping out her warrant card and flashing it through the windscreen, as she pointed for the driver to back off. It only took seconds for the woman to become extremely apologetic and reverse to allow Jade to pull in.

Jade turned towards Karen, a look of feigned disgust on her face. "That was really naughty of you! I can't believe you did that."

"Yeah, I know. But buggered if I was going to sit in this car park any longer. Besides, we are on official police business. So tough shit," Karen grunted as she pushed open the door and stepped out of the car.

Jade caught up with her as they went through the entrance of the hospital and searched out Lesley Skinner's ward. "You don't have a lot of patience do you?" Jade teased as Karen held the door open for her.

Karen rolled her eyes. "That's why I hate hospitals. It's those bloody car parks. They suck the life out of you and raise your blood pressure at the same time. I'm sure they do that deliberately, so you end up being a patient at the hospital," she said, laughing.

After asking one of the nurses to point them in the right direction, Karen and Jade made their way towards the far end of the ward, and the last bed on the left. As they peered around the curtain, they found a frail-looking woman propped up on a few pillows. Her grey hair was thinning, lank and greasy. Her cheeks were sunken, and her arms which rested on top of the bedsheets were thin and leathery. An oxygen mask covered part of her face, and the gentle hiss of air filtered through the mask as Lesley Skinner took short and raspy breaths.

Her eyes flicked between Karen and Jade as they stood to one side of her bed.

Karen pulled out her warrant card. "Hi, Lesley, I'm Detective Inspector Karen Heath and this is my colleague Detective Sergeant Jade Whiting. Your name has come up in an investigation that we are involved with, and we wondered if you'd be able to answer a few questions?"

"What is this about?" Lesley asked, her voice gravelly and coarse.

Karen moved in a little closer so other patients couldn't hear their conversation. "We are investigating the murders of Annette Buckley and Martin Shields. We understand that you knew them?"

"Murders…?" Lesley asked. The news surprised her, as she began to cough and splutter.

Karen took a step back to give the woman space. "Yes, we've discovered their bodies and have launched a murder investigation. We are keen to talk to everyone who came into contact with them. Our lines of enquiry have identified that you once worked at the children's home?"

Lesley nodded and stared up towards the ceiling, her chest heaving through a combination of a lack of oxygen, and the anxiety that crept up upon her after hearing the news. She tried to mouth a few words but struggled as her weakened air sacs wheezed and coughed in protest. She pulled her air mask away and coughed mucus into a tissue as her lungs rattled.

Karen winced and turned towards Jade who looked equally distressed and had repositioned herself to the foot of the bed where she could grab more hand sanitiser gel from the dispenser hanging off the bed frame.

"I'm really sorry to ask you these questions at a time when you feel so unwell."

"It don't matter. I'll be dead soon. This is the third time I've been in here in a year. And I've been stuck in this bed for three weeks. They've taken me off the steroids because it's not helping. Every time they reduce my oxygen levels, the oxygen saturation in my blood drops into the seventies. I don't think I'll be leaving this bed and going home again, do you?"

Karen shrugged, not knowing what to say. The woman had already come to terms with the fact that she was approaching her end-of-life. "You're in the best place. The nursing team here are fantastic, and I'm sure with the right treatment, you'll be out of here and back home, even if you have to have oxygen at home."

Lesley tutted.

"What can you tell us about the Lighthouse Children's Home?"

Lesley took a couple of heavy drags of oxygen, allowing it to penetrate the deepest parts of her lungs before she continued. "It wasn't a very nice place. How it was allowed to continue to run is beyond me. I'm not surprised that Annette and Martin are gone. Martin was a vicious character. He ran that place like it was a borstal. He was strict with the kids."

"How strict?"

"Every time they misbehaved he would lock them in their bedrooms. He'd punish them by telling them to go to bed without dinner. And that's just the beginning of it." Lesley looked at Karen, a mixture of silent pain, both emotional and physical, pouring from her eyes. "I felt sorry for those kids, but there was not a lot I could do. There was no way I was going to go against Martin. I would have lost my job."

"Did you witness any threats being made towards either Annette or Martin whilst you were there?"

Lesley shook her head.

"Can you think of anyone who'd want to harm them?" Karen asked, softening her voice.

"I don't know."

"What did Martin do that was so bad? And you said he ran it like a borstal. Did you witness anything?"

"Just leave it. They are gone now. It's better that way. Let the memories fade with them," Lesley said with a stutter as she gasped for breath and coughed violently, her torso lifting off the bed with each violent hack.

Noting Lesley's discomfort, a nurse approached the bed and checked on her patient. She checked Lesley's saturation levels before turning to Karen. "I think Lesley needs to rest. The more she talks, the more it aggravates her chest. If it's really urgent, perhaps you can come back later today or tomorrow and continue with your questions?"

Karen reluctantly agreed, leaving Lesley's bedside as a nurse pulled the curtains around to give the woman privacy.

It was only when they were back in the corridor outside the ward that Jade breathed a sigh of relief. "No wonder people fall ill when they come into hospital. Patients coughing and spluttering, who knows what germs are circulating in the air, and I'm sure the woman in the next bed had shit herself, either that or had bad guts," she said, gagging whilst furiously pumping more hand sanitising gel into the palm of her hands from the dispenser on the wall.

Karen rolled her eyes. "She had emphysema, not the bubonic plague, you doughnut! After what Lesley said, I'm almost certain that the children's home had something to do with this now. Whatever happened there was directly or indirectly responsible for the deaths of both Annette Buckley and Martin Shields."

36

Wintry air swirled around Karen as she walked up the path towards the communal door, taking every lick of warmth it could. The fall of daylight had led to the fading of what little heat there was. She wrapped her arms tighter across her chest, pulling her coat closer and tucking her chin downward into the collar. Her breath was now only visible under the sporadic street lights, the few which still lit up the street.

Their visit to Amy Burchill had thrown up nothing of significance. A common theme surfaced, as many of those that they visited appeared to have little or nothing to say. Their reluctance concerned Karen, and she sensed that both Jack and Amy were holding back. Questions about what they had to hide sat uncomfortably with her. Karen had called the office to get her team to run checks on both of them for completeness. The fact that both came across introverted, hesitant, and socially awkward wasn't a coincidence. Karen's questioning hadn't been intense, nor aggressive in her mind, but both displayed qualities that she would have expected from interviewing children or teenagers.

"Why are we always visiting tower blocks?" Karen huffed as she searched out the apartment number on the row of buttons and pressed the buzzer.

Jade shrugged and didn't answer, as she stamped her feet, trying to keep warm.

The intercom crackled into life, and a timid voice replied. "Hello?"

"Is that Kelly Roberts?"

"Yes. Who is it?"

"It's Detective Inspector Heath from the Met Police. We'd just like to come in and ask you a few questions. Would you mind opening the door?" Karen asked. There was a pause for a few seconds, as Karen raised a brow in response.

Without an answer at the other end, the door buzzed, and the locking mechanism released. Luckily, Kelly's apartment was on the third floor, so Karen and Jade didn't have far to travel in the lift, which repulsed both of them. The smell of weed, urine, and stale air had them shielding their faces from the worst of it.

Kelly Roberts was waiting for them in her doorway as they approached. Karen and Jade held up their warrant cards before Kelly invited them in and through to the lounge.

Karen and Jade both grabbed an armchair each, leaving Kelly to sit in the middle of the sofa, looking like a forlorn soul.

"Can I get you something to drink like a tea or coffee?" Kelly asked, her voice soft and meaningful.

"No, thank you. We won't keep you too long. We know it's getting late, but we wanted to ask you a few questions," Karen replied, glancing around the room. A modest-sized TV sat in one corner, showing a series on Netflix. There was a similar theme to what she had seen at Jack's place. The apartment was sparse, with not many creature comforts. A stack of magazines rested on the dining table that had been pushed to one side. A little midi system sat on a shelf behind the door, the likes of which she hadn't seen for many years. Everything looked second-hand, but the room was tidy and well maintained. The wallpaper wasn't to Karen's taste, but she imagined that it had been up for many years, and the council hadn't been bothered to replace it.

Karen noticed that even though Kelly dressed down, she had a natural beauty with a flawless complexion. She wore tight black jeans, an oversized jumper, and brown UGG boots, which no doubt were needed in the apartment, as Karen noticed the slight chill. Kelly had long dark hair hung loosely down the middle of her back. It was clear to Karen that Kelly looked after herself, and had a softness about her rounded face, especially when she smiled. She reminded Karen of Katie Holmes in the film *First Daughter* that she'd recently watched on Netflix.

Kelly's brow knit together. "What's this about?"

"There isn't an easy way of saying this, but we are investigating the deaths of Annette Buckley and Martin Shields. And as part of our investigation, we are contacting all former employees and residents to build a bigger picture of both the care home, and the two deceased." The second

Karen mentioned their names, she noticed a change in Kelly's demeanour. It was as if she was witnessing the same reaction seen in Jack Dobson. Her shoulders rounded, she dropped her head and stared towards the floor, clenching her hands into a tight ball before burying them deep between her thighs. Karen looked across at Jade, who hadn't taken her eyes off Kelly.

"I wondered if you'd be able to tell us about your time at the Lighthouse Children's Home?" Karen asked.

Kelly didn't look up but shook her head in reply.

"Kelly?"

Her long hair haloed around her as she shook her head. "I don't want to talk about it. It's a part of my life I'd like to forget. I'm sorry I can't help you."

Karen picked up on the anguish in her voice, a silent pain. She softened her voice and leant forward in the armchair. "Kelly, we really need your help. We've spoken to a couple of ex-residents, but everyone has been reluctant to say much other than it wasn't a nice place. Please help us to understand what happened there. Yes, we are investigating the murders of Annette Buckley and Martin Shields, but we also have a duty of care towards you and all the ex-residents." Again, Karen noticed the impact at the mere mention of their names. Karen signalled for Jade to try.

"Kelly, Karen's right. We do need your help. But we need to understand more about Annette and Martin, and the care home if we are going to crack this case. Regardless of what Annette or Martin were like, they both deserve answers."

Kelly erupted and threw her head back, staring at the ceiling for a few seconds before levelling her eyes with

Jade. Tears streamed down her face, spittle dribbled off her lips, and her eyes appeared inflamed with anger as her face contorted. "That woman deserves nothing. Death is too good for her. She needed to feel the pain that we all felt. Don't you see that? Don't you fucking see that?" she screamed, thumping her fists on her thighs.

The unexpected reaction took Karen and Jade by surprise as Karen looked around the room and spotted a box of tissues on the dining table. She grabbed a few before handing them to Kelly and planted herself down beside her.

Jade continued. "I'm sorry that it's upsetting to bring up your history, but what happened? We're here to help. If something's happened, we are here to get you justice."

"How can you give me justice when that man is dead? Don't you get it? Look at me. Just look at me!" Kelly replied, jabbing her own finger into her chest. "All you can see is me on the outside, but you can't see what happened to me on the inside, can you?" she added, now jabbing her finger into her temple. "They fucked me up!"

Karen headed off to the kitchen to make them all a drink before returning and placing a hot cup of sweet tea in Kelly's hands. "Drink this."

Jade waited for Kelly to compose herself, before trying her luck again. "Whatever's happened, you can't bottle it up forever. Tell me about it and maybe we can help."

Kelly took a few sips of tea, savouring the warmth on her lips as her eyes darted between Karen and Jade. She sniffed and blew her nose hard into the tissue, before wiping the snot from her top lip.

It seemed an eternity before Kelly spoke again. Her eyes

were fixed on the wall opposite her, flicking wildly as she gathered her thoughts and took a few deep breaths to compose herself.

"I… I…"

Jade noticed the quiver in Kelly's voice. "It's okay, in your own time."

"I… was raped by Martin Shields when I was thirteen years old."

Jade shook her head ever so slightly as she looked in Karen's direction. A combination of sadness and disgust in her eyes.

Another sniffle and a heaving breath. "That's why I am not sad that he's dead. I was thirteen years old. And it didn't happen once. It happened every few months for as long as I can remember. He would give me a pill to swallow. It used to make me really drowsy, dizzy, and sleepy. I was out of it most of the time."

Karen jotted down a few notes as Jade listened.

"I was taken to what was called the black room. I was locked in there and raped in pitch blackness. Eventually I would come around and be in total darkness."

"And did anyone know about this?" Jade asked.

Kelly shrugged. "If I raised my voice or screamed to be let out, he'd come back to rape me again. He would only let me leave when he was ready to let me out."

"I'm so sorry," Jade said, as she gave Kelly's hand a squeeze.

"That's just the half of it. I fell pregnant. I lost the baby as the abuse continued. He would take me to the black room and kick me in the stomach over and over again until one day I aborted," Kelly added, as she began to sob into her hands, grief consuming her as her shoulders shook. The cries that came from her throat sounded like those of a wounded animal fighting for its life. A mixture of guttural screams that punctured the silence of the room.

"Surely others must have heard this, what about the other staff?" Jade asked.

"The kids all knew about it, but we were all too scared. I'm sure it happened to others, but everyone was too frightened to say anything. We were just kids. We didn't have parents to protect us. The people who were there to protect us either didn't care, or hurt us more…" Kelly said, as her voice quietened.

Jade felt waves of nausea washing over her. Child abuse was something that every officer had dealt with at some stage in their career, but it never got easier to handle or to hear.

"Did you tell anyone about this?" Jade asked, holding Kelly's hand again.

"Just one person. Jack Dobson. He was the only one that cared. He was like my big brother. The more he tried to protect me, the more he was singled out for punishment. Martin was awful to him. That man robbed us all of our childhoods and most of our adult lives as well. Look where I've ended up…" Kelly said, as she waved her hand around the room. "A one-bedroom council apartment. No one wants me."

Jade whipped out her notepad and pen and wrote down something before handing it to Kelly. "This is a unit that we've dealt with on many occasions. They help people like yourself to deal with the things that you've experienced. I'll get in touch with them for you, so hopefully you'll hear from them soon."

"I'm not a basket case," Kelly replied, waving the piece of paper in the air.

"I'm not saying that you are. But they are really good at dealing with people who have been the victims of sexual abuse. You can't keep this locked up forever, because it will do you more harm than good. At least speak to them when they call you, and it's up to you whether you decide to accept their help or not. Okay?"

Kelly nodded and sniffed loudly.

37

Karen hammered on the door and rang the doorbell several times. The light came on inside as footsteps hurried along the hallway. The illumination crept up the front drive as Jack Dobson open the door. Karen and Jade barged in without giving him the opportunity to object.

"I think we need to have another chat, don't you, Mr Dobson?" Karen said firmly as she walked into the lounge.

Dobson hurried in behind her open-mouthed, a mixture of shock and consternation leaving his eyes fixed wide. Jade followed behind him, making sure he didn't make a run for it.

"What's this about?" he said in a hurry, his movements animated and edgy.

Karen turned to face him and stuffed her hands in her pockets. "I don't think you've been very honest with us. You see, I believe you know a lot more about what happened at the children's home then you're letting on. Would I be correct in assuming that?"

Dobson shook his head in a hurry, as he hovered on the spot, unable to stand still. "I told you everything."

Karen dropped her head to one side. "Really? You used the words brutal punishment and discipline on our earlier visit. Why would you say something like that if you didn't have evidence to back it up?"

"Dunno. I guess it's based on what I picked up from other people. Nothing happened to me."

"So you said, Mr Dobson," Karen replied, crossing her arms. "When we asked you about the bullying, harassment, and whether you had heard of anyone being on the receiving end of it, why didn't you say anything?"

Dobson shrugged a shoulder. "I didn't clam up. I dunno what you mean."

Karen decided to drop the bombshell, having listened to enough of Dobson's excuses. "Kelly Roberts." She let the name sink in, whilst registering Dobson's reaction. He stiffened at the mention of the name.

"We've just been to see Kelly Roberts, and we know what happened. You knew more than you were letting on. Why?"

Dobson remained silent, staring at Karen, a pained expression etched in his features as his brow furrowed.

"Mr Dobson, we are not here to give you a hard time. We are trying to find out the facts, and background to the cases we are investigating. Why didn't you tell us about Kelly?"

Dobson bowed his head and looked exhausted as he stepped back and dropped into the sofa.

Karen pushed him again.

"Who was going to believe us after all these years? We were kids then. It was our word against theirs, even as adults. I saw the deaths being reported on the news, but who could I tell? If I had said something, you lot would have pointed the finger of suspicion at me."

"Why would we do that, Mr Dobson?"

"Because of what he did to Kelly and because I had a few run-ins with him. She was like my little sister, and I tried to protect her from him. But anyone who stepped out of line was taken straight to the black room."

Karen narrowed her eyes. "Tell me about the black room?"

"It was a room in the attic. If we saw anyone being marched up there, we knew they were in trouble. He didn't go up there for any other reason. No one could hear you scream when you were locked in the black room. There were no windows and no light. Everything was black in that room. The walls, the floor, and the door. Everything. You had no concept of time when you were up there. It was just you, your tears, and the sound of your heartbeat hammering in your ears."

"It was a council-run care home, so surely when it was visited by council staff, they would have known about the room in the attic?" Karen asked.

"No. The whole front of the room was hidden behind a huge stack of boxes that Shields always put in the way when he knew they were going to get a visit. No one ever knew it was there. There was a little tin box and a pair of pliers on a shelf just outside the door to the black room. If we had a tooth that was falling out, or needed fixing,

Shields would give us a tablet before tying us to the chair and pulling it out himself rather than taking us to a dentist."

On hearing that, Karen felt a wave of anger ripple through her muscles as her hands curled into tight fists. "You were taken to the black room every time you tried to stick up for Kelly?"

Dobson nodded. "Occasionally, he would drag me to the toilets and put my head down the bowl before flushing it. He said I deserved to be flushed down into the sewers and left to the rats because I was nothing more than a piece of shit."

Karen shot Jade a look of concern and then encouraged Dobson to continue.

Dobson fidgeted on the sofa before returning his gaze towards Karen. "I was locked in the black room on lots of occasions as a punishment. For twelve hours at a time. There was a solitary chair in the middle of the room screwed to the floor. There was no toilet in there." Dobson winced in embarrassment. "If you weren't tied to the chair, you'd piss or shit on the floor. And then when Shields came back in, he'd make you clear it up so that it was ready for the next person. To know that was the same room where Kelly…" Dobson couldn't continue as his eyes misted, and his jawbones flexed.

"I'm sorry to hear that. They must have been terrible experiences for someone so young," Karen muttered.

"Yep, they were. I'm not sad that they are dead. They deserved it. They were more unfit to look after us than our own parents."

"What happened to yours?" Karen asked.

"Mum was single. Dad took off. And she wasn't the maternal type. She gave me up. There's not much to say other than that."

Karen checked her watch; it was gone nine p.m. "Are your wife and child back?"

"No."

"It's gone nine p.m., so surely your daughter should be tucked up in bed by now?"

He ground a toe into the carpet. "They're not here. And never will be."

Karen's eyes widened. "Excuse me? What do you mean?"

"My wife left me a few weeks ago and took Annie with her. She couldn't cope with my mood swings. One minute I was sad, the next happy, the next angry and wanting to put my fist through a wall. It was too much for her. To be honest, I don't blame her." Dobson sounded dejected.

Jack Dobson's broken life unravelled in front of Karen's eyes, and the more he spoke, the sadder he looked.

Karen and Jade left Dobson not long after, leaving Dobson with his haunting memories.

"Blimey this is a nightmare," Karen sighed as she settled into the passenger seat of Jade's car. They sat in silence for a few minutes, reeling from what they had heard.

"How can this go on in modern-day society and not be picked up?" Jade said, airing her thoughts. "This was a council-run property, and the owner and manager were able to pull this off under their eyes."

Karen stared out through the windscreen into the darkness. The revelations from Kelly Roberts and Jack Dobson had blown their case wide apart. It had given her potential motives, but as yet she was no clearer at identifying the suspect. The whole evening had been difficult for her to accept. During the conversation with Kelly, she had spoken about how the abuse had affected her ability to trust men, with a string of failed relationships behind her. Kelly was introverted and scared, even though she wanted so much more from her life, but the memories of the past kept coming back to haunt her.

It was particularly difficult to hear that the level of abuse Kelly had suffered, and the later aborted pregnancy had left her with internal damage and the inability to have children. Karen shook her head in disbelief. How could someone who had been through that ever move on? The dreams of a happy life, and a family life that Kelly had briefly mentioned were just that now, dreams that would never be fulfilled. Karen felt for the woman as her pain tugged on her heartstrings and filled her with sadness.

"I think we should list Jack as a potential suspect. He has more motives than anyone else. His own abuse, Kelly, a broken marriage, and above all else, guilt."

38

It was still dark when Karen arrived at the office, having given up on the idea of getting a good night's sleep. Upon arriving, she made a strong coffee, before touching base with her team covering the night shift.

She'd struggled with sleep during the night. Her head was filled with dozens of thoughts and "what ifs" that constantly flooded her mind. Scrolling through her Instagram feed, trying to tire herself out hadn't worked. She'd succumbed to sleep when she dozed off around three a.m. but had woken less than two hours later with bloodshot eyes and heavy black creases which she hid with a ton of concealer before leaving the apartment.

With a second coffee by her side, Karen sat on the floor in one of the spare rooms, surrounded by boxes recovered from Annette Buckley's house. She had spent the last thirty minutes sifting through the files. For the first time in many years, she felt personally affected by the revelations from the night before. As police officers, it wasn't uncommon to witness the sharp end of child abuse. But like Karen, many officers kept emotions out of it, and saw the children as either victims or witnesses. But the stories from last night affected her at a deeper level, and she found herself tossing and turning during the night as her mind conjured up images of children crying, the black room, and the vicious assaults the children must have endured.

Around her were several Manila folders, each one containing the notes of a child resident, along with a photo of them pinned to the outer cover. As she scanned the innocent faces, her heart squeezed in her chest, they looked so weak and defenceless. Not one of them smiled for the camera, and knowing what she knew now, it was no surprise.

She flipped open one folder and studied the handwritten notes. Charlie Atkinson, aged nine. His notes referred to him being a constant bed wetter. The instructions given to staff were that he was to not receive anything to drink after six p.m. But what Karen found more upsetting was the note that his bedsheets were to be changed only once a week as he needed to learn to control his bladder. Karen shook her head and tutted in disbelief.

The next folder she picked up belonged to Megan Harris. Megan appeared to be on the receiving end of the punishment regime. She was categorised as being unruly and disobedient. There was a reference to her stealing strawberry laces from a newsagent. Karen's eyes widened as she read further. Megan was caught with sweets under her pillow. Her punishment was no food for twenty-four hours.

The case files were littered with stories of misery and harsh punishment. She would have expected it in the workhouses in the eighteen hundreds, not modern society.

Another file belonged to a sixteen-year-old called Aidan McLeish. His notes painted a picture of a troubled youth, who had run-ins with the staff and local residents. He had been caught on several occasions stealing cigarettes from an off-licence, before being returned under duress to the children's home. Karen's eyes widened when she read an entry that he had threatened Martin Shields with a knife during one altercation. Aidan remained at the home for a further seven months before running away. The notes indicated that police were unable to trace him. She was torn from her thoughts when Jade popped her head around the door.

"Morning, you're in early."

Karen yawned and stretched her back before checking the time on her phone. "I could say the same about you, since you weren't due in for another hour."

Jade came in and knelt beside Karen as her fingers trailed over the folders. "I couldn't sleep to be honest. I kept thinking about Kelly most of the night. I don't understand how she'll ever be able to rebuild her life."

"I know. I think that's just the tip of the iceberg. I've struggled to find anything positive in these files. There are no words of encouragement, no successes, not even an achievement. It's like these kids were forgotten." Karen briefly outlined the evidence of abuse uncovered in the files.

Jade shook her head. "No wonder Kelly said she was pleased that they were dead. It makes you wonder what was missing in their lives."

"That's easy. Love. They needed a loving home, loving parents, and the chance to just be kids!" Karen's mind wandered as she imagined the difference those simple things would have made. "The chance of having a normal family life, playing in the garden, dinner around the table, silly family arguments, even opening Christmas presents on Christmas Day."

Jade agreed. "It's left more broken people than fixed ones. These kids needed to feel safe, warm, and loved. They've been left with a tainted past, nightmares, and mental and physical scars."

Karen reflected on Jade's words. She thought about Jack's description of the black room. Everything black, which summed up his mood. Jack told them about how the chair was screwed to the floor in the middle of the room. And what alarmed Karen was the presence of leather wrist and ankle restraints for the unruliest. Jack mentioned that most children incarcerated in the black room soiled their underwear rather than the floor to avoid cleaning it up.

Karen picked up the small tobacco tin discovered amongst the boxes. She conjured up an image of the pliers alongside the small tin and realised why it sent so much fear through the kids. It was the most barbaric thing she could think of. Jack revealed that if any child struck one of their adult carers, the child was strapped to the chair in the black room, and a tooth was pulled out as punishment. As she opened the lid, her breath stuck in her throat when she realised how small the teeth were. They looked no bigger than baby teeth. Karen sniffed and cleared her throat as she felt sadness well up inside her.

"We live in such a sick world, Jade."

Jade appeared lost for words and offered nothing more than a nod in agreement as her eyes misted over too.

39

Karen stabbed the doorbell to the small terraced house in Ealing and stepped back. A thin, stooping black man with a grey goatee beard and matching Afro answered with a slight smile.

Jade had made an appointment for them to visit Tracey Danbury, a retired care worker for the council who lived with her husband. It offered an opportunity to get away from the misery and sadness uncovered as they read through more files.

"Good morning, we are looking for Tracey Danbury," Karen said, as she held up her warrant card. "I understand my colleague Detective Sergeant Whiting here called ahead, so she should be expecting us."

The man nodded and waved his hand. "Come in, ladies, come in. My wife is in the lounge." His strong Jamaican accent sounded jovial and light as he led them through to the front room.

"Tracey, these lovely ladies are here to see you. I'll leave you to it. Can I get you a refreshment?" Tracey's husband asked.

Karen thanked him but declined the offer.

Tracey was in her late fifties, short in stature, but with a big smile that showed off sparkling white teeth. Her hair was in cornrows, a mixture of black and grey that aged her prematurely. She introduced herself before offering Karen and Jade a seat.

"Thank you for seeing us, Tracey. I'm Detective Inspector Karen Heath, and I believe you've already spoken to my colleague Detective Sergeant Jade Whiting?" Karen said, looking across to Jade who sat beside her on the sofa.

Tracey nodded and greeted them again with a smile. "What can I do for you? I understand you wanted to know about the Lighthouse Children's Home?" she asked, searching the faces of the officers.

Jade took out her notepad and pen, before resting it on her lap and looking around the room. It had a bright and airy feel to it, laminate flooring, and oatmeal coloured walls. A small fireplace provided a central focal point on the chimney breast, with original decorative tiles framed inside a wooden surround. There were photographs on the wall of coconut trees, and pictures taken on a beach which Jade assumed might have been somewhere in the Caribbean. The room wasn't modern but clean and tidy.

"Yes, that's right. Sadly, we are investigating the deaths of Annette Buckley and Martin Shields. And as a result, we're contacting everyone who was either at the children's home or had dealings with it. From our records I understand you were one of the care workers assigned from the council to liaise with the care home?"

Tracey rested her chin on her upturned palm. "I saw that on the TV. That's absolutely awful news. Yes, I was one of the care workers. My findings, along with others, were responsible for the eventual closure of that place."

"What can you tell us about it?" Karen kept it deliberately vague, not wishing to steer the woman in any particular direction.

Tracey took a long, deep breath before pursing her lips and sighing. Her shoulders sagged as she looked at Karen. "It wasn't a very nice place. They were just kids and didn't want to be there. They wanted to be as far away as possible, so they were always finding ways to get out."

"Why did they want to get away?" Karen asked.

"They said they felt sad being there. They were bored. They didn't like the way they were being treated, and they were never allowed to play games. Many of the boys had never had an opportunity to kick a ball around the backyard like boys do up and down the country. They were denied such simple pleasures."

"I understand a few fell in with the wrong crowd?" Karen probed.

"A couple did, yes. Sadly, they indulged in drinks, fags, and theft. There were quite a few dares going on, and obviously the younger boys wanted to act a bit older, so got involved."

"Like what?"

"Mainly stealing. Walking into newsagents and grabbing a load of biscuits or cans of drink and running out. They wanted acceptance and to feel part of the crowd, so they did silly things like that. All it did was get them in more trouble," Tracey tutted.

"Did any of them confide in you?" Karen asked.

Tracy shook her head. "I tried to get them to talk to me. But they wouldn't always tell the truth. They painted a completely different picture rather than tell me what I should have heard."

Karen gave a pointed look. "Did you see any evidence of bullying, or physical, or sexual abuse?"

"Oh Lord, don't tell me that you've uncovered evidence of that?"

"It's a line of enquiry that we are looking at. Allegations have been made and we have a duty to investigate them. I just wondered if you'd seen any evidence of that?"

"No. I wish I had. I could have acted on it. But in hindsight, the kids were so terrified that they were scared to tell me the truth. They would rather gloss over bad bits and tell me that everything was okay. I did have my suspicions, and raised them, but whenever we investigated, we found no evidence. All I could do was report on them and log my observations."

"In your dealings with the children's home, how did you get on with the staff there?" Karen asked.

Tracey shrugged. "Okay. They were a mixed bag. Some were lovely, and despite the poor wages and crap conditions, they did the best they could. Others on the other hand could frighten the pants off a corpse."

Confusion creased Karen's brow as she prompted Tracey to continue.

"A lot of the staff were just as tight-lipped as the kids. They appeared to come in and do the job and look forward to getting paid. The manager on the other hand was someone I never got on with. Martin was very cold and abrupt. I think I put him on edge every time I turned up. I got the impression he didn't like having me around."

Karen gazed at the woman. "What do you mean?"

Tracey pinched her eyebrows together. "Well, I remember on several occasions when I asked if it was okay for me to wander around and just check up on the building and make sure that facilities and services were adequate, he would always tell me that something was wrong and maintenance were due any moment. He didn't want me to hurt myself. He would fob me off with excuses like that."

"And did you see his interaction with the children?" Karen asked.

"Only a few times. I mainly had my conversations with him in his office. But I do recall a couple of occasions that whilst walking along the corridor with him, if any children appeared ahead of us, the poor little things would turn around and scurry off in the opposite direction."

Karen asked a few more questions before thanking Tracey for her time and reminding her to get in touch if she thought of anything else that may be of interest.

40

Karen gathered her team and whilst she waited for them to assemble, added photographs of children retrieved from the Manila folders. The sound of chairs being dragged, computer screens being locked, and conversations flying in all directions echoed around her as she stepped back to take in the collage of photographs.

"Okay, team. I thought I'd add images of the other children for one simple reason, each one of these may have suffered physical and/or sexual abuse during their stay in the children's home. I want you all to redouble your efforts to track down as many former residents as possible. We've dealt with all the London ones, and as you know, having read the reports on the database, their experiences were nothing short of horrific."

The look on their faces suggested that they were just as horrified, as Karen scanned the room of nodding heads. "We drew a blank with Alan Clark. He didn't give us any further information. We can now target everyone outside of

London and then extend our search worldwide until we've spoken to every single person."

"If we do find others who have experienced physical or sexual abuse at the hands of Martin Shields, it's a bloody shame that we can't hold him accountable," Jeff said, as he threw his pen on the table beside him, and crossed his arms in disgust.

Others murmured in agreement.

"I agree, Jeff. So far Martin Shields is the only one we can hold accountable. But what we can do is give his victim's closure," Karen added.

"And help them get professional support," Jade chipped in.

Karen agreed as she gave Jade the thumbs up. "In the meantime, we still need to crack on with identifying any other staff members who worked there for any period, as well as anyone else who interacted with the children's home. Have you got any updates on that?" Karen asked as she raised her hands, palms up.

Steve waived his pad in the air, before flicking through it. "We are still trying to contact one other member of staff. An assistant called David Simpson, who left London in 2011. His last known location was Coleraine in Northern Ireland. We've got local units going to see him today. I should be able to give you a further update within the next few hours."

"Excellent work, Steve. Keep me updated."

Steve continued. "We've also traced Angie Jones, a senior care assistant. She worked there for about seven years, possibly longer. She lives over in Ilford now. Brad and me are going to visit her this morning."

"Is that all the staff?" Karen asked, adding both of those names to the board.

"As far as we can tell, boss. I don't believe they could have had any casual staff without going through the proper checks. But then again, knowing what we know about that children's home now, anything is possible," Steve added.

"Is there any way of finding out if they had any casual staff who may have worked there on a temporary basis?" another officer asked.

"Only if it was recorded in their financial details. Annette could have paid them cash in hand. That being the case, then there may be no record of them." Karen realised the safety implications and the risk to the children if Annette had employed migrant workers who left no audit trail.

Chris, one of Karen's female officers, provided the rest of the team with feedback on a maintenance guy who used to fix any problems with the building. He recalled that the place felt cold, not just in terms of temperature, but atmosphere. In his words, "it was always missing something… laughter". He had gone on to say that as he walked past rooms, he would see children sitting on their beds in silence staring at their books. Occasionally one or two would look up at him, but he said the children looked odd. When Chris had pushed him further, the man had gone on to say that their eyes looked empty and dark. He wasn't even sure they were reading the books, more like staring at them like zombies.

Chris's comments had left many of the team conjuring up their own interpretations of what the man had seen.

DC Craig Martin was the next to speak. "I managed to speak with the catering suppliers. They were always asked to deliver items such as rice, cereals, bread, and pasta. There was little in the way of fresh produce other than tomatoes. One thing the suppliers did mention was that orders appeared smaller than expected for the size of the place. They put it down to the children's home, ordering extra supplies from elsewhere or possibly growing their own."

Karen grimaced. "Did they order much in the way of fruit and vegetables?"

Craig shook his head. "He said they never ordered any fruit, ever. Vegetables were mainly potatoes and onions."

"Hardly a nutritious shopping list, hey?" Karen muttered as she slowly paced up and down in front of her team. "There was something that Jack Dobson said when Jade and I visited him that makes me think it's worth pulling him in for another chat whilst we search his apartment. Let's get that done today and bring him in for this afternoon."

Karen was adamant that the killer was connected to the Lighthouse Children's Home and shared her thoughts with the team. She wondered if it was a parent who carried guilt about not only having the child taken away from them, but any abuse the child had experienced. She considered whether it was a former resident which was why she was keen to speak to Jack Dobson again.

"Could the killer be a local resident? Someone who was pissed off about the children's home, for whatever reason?" an officer speculated.

"It's a bit extreme," Karen answered. "And why now? It's been shut for eighteen years. Annette Buckley was nearly eighty years old, and Martin Shields was in his sixties. If they were pissed off about something, they could have done this sooner."

The questions caused a series of mini conversations to break out amongst the team as they debated various motives.

"Any news on the car or further sightings on CCTV?" Karen asked, more hopeful than anything else.

"No further sightings, boss," Brad offered. "We've set up an alert on the ANPR, and we're just waiting for those plates to flash up again. It's like the car has gone to ground."

"Okay, keep me updated. In the meantime, continue tracing and contacting all other ex-residents. Someone must know something that can give us the breakthrough," Karen said, tapping her marker on the whiteboard.

An officer towards the back of the crowd raised his arm, and Karen signalled for him to speak up.

"Do you think it's one person who has committed both crimes?"

Karen weighed up the question. She wasn't sure herself. "That's hard to say, especially because the MO was different in both crimes. Generally, we'd expect both victims to have been killed in a similar way. Dr Rai did mention that a killer often becomes bolder, and more dangerous as the killing spree continues. It's possible that one person committed it, but at this stage, it's worth keeping an open mind to the possibility that more than one perpetrator committed these acts."

The team were about to split off back to their desks when Karen called them back.

"I want you all to do one thing for me. When you have a moment, I want you to read the case files on the other children who were in the care home. The Manila folders are in the spare interview room. What I read this morning really hit home as to how painful their experiences were, both emotionally and physically. You can't help but be touched by their plight."

Karen looked at the sullen faces of her officers. "We need a result for them. Let's get it," she said, as she watched her team continue with their day, a sense of urgency in their actions.

41

Karen strummed her fingers on the desk as she clicked through the various entries on the HOLMES2 database. It had been a hectic few days, which meant she hadn't found the time to review the case files, and the evidence gathered. She scanned through the compiled reports on the children's home, as well as the press articles that detailed the objections from local residents. Her team had followed up with those named in the articles, and their statements added.

As she read them, it was clear that tension had simmered between the home and local residents for many years. Statements from local shop owners catalogued thefts that had taken place on a weekly basis, and with their patience stretched, residents had decided to protest.

Whichever angle she approached this from, there appeared to be aggrieved parties. Local residents, local businesses and the ex-residents. All of them had a grudge to bear, but who was prepared to kill?

Karen found it hard to concentrate today, although she couldn't be certain as to the reason. In part, Karen knew it was down to the case, and the harrowing stories uncovered. But also recognised that much rested on her shoulders about the hijacking. If she didn't do something soon, she risked losing Barbara. Karen feared there was only so much the woman could take, her nerves were already frayed.

Karen's thoughts also turned towards her sister as guilt washed over her. She hadn't been to see Jane in over a week. She had visited more often in recent weeks until this case landed on her desk. Karen chewed on a fingernail whilst she considered her options before she grabbed her phone and called Nurse Robyn Allen at the Broomfield Residential Care Home. After getting through to the receptionist, Karen waited patiently whilst they called Nurse Allen.

"Karen! Really lovely to hear from you. How are you?" asked Robyn.

Karen loved the excitement and exuberance in Robyn's tone every time they spoke. Despite her challenging role, Robyn carried a cheerful disposition that exuded optimism and happiness even in the darkest moments.

"Hi, Robyn. I'm really good, thanks, How's you?"

"I'm tickety-boo, thank you. We haven't seen you for a while, have you been chained to your desk?"

Karen let out a deep sigh. "Something like that. I've got a really heavy case on at the moment, and it's been non-stop for the past eight days. I'm not getting much sleep, and by the time I leave here, it's too late to see Jane."

"Eight days, hey? Are you involved in that human remains case on the news?"

"Yep. I'm leading the investigation on it. It's not a pretty one."

"I bet."

"Anyway, how is Jane? Can I see her?"

"Jane is fine. There's nothing for you to worry about. There hasn't been any change in her condition, and she's still getting daily physiotherapy sessions and regular check-ups on brain activity," Robyn replied. "Let me hang up, and I'll call you back on WhatsApp video in a couple of seconds when I get to Jane's room."

"Great, thanks."

A couple of minutes later, Karen's phone buzzed, announcing the arrival of the video call. Karen accepted and saw Nurse Allen's smiling face staring back. Karen found it warm and reassuring. Robyn stood beside Jane's bed and swivelled the camera around in Jane's direction. A few minutes of silence followed as Karen studied her sister's features. Jane's hair had been combed nicely, and moisturiser had been applied to her face. An air of melancholy surrounded Karen as she looked at the screen. Her sister looked peaceful, like she always did. But it didn't feel the same as sitting beside her, holding her hand, telling Jane about her day and what she had been up to.

"She looks lovely, Robyn. I probably don't say this enough but thank you so much for the way you look after her."

Robyn turned the camera to face herself. "It's my pleasure, you just need to make sure that you get back over here as soon as you can. Someone's been asking for you."

Confusion spread across Karen's face as her brow furrowed. "For me? Who?"

"Kevin Fenn. Sadly, his wife is deteriorating, and on his last two visits, he asked if you had been in."

Karen knew what Kevin was going through, and she missed chatting to him. It seemed like they welcomed a level of moral support from each other. Karen knew how lonely it could get, especially when she didn't have a shoulder to lean on. "I'll try to make it there in the next few days, but I don't want to make a promise I can't keep. Is his wife Claire really bad?"

"I'm afraid so. It could only be a few more weeks now, but we remain hopeful. The main thing is that she is stable."

"Okay, well keep me informed. I need to crack on."

Nurse Robyn Allen agreed before she hung up.

Karen leant back in her chair and stared at her computer. It felt like a long day already, even though it was only lunchtime. Breakfast seemed a distant memory as her stomach creaked and rumbled in protest. Lunch would have to wait as Jade popped her head around the door to let Karen know that Jack Dobson had been picked up and was awaiting interview downstairs, along with new information relating to him.

By the time Karen made it to the interview room, Dobson sat slumped in a chair, his hands in his pockets. Karen and Jade positioned themselves opposite, and the uniformed officer stood at the door.

Dobson stared at the desk, occasionally glancing up at Karen, before averting his eyes again. Jade did the introductions and formal caution for the benefit of the recorder before Karen continued.

"Am I under arrest?" Dobson asked.

"No, Jack. Should you choose to leave here at any point, then that's your prerogative, as is your decision not to have legal representation."

Karen began by asking a few basic questions and recapping the information he had given them relating to his experiences at the children's home.

"Jack, it's come to our attention that you were formally cautioned a few years ago. You got involved in a fight. What happened?"

Dobson took a sip of his water before looking at Karen. "I had a bit too much to drink in a pub, and someone pushed me, and then it turned..."

"Just because they pushed you?" Karen interrupted.

"Yeah. I mean, no. I spilt beer down my front, and I saw red mist. It kicked off. I'm not normally like that, but as I said, I'd had a bit too much to drink."

Karen nodded. "It doesn't take much to get you angry?"

"I didn't say that," Dobson replied, shaking his head.

Karen probed further about his life at the children's home, and his relationship with the staff. Dobson was guarded in his responses and played down the anger he felt about his treatment.

"I appreciate it was a difficult point in your life whilst you stayed there, but surely you must have been incredibly angry at the way Martin Shields treated you, and ultimately Annette Buckley?"

Jade remained silent as she took notes and studied Dobson's mannerisms and behaviour, looking for any signs of incongruence.

Dobson threw a hand up in the air. "Hold on a minute. You can't blame their murders on me. It was nothing to do with me."

"I didn't suggest that you did. I'm merely trying to understand how you felt towards them after everything you said to me."

The man let out a disgusted snort. "Yeah, I fucking hated them for what they did, and what they did to Kelly. But I'm not capable of murder. That's not me."

"You see, you mentioned and I quote, 'He said I deserved to be flushed down into the sewers and left to the rats because I was nothing more than a piece of shit,' and that's exactly where Martin Shields ended up. Left in the sewer to the rats. Now it might be a coincidence, but I don't believe in coincidences. I'm asking you; did you have anything to do with his death?"

Dobson tipped his head forward into his hands and shook his head. "No, no, it had nothing to do with me," came a muffled reply from behind his fingers.

Karen changed tack. "Are you into your cars, Jack?"

Dobson shrugged but didn't reply.

"For the benefit of the tape, can you verbalise your responses, Jack?"

Dobson sighed. "No, I'm not into cars. I drive an eight-year-old Ford Focus. But then if you checked, you would know that."

"We do. But I just wondered if you'd ever driven a BMW?"

"No."

Karen was just about to continue when there was a knock on the door, and a police officer appeared, beckoning Karen into the corridor.

Karen returned a few moments later and placed a long plastic tube on the table between them, before taking her seat. Dobson stared at it for a few seconds before looking at Karen.

"This machete was discovered under your bed by officers following the search of your apartment. Why would you need one of these?" Karen asked as she crossed her arms across her chest and leant back in her chair.

"Dunno. Protection, I guess."

Karen narrowed her eyes. "Protection?"

"It's a dangerous place out there, and after what I've been through, I don't feel safe. It's purely for my own protection."

"What do you think our forensic unit will find when they do a detailed analysis of this weapon? Do you think they'll discover evidence linking it to the murders of Annette Buckley and Martin Shields?"

Dobson shook his head wildly in denial. "No. I'm telling you I've got nothing to do with them. You can check my whole apartment and you won't find a single shred of evidence linking me to those murders."

Karen was hoping that that wouldn't be the case, especially after officers found a scrapbook. Articles relating to the children's home had been carefully cut out and taped inside. Karen retrieved photographs from an envelope the police officer had given her. She pulled them out and placed them on the table so Dobson could see them. They were pictures of Annette Buckley standing on the steps to the children's home. In one picture, Annette's image had been cut into two, and stuck into the scrapbook, her head separated from her body.

"What can you tell us about this picture, Jack?"

He glanced away. "No comment."

"Had it always been your intention to attack Annette Buckley and dismember her like in this picture?" Karen asked, tapping the image with her finger.

"No. I'm not like that. The scrapbook is so old. I don't know what I was thinking when I did that."

Karen skirted around a few more issues, before terminating the interview and bailing him pending further enquiries. The machete, clothes retrieved from Dobson's apartment, his shoes, and trainers, along with a buccal swab would be sent for analysis. Police officers reported no evidence of a meat cleaver in the apartment, and the machete wasn't sharp enough to inflict the damage that Wainwright had pointed out. But with blooded footprints discovered in Annette's house, the task would be to reference them against the items of footwear recovered.

42

"Oh my God, that smells delicious. Hope you lot have saved us some?" Karen shouted across the incident floor as they returned from interviewing Jack Dobson. The smell of pizza filled the air after her team had ordered an early dinner.

Karen helped herself to some pepperoni pizza. Jade nabbed a few chicken feast slices before dashing off to the safety of Karen's office.

Karen shut the door behind them and dropped into her chair with a big smile on her face as she stared at her food. Other than a bowl of cereal that morning, and a KitKat, Karen hadn't found the time to grab anything else. She picked up a slice off her napkin, and took a large bite, savouring the spice of the pepperoni, the crunch of the green peppers and gooeyness of the melted cheese. She closed her eyes and enjoyed the sensation.

"This is so good," Jade muttered with a mouth full of pizza. Her face lighting up in ecstasy.

They both ate with a greed as if they hadn't eaten for a week, the murmured sounds of contentment breaking the silence between them.

"I don't know what it is about pizza, but it's so bloody moreish. There is absolutely no way that I can eat a pizza slowly," Karen added, as she polished off her first slice and moved on to her second.

Jade nodded in agreement as she wiped tomato sauce from her lips. "What did you make of Jack Dobson?" she asked, turning her attention back to work.

Karen shrugged. "It's hard to say to be honest. I'm not sure he is capable of murder, but he does have a motive, and he is angry."

"There was no DNA recovered from the scene, and the only thing we have are the footprints. What happens if they don't match up to any of the footwear that Dobson owns?"

"He's angry, but he's not stupid. It's unlikely that the machete was involved in the attacks. If there's no evidence of a meat cleaver, I doubt we'd find proof of matching footwear. He could have easily discarded both items, and they could be in a landfill site somewhere in Essex."

"If Dobson was trying to protect Kelly when they were in the children's home, what if they committed these acts together?" Jade speculated.

Jade raised a good point in Karen's opinion. They had both been mistreated. There was a possibility that they both decided to seek revenge.

They continued to throw about theories when Karen's phone rang.

Karen checked the screen to see who it was before putting the call on loudspeaker. "Hi, Steve, where are you?"

"Boss, Brad and I are in Ilford. We've visited Angie Jones's address, but unfortunately, she was out. We spoke to her neighbours, and one of them mentioned hearing her door being closed earlier on today."

"Okay, Steve, knock it on the head for today, and get yourselves home. Can you agree between yourselves to visit her again tomorrow morning?"

"Yep, we'll go first thing, and then make our way to the office."

"Great, have a good evening and I'll see you tomorrow," Karen replied before hanging up.

Jade washed down her pizza with a gulp of Coke before she placed a hand over her mouth to stifle a burp. "We've nearly spoken to everyone connected to the children's home. We're running out of options here."

"I know. There's a tenuous link with Jack Dobson and that's about it at the moment." Karen's mind wandered through a myriad of thoughts, the things she had seen and read relating to this case. "Tomorrow morning can you check a name for me, Aidan McLeish. I remember from the files that he had threatened Shields and then run away not long after. The police hadn't been able to track him down. Grab his file and do a search on him."

Jade stood up and threw her napkin in the bin. "Right. I'm off for the evening, a long hot soak in the bath, a glass of wine, and an early night is on the cards. How about you?"

Karen pursed her lips and stared up towards the ceiling in contemplation. "Do you know, that doesn't sound like a bad idea," she said looking at the time on her phone. "It feels like ages since I've been home early. I've got a ton of washing to do, so I can let that run whilst having a soak, and then spend an hour chilling with the cat before he disowns me." She laughed, logging off her PC and grabbing her coat and bag. "See you tomorrow morning."

43

Karen paced up and down the pavement, nervously checking the time on her phone. She knew he would arrive any minute, and yet hadn't figured out what to say, nor how he would react. The chill of the early morning found its way through her clothes and tickled her skin. Each exhale left a white cloud as she stamped her feet to keep warm.

Karen knew that once she had said it, there was no turning back and she would have to follow through to the end regardless of the consequences. Karen had spent the night drifting in and out of sleep, battling with her conscience, visualising the many outcomes, and reflecting on what it might do to her career. But something inside willed her on. Having spent over a year thinking about the impact that the hijacking had on her life, like shackles bound to her ankles, it slowed her down, and dragged Karen back countless times to that eventful day.

She scanned up and down the street, looking for him. Karen couldn't decide what she felt. There was a tinge of excitement, but mainly fear that sat on her like a pillow over her mouth and nose. Enough air could get in, allowing her body to function, but it crippled her all the same.

She froze on the spot, as her stomach did somersaults. The fear spoke to her in its cackling voice. It told her legs to go weak, her stomach to lurch and her heart to ache as she finally caught sight of him across the road. It was now or never as he was just yards away.

"Karim Malik?" Karen said, as she crossed the road and moved alongside him.

The man stopped in his stride, confused at the randomness of the approach.

"You're Karim Malik aren't you who works in our IT department? I work in MIT."

Karen's introduction did little to ease the man's confusion.

"Yeah, I'm Karim…"

Karen still hadn't figured out exactly what to say, and just went with whatever came to mind. "Sorry, I was just heading into work when I spotted you across the road, and thought I'd grab you as I need some help. I spoke to IT support, and whoever I spoke to recommended that you'd be able to help me with a database problem that I have. I'll fill you in as we head upstairs."

"Ah, right. Why did my name come up?" Malik replied, slightly guarded as he continued to walk again, and turn into the car park at the back of their offices.

Karen brushed it off with a wave of a hand and tried to act clueless. "I don't know. I'm so not techie. It's just that when I explained the problem, the woman on the other end of the line said, 'oh, Karim should be able to help you with that,' so it's quite handy that I bumped into you, because I was going to pop into the IT department this morning. Seeing you has saved me the trip."

As they made their way into the back of the building and towards the lift, Malik asked her to describe the problem she was experiencing. Karen continued with the act, describing the nonsensical problems that she was having, that included the screen freezing, certain applications crashing whenever she tried to access them, and so on.

They stepped into the lift together, along with one other person, who got off on the next floor. Karen had already decided where she would confront him. She had chosen the second floor, which housed their training centre as it was the least used, and the floor before Malik would normally exit. Karen casually pressed the button for the second floor and smiled politely at Malik. As the lift stopped at the second floor, she turned to Malik and said she would fire up her computer and give him a call, to which he agreed.

As the doors opened, Karen stepped in behind Malik and shoved him in the back with all her might. It sent him stumbling into the corridor. He spun around in confusion, as she barrelled towards him, and grabbed him by his arm, before yanking the door to the nearest training suite and shoving him inside.

"What the fuck?" Malik yelled.

Karen slammed the door shut and blocked it with her body as she jabbed a finger in his direction. "You fucked with the wrong person. I know all about you and what you've done."

"What the fuck are you talking about?" Malik screamed in confusion and anger.

Karen's eyes widened, her cheeks reddened, and her hands clenched into tight fists. Every part of her wanted to lunge towards him and batter him to the floor. Every cell of her being wanted to release the pent-up anger and frustration that had haunted her for over a year. "I know you have been manipulating and deleting official police records. You're fucked, buddy."

Malik desperately tried to hide his growing fear. He could control the tremor in his voice to a degree. He could make himself smile somewhat, even if it looked pasted on. But his perspiration was a law unto itself, and in no time at all beads of sweat trailed down his forehead. "You've got it all wrong. Someone's fed you a load of bollocks. I don't have access to that stuff."

"I don't think so. I know it's you. And I know you have access to *that stuff.* You've been very clever in trying to hide your tracks, but I've got documented proof about your IP address, and your access gateways that have been used to manipulate the data." Karen could see the swell of panic rising. He looked like a feral cat trapped in a corner, desperately seeking a way out. His eyes darted over her shoulder towards the door. "Don't even think about it. I'll have you kicked out of here for assaulting a police officer quicker than you can take a piss."

Karen noticed Malik's glazed, bloodshot eyes, and how he furiously licked his dry lips. His movements dipped between bouts of nervous fidgeting and slow-motion reactions. He kept running his hand over his long hair, which was tied in a ponytail at the back.

Karen strode towards Malik and shoved his chest, pushing the man backwards. She continued jostling him until he was backed up against the wall. "You've taken something. I can see it in your eyes. You're already drugged up to the fucking eyeballs. What did you take this morning, a bit of charlie? Smoked a joint on the way to work? How about if we conduct a drug swipe on you now? What do you think it will throw up?"

Malik shook his head violently, the fear spreading from his eyes down his face as his teeth snarled, forcing a grating whine from his throat.

"Look at the state of you. You're twenty-eight years old. I know everything about you already. You graduated from City University with a two one degree in computer sciences. You live with your parents in Hounslow and have a twenty-five-year-old sister who works for Credit Suisse in Canary Wharf. I wonder how they'll take it when they find out you're going to prison?"

"Please. Stop. Enough. I had no choice."

"You always have a choice. And you have two choices now. You either confess or get arrested for tampering with official documents. What is it going to be?" Karen said as she jabbed her finger into his chest.

He sucked in a ragged breath. "I…"

Karen whipped out her phone saying, "You have ten seconds to make up your mind before I call this in and your life changes forever."

Unshed tears turned Malik's eyes glassy. A sheen of perspiration coated his face as he stared wildly at his surroundings, as if the walls were closing in on him. "Okay, okay. It was Skelton. It was DCI Skelton who asked me to do it. It was a favour I had to return."

"Return? What?" Karen hissed.

"I got arrested for being in possession, and Skelton made the charges disappear."

Karen stepped back and felt like she'd been kicked in the stomach. Her mind tried to make sense of what she had just heard.

"I swear, I wanted to get out. I didn't want to do it. I was too scared of him. I didn't know what else to do, especially when he said there were dangerous people who needed this information to disappear."

Karen ran a hand through her hair whilst her mind searched for a way forward. "Listen, Karim, it's not you that I want. It's Skelton. I have a duty to uphold the law, and with my DCI being a police officer, it's even more important that I bring him to justice. You have been a victim of a crime. Christ, we both have. Now, he's blackmailing you. He's done wrong to both of us."

Malik shook his head, and Karen couldn't tell if any of her desperate words had hit home. Karen called his name a few times, but he didn't respond, lost in his own confusion.

"Karim!" Karen shouted. "Pay attention. I'm not after you. I need to deal with my DCI. Here's what I want you to do, I need you to stay out of the way, so go home and stay there. Wait for my call. As soon as this is over, and I have Skelton, I'll let you know." Karen tried to sound forceful, but panic sucked the air out of her lungs.

"And then what?" Malik muttered.

"And then you can put your side of the story across and explain how you were a victim of Skelton's blackmailing, and what he threatened to do if you didn't comply."

The man's lower lip quivered. "And… and will that help? Will I be in the clear?"

Karen offered nothing more than a nod in return, knowing that she would deal with him anyway.

Malik scrambled around the desks and charged at the door, grabbing the handle, and yanking it open before racing down the steps and out of sight.

Karen's knees buckled as she grabbed the desk to steady herself. It felt like someone was standing on her chest as she gasped for breath. Waves of nausea washed over her, as bile scorched the back of her throat. She turned to her left, and ran towards the wastepaper bin, before heaving violently into it. A mixture of acidic bile and cereal left a bitter and sour taste in her mouth as she wiped puke from her lips.

Karen's mind swirled as her stomach lurched again. She dropped to the floor, fell forward on to her hands and knees, and stared at the carpeted floor. White flecks danced in her vision as the periphery darkened. Karen gasped for air.

Skelton.

44

Karen slipped into her office and closed the door before dropping into her chair. Exhaustion and tiredness racked her body. She had retreated to the ladies' toilets on the second floor and locked herself in a cubicle following her panic attack. She looked a mess and felt it too. After washing her face in cold water and straightening her hair, she'd returned to her office to retrieve her toothbrush and toothpaste. A quick clean of her mouth washed away the metallic taste, and the smell that reminded her of baby puke.

The startling revelations hadn't quite prepared her for the reality of hearing it. She knew Skelton received alerts every time she accessed the file. But to discover that he had been responsible for the disappearance of vital evidence and witness statements left her beyond shell-shocked. Her mind felt exhausted and her body felt weak from the earlier surge of adrenaline that had raced through her veins. She needed time to figure out how to handle the situation and the new information. But Karen knew that time wasn't on her side.

Karen jumped when her phone rang. It was Steve. Upon answering it, her mind switched back into work mode with news of a disturbance at Angie's house and Angie missing.

THIRTY MINUTES later Karen stepped out of Jade's car and they proceeded towards Angie Jones's house in Auckland Road. She had tried to update Skelton before leaving the office, but he was nowhere to be seen. A call to Skelton's phone hadn't helped either, having gone to voicemail.

"What have we got, Steve?" Karen asked as she met him at the front door.

"When we arrived, there was no answer again. We couldn't see anything through the windows, so when I peered through the letter box, I saw that…" Steve replied, pointing to the hallway.

Karen looked beyond their huddle. A small table lay on its side. Pieces from a broken vase littered the carpeted floor. A row of shoes had been thrown into disarray. "Was anyone inside?"

Steve shook his head. "We checked every room. There were no signs of a struggle anywhere apart from the hall. My guess is she answered the door to someone, and an altercation ensued."

"Where is Brad?" Karen asked as she entered the house, avoiding the broken vase pieces on the floor.

Steve pointed out towards the road. "He's doing door-to-door enquiries."

Steve and Jade followed her as they moved into the lounge.

Karen took a moment to take in the room. It felt cosy, with grey sofas, a brown carpet, and decorative prints on the walls. A trendy nightstand lamp stood in one corner, with a larger-than-life shade in cream. Nothing appeared to be disturbed with no signs of a robbery. They wandered through to the dining room before ending up in the kitchen. Whatever happened had been confined to the hall.

The team gathered in the front garden. Karen instructed Jade to get SOCO down to dust for prints.

Steve flicked through his notes. "Boss, the resident next door said she heard loud voices. It sounded like an argument in the early hours of this morning. She heard Angie shouting, 'no, David!' And then there was a thud."

Karen looked perplexed. "Why didn't she call it in?"

Steve shrugged. "Apparently it's the norm around here. Raised voices, arguments and fights are commonplace. Just four days ago she was woken by *our lot* kicking in a door five houses down at five a.m. According to local residents, it was full of troublemakers with people coming and going at all times of the day and night. She didn't think anything of it."

Karen shook her head in disbelief. *What is happening in this world that even the sound of a disturbance doesn't bother people?*

"What do we know about Angie Jones, Steve?"

Steve checked his notes. "Angie is single and works part-time in Ilford. She kept herself to herself and didn't chat with neighbours, even when putting out her bins. She was known for having a permanent scowl."

"Nice. Any other family?" Karen asked.

Steve confirmed that there wasn't.

"And do you have any idea who David is?"

"Unfortunately not, boss. Because she kept herself to herself, her neighbours didn't really see her with anyone. Unless David was local? Maybe he worked with her in town?"

Karen rubbed her temples. She was already too tired for this; the events of this morning had wiped her out. The fact that no one had seen David either didn't help. Angie's neighbour had commented that it was none of her business and far too early, and if she stared out of the window every second she heard a sound, she would never get anything done.

Karen moved out on to the road and glanced up and down the street. It was a long road full of nineteen forties terraced housing which she imagined had appeared quite pretty once. From where she stood, the gardens now looked unkempt, cars were crammed into spaces designed for just one car, and windows appeared to have not been cleaned in years. One or two of the properties appeared in disrepair and reminded her of Onslow's front garden in the TV sitcom *Keeping Up Appearances*.

Angie's property was on the end of the terrace, and on the intersection between two roads. She walked to the corner and peered down a side street called Brisbane Road. The road sloped down to a park in the distance. Karen turned when Jade called out to let her know that Brad had discovered something on a neighbour's CCTV.

Moments later Karen, Steve and Jade crammed into the living room of an elderly gentleman called Frank Moreland who was being cared for by his daughter Christine. The room smelt musty and dated in comparison to Angie's lounge. There were far more memorabilia, and old photographs that crammed the windowsill, the fireplace shelf, and standing cases that nestled in the alcoves either side of the fireplace.

The extra commotion in his lounge appeared to unsettle Frank, who remained seated in his wing-backed chair, with a thick tartan blanket thrown over his lap. Karen glanced over to him and tried to appease him with a warm smile and her thanks. He looked over the top of his glasses and down his nose at her before muttering about the inconvenience as he read his newspaper.

"You'll have to excuse my dad. I'm really sorry," Christine said apologetically. "He's not used to a lot of visitors, and he likes to stick to his routine. He normally spends his mornings reading the newspaper, and that's enough to let him fall asleep for the afternoon."

"Hey, no need to apologise. We'll try to get out of here as soon as we can. We need to look at the footage and take a copy if that's okay?" Karen offered in reply.

Christine nodded enthusiastically and returned to her seat beside her dad whilst Karen turned to stare at the TV.

Brad pressed the button on the mouse to replay the footage. It showed Angie being pushed through a side gate in her fence before being bundled into a car. That in itself was enough to set alarm bells ringing. The fact that the vehicle was a light-coloured three series BMW raised the risk level further. It had taken place under darkness, so it was hard to figure the exact colour and number plate of the car.

Karen leaned in closer. The man in the footage wore a thick coat with the hood up. All she could make out was that it was a white male. Through the short clip, he kept his back to the camera. *Clever!*

"We've just witnessed Angie's abduction," Karen whispered. "Brad, get a copy of this over to digital forensics to see if they can enhance the images. Steve, find out Angie's mobile number. It's a slim chance, but if she's got it with her, we can do a phone triangulation to identify where she might be. Jade, can you get an ANPR trace on this please?"

45

Skelton turned off the A13 and into the industrial estate. Nerves fluttered in his stomach like a thousand butterflies. He'd been here before, and the outcome had shocked him to the core. Flashbacks of seeing Two-tone Charlie shot dead in a shipping container assaulted his senses. This time he felt reassured as the estate was busy. Delivery vehicles trundled past, pallets were being loaded on to flatbed lorries, and the bleeping of forklift trucks sounded from all directions. Workers milled in and out of open doorways, swapping paperwork, having a sneaky fag, and exchanging laughter.

He weaved through the flow of traffic of parked vehicles until he reached the unit and stopped a few yards from it. Signage above told him it was Trafalgar Wholesale Wine Importers. He knew it was a clever front for the Connells money laundering business. One of Sally's men loitered by the entrance to the loading bay as Skelton approached. He stepped into Skelton's path before guiding him to the side and giving him a pat-down. Satisfied that Skelton wasn't carrying any weapons, he nodded for Skelton to go ahead into the darkened warehouse.

Though it was a large unit, it was eerily quiet. Boxes of wine from across the globe were stacked thirty feet high. Ahead in the shadows stood Sally Connell, her brothers on either side of her. None said a word as Skelton walked towards them, his footsteps slow and measured, as his eyes scanned his surroundings. Something wasn't right. Usually Sally had a small entourage with her, thickset men with stubbly faces, and cold menacing eyes. Their absence worried him.

An awkward silence dragged on for a few minutes as both parties weighed up their opponent. Sally dragged on a cigarette, and slowly exhaled, leaving a smoky halo that lingered above her.

"I'm feeling kind today, Skelton. Rather than make this messy, I wanted to give you one more chance to hand over Heath. We both know that I could have had her eliminated weeks ago, but I gave you a chance to sort out your mess. Sadly, you haven't."

Skelton shook his head, unsure what to say to pacify the woman. "I'm trying my best… I just need to persuade her somehow."

"Your best isn't good enough. You've had your opportunity to try to persuade her, so it's our turn to do the *persuading*. We gave her a warning, and she didn't take it. She's made her bed."

"Sally don't do this. You've got a really cushy number at the moment, and with me being in the middle, I'm keeping the heat off your back."

"Do you think that bothers us? You're replaceable... We have others who can do a much better job than you and need less persuading. Set it up, Skelton, or it's over."

Skelton grimaced. "Don't do this. I beg you. Don't do this."

Sally smiled as she plunged her hand into the pocket of her coat, forcing Skelton to flinch. She pulled out a phone and searched for something on it before closing the gap between them and turning the screen to face him. Skelton swallowed hard, his eyes refusing to believe the moving images. The video showed him at the casino facing the camera that appeared to be situated behind the bar. The Connells had their backs to the camera, and he watched as a packet of drugs was handed to him.

Cold sweat glistened on his furrowed brow. He clasped his hands tightly in front of his stomach and fiddled with his knuckles, weaving his fingers in and out of each other.

Once the short clip had finished, Sally retreated and smiled at Skelton. "Your time with us has come to an end. You are surplus to requirements. We'll deal with Heath before the day's out. Skelton, you have been a waste of time and messed with the wrong people."

Dread crept over Skelton like an icy chill, numbing his brain. In the frozen state his mind offered him only one thought. *It's today. There is no avoiding it.* He felt like a cow being herded into a truck for the slaughterhouse, only the cow didn't know where it was going, and he did.

"Choose your destination, Skelton. Where do you want your container to end up before they open the doors to find you?"

Skelton felt his sphincter muscle twitch, the threat of shitting himself only added to the fear that engulfed him like an inferno. His mouth fell so dry, he couldn't swallow. A part of him wanted to fall to his knees and cry like a little boy begging for forgiveness, another part wanted to plead for his life. Even if he couldn't save himself, he needed to warn Karen before it was too late.

"Sally, I'm sure we can work this out. We've been good for each other. You've built your business because of what I've done for you. Doesn't that count for anything?" Skelton uttered as his mind raced through his options.

"No." Sally's reply was as cold as her icy stare.

"How can you say that? I've covered up so much for you. I've made sure that you were able to bring in your deliveries without attracting attention from the police. I have created distractions for you and evidence has disappeared. Who else is going to do that for you?"

Sally rested her chin on her hand and let her eyes travel towards the ceiling in mock contemplation. "Let me think… Oh, at least three others that I know, and all three of them hold senior ranks to you."

Skelton shook his head when several of Sally's men appeared from the shadows behind her. He knew he was moments away from a bullet. It was now or never. He turned on his heels and raced for the loading doors. He heard the shouts and heavy footsteps that came in pursuit. The lump at the door who had his back to the warehouse didn't react in time as Skelton raced past him and into the open. The sounds of everyday life drowned out the thumping pulse in his neck as he charged towards his car, avoiding the delivery truck that passed the Connells's loading bay.

He hastily fumbled for his keys, his hands trembling so violently that he couldn't keep a firm grasp. The keys fell, and he watched them like a slow-motion film fall to the floor. His eyes widened in panic and fear as he bent down to grab them. Everything happened in just a few seconds, but it felt like minutes, as he jumped into his car. He glanced over his shoulder to see the Connells and their men standing in the loading bay watching him. They were keen to avoid any attention, as people milled around, and cars and vans passed by them.

Skelton started his ignition and accelerated away, his breath coming in gasps, and the sound of fear screeching from his throat.

Sally watched Skelton disappear into the distance before she retreated into the warehouse. It was a minor inconvenience, but one she needed to rectify. She flicked through her contact list before finding the number and waited for it to connect.

A man with a flat monotone voice answered. "Yes, Sally. Do you have instructions for me?"

Sally lit a cigarette, before taking a deep drag into her lungs, and blowing out smoke rings. "I need business taken care of. Clean and quick. Make sure it's in public, I need to send a clear message not to fuck with us."

A pause. "Consider it done. Send me the details. It's five grand a pop as usual."

"Done," Sally replied before terminating the call.

46

Karen paced anxiously. Whilst her team were busy on their phones, chasing down leads and information, she took the opportunity to have a few moments alone to sort out her thoughts which felt like a tangled mess of wires in a box. The problems and revelations around Skelton only added to the hazy mist of confusion that clouded her mind. She wondered why he wouldn't be in today, and what she would say to him tomorrow. Karen needed to tread carefully, as she didn't know how much Skelton knew about Malik. For the time being she needed to concentrate on finding Angie Jones.

Following the risk assessment and the heightened risk to life, Jade had organised local units to attend. With more police cars arriving by the minute, their presence had attracted the attention of residents, who spilled from their front doors and looked on quizzically.

"Terrific," Karen tutted as she made her way back towards Steve. He was hanging up from a call and waved to get her attention.

"Boss, we've heard back from the police in Coleraine. They had no joy contacting David Simpson. According to his neighbours, Simpson hasn't been seen for about two weeks. His car isn't there either. Check this out. He has a three series grey BMW."

"What model of three series?"

Steve held up an image that had been sent through to him by officers in Coleraine.

Karen drew in a sharp intake of breath through clenched teeth and shook her head. "It looks like the same vehicle that we're looking for."

"Do you think it's Simpson?"

Karen shrugged. "It's possible. Equally, someone could have taken out Simpson, and then used his car to come over here to take out Buckley and Shields. And Angie Jones was the next on the list…" Karen speculated, nodding towards Angie's house.

"That would explain why the BMW is running on stolen plates. If it's the same one from Ireland, it would be running on Irish plates which would stand out like a sore thumb."

Steve's point was valid as Karen thought it through. "What do we know about David Simpson?"

"He's the last member of staff unaccounted for. He started at the age of eighteen years old, in 1992, which I think was four years after the children's home was set up. He was employed there till 2001 and left at the age of twenty-seven. That's all we know about his employment at the moment," Steve continued, as he trawled through the emails that were coming through thick and fast from their colleagues in Coleraine.

"There's a large gap in his CV that we can't account for at the moment," Karen said.

"They've informed me that he was arrested in Coleraine for being drunk and disorderly. He was hospitalised once for alcohol poisoning. According to residents, he would pop into the local pub most afternoons for a couple of pints. None of the door-to-door enquiries were able to confirm if he had a job or not, as he appeared to be in and out most days. But they also said he spent a large amount of time in a workshop around the back of his house. He was into his woodworking."

Karen instructed Steve to check David Simpson's bank records, in case large sums of money had been withdrawn either voluntarily or under duress in the last few weeks. If under duress, the cashpoints or banks he visited might have CCTV. She also instructed him to contact the mobile phone companies to see if they were able to get mobile mast data. With it, she hoped to track his movements over the past few days.

Jade stood in the front garden of a house further down the street making notes having spoken to the resident of the property. It was the shouts from a local officer that stopped everyone in their tracks. Jade ran back towards Angie's house, where the majority of officers convened in a large group, with Karen pushing her way into the middle as they blocked the pavement.

Reports had come in of a series of pings on the ANPR system. The BMW had been seen on the A406 in Barking, as well as Bow Road, then in Stoke Newington Road, and lastly in Commercial Road. Karen checked those locations on Google Maps, but it was hard to distinguish the direction in which the car was travelling because of the erratic nature of the alerts.

"He's giving us the runaround. These alerts don't make sense. One minute he's here, and the next he's there," Karen added, jabbing the different points on her phone.

"The last known ANPR trace was on the A107 in Hackney," the officer added. "Shall I put out another alert, and order police units with ANPR to scour the area?"

"Yes, do that if you could. And keep us updated. We'll head over towards Hackney now."

Karen and her team raced back towards their cars and headed off in convoy. Time wasn't on their side and Karen knew that. There was a strong probability that by the time they reached the general area, the car would have gone to ground, or worse, left the area entirely. They were twenty-five minutes away, but if they pushed it, they could make it in fifteen on blue lights.

Karen needed to find that car and Angie Jones before her fate was sealed as well.

47

Traffic snaked down the road, a single line of cars and vans, each averaging less than five mph in their stop-start fashion. It was gridlocked in both directions. Karen tapped the dashboard in frustration as Jade weaved through the traffic. With nowhere to go, vehicles in front of her had begun to turn off their engines, with drivers stepping out of their vehicles and looking up and down for clues.

Sirens erupted behind her, and in quick succession police cars, an ambulance, and a fire engine appeared from different directions, and headed to a point somewhere ahead of them. The hypnotic whipping of the air spelt trouble for Karen, as a red air ambulance flew low overhead, looking for a suitable place to land.

"Get out of this, Jade. In the next few minutes this place will become jammed and we'll be stuck."

Jade didn't need to be told twice, and darted around a few vehicles, before cutting across them and turning left into a side street. With a punch of the pedal, she accelerated away, the underside of the car colliding with the speed bumps that vibrated through the whole vehicle. Karen gritted her teeth and held on to the grip handle above her, as her radio crackled into life. Further vehicles flooded the area, and as they approached Hackney, the area wasn't lost on Karen. It was less than two miles away from where the limbs and torso had been discovered. Their killer was returning to a patch that they were familiar with.

A few minutes later they cruised the streets of Hackney, their eyes peeled for a grey BMW. Steve and Brad had taken a different route and were a few roads away. Jade stopped each time they came across another patrol vehicle and exchanged an update of the areas that they had covered to avoid repetition, before moving off again.

"Karen, they could be absolutely anywhere. It's too big an area for us to cover. For all we know, the car could be off the road now parked in a garage."

She understood Jade's concerns and shared them too. Her request for NPAS had proved unsuccessful. The nearest helicopter was on the other side of London dealing with the fallout from a pre-planned stop on a vehicle suspected of being involved in a county lines drug operation.

"We have to try. If there's a chance of saving Angie Jones, then we need to keep looking until we find her. Ideally alive."

Karen's heart quickened and her eyes widened in excitement as reports came in of a marked unit trailing a vehicle matching the description of the grey BMW. Karen pushed Jade to get them to the area as quick as possible. Jade dropped it down a gear and flicked on her sirens to speed along the narrow streets. Karen told Steve to make his way to the location as well. Cars pulled into narrow gaps to allow Jade to squeeze through. Pedestrians jumped back between parked cars as she raced past. All the while Karen hung on, as her stomach flipped each time Jade took a corner too fast and the tyres screeched across the tarmac.

The officers in the marked vehicle following the BMW then confirmed they were in pursuit as the suspect's car sped away. Officers gave a running commentary on the airwaves, confirming that the target vehicle was travelling at five four miles per hour in a thirty zone, and had just gone through a red light, narrowly missing vehicles approaching in the other direction, and a mother crossing whilst holding her child's hand. That in itself worried Karen, as whoever was driving was prepared to take extreme risks and risk injury to others.

With unmarked and marked vehicles approaching in all directions, it appeared as if the suspect vehicle would soon be cornered, especially with the news that officers were lying in wait ahead of the BMW to deploy a stinger.

With the sound of Jade's engine screaming and her sirens on, Karen listened into the running commentary.

"Stinger deployed, Stinger deployed, suspect vehicle has mounted the pavement to avoid it, and hit a pedestrian," shouted an officer during his commentary.

"Shit… this person is a lunatic," Karen hissed.

The senior officer monitoring the pursuit from the control room had given the authorisation for the vehicle to be brought to a stop with controlled contact. Karen knew that this would mean that other units specialised in TPAC would need to take the lead in the pursuit. The use of tactical pursuit and containment wasn't a decision taken lightly, as it was both a dangerous manoeuvre and risked damage to police vehicles. But with the suspect vehicle having hit a pedestrian, the control centre had decided to end the chase.

"Speed is six one miles per hour. Vehicle has crossed over and is driving on the opposite side of the road. Oncoming vehicles. Impact, impact. Target vehicle has collided with another car and left the road. Decamp… Decamp."

They were minutes away, as Jade did a quick U-turn and headed in the direction of the collision. As they arrived, the area swarmed with police cars. The scene was total carnage as Karen exited Jade's car. The suspect BMW had clipped the front of another car causing it to tailspin. The BMW had then mounted a central crossing, taking out the two white bollards in the process. The wheels had whacked the pavement on the other side, causing it to flip over and crash into a brick wall.

As Karen approached, she could see commotion centred around the rear of the car whilst other officers scaled low walls and disappeared into the woodland beyond in pursuit of the suspect. As Karen peered into the rear of the vehicle, a woman lay bound and hooded, her body trapped where the rear bulkhead had caved in from the impact. An officer from the other side of the vehicle reached in and carefully peeled off the hood to show a bloodied face. From where Karen stood, it appeared to be Angie Jones.

Karen instructed local officers to put diversions in place to keep traffic away from the scene for when the fire brigade arrived. There was nothing she could do for the woman until she was released, so Karen turned her attention to the driver who had made off. She listened in on her radio as officers continue their search. With NPAS still unavailable,

Karen put in a request for a dog unit and specialist officers who could send up a police drone to scan the woodland.

More officers flooded the area to form a cordon around the woodland to keep the driver contained.

Now it was a waiting game.

48

With the day closing in, and twilight fast being replaced by a blanket of darkness, Karen and her team held back whilst uniformed colleagues extended their search through the woodland looking for the driver. The tree canopy was dense, and the undergrowth was thick, which hampered search efforts. With Karen remaining by the roadside, it provided her with the opportunity to listen in on the commentary as they searched in less than favourable conditions.

Karen watched as fire crews used cutting gear to free Angie Jones. Large pincer claws on their equipment made light work of cutting through the steel body of the car. With arc lights set up to provide a source of light, a blue screen had been erected around the car to stop prying eyes.

"It doesn't look good," Jade said as she stood alongside Karen. "I've just spoken to the paramedics, and her stats are stable, but she's bleeding out from an injury to her abdomen. A piece of the rear bulkhead tore away and pierced her side."

"Have they managed to contain the blood loss?"

Jade winced. "As best as they could. The fire service wouldn't let the paramedics stay in the car for longer than necessary. I think they did a bit of a patch job. The sooner they get her out the better."

Karen sighed and clenched her fists. "We need her alive."

It was a long-drawn-out wait whilst Karen asked for news from the search. As each minute passed, the greater the risk grew that the driver had slipped away. With the woodland surrounded by a three-foot-high wall, he could have hopped into the woods and reappeared several hundred yards down in an adjoining street. Karen's efforts to place a cordon around the area may have been a little too late. Specialist officers with a drone had finally arrived. It took them less than a few minutes to get their equipment up in the air, and a constant droning noise could be heard in the darkness. To Karen, it sounded like a swarm of bees hovering not far from her. The drone had been fitted with a thermal imaging camera to see if it could pick up a heat source.

Karen could tell from the noise that the drone was taking sweeps from left to right as it faded from one side of her, only to reappear on the other. Karen's impatience grew as hopes faded. Just as she was about to resign herself to the fact that they were too late, her radio broke into life. The drone operator had picked up a stationary heat source. It was too large to be a small animal and unlikely to be anything like a deer, certainly not so close to this built-up area. Officers on the ground were guided towards the heat source.

The operator provided further updates. "Yes. Yes. Yes. We

can confirm that the heat source is a person. They are on the move again. Officers on the ground, if you can move in the direction of eleven o'clock from where you are standing. The suspect is about fifty yards ahead of you."

Karen felt the first feelings of excitement, as the hairs on the nape of her neck stood up. With it being dark, Karen had retrieved her coat from the car and pulled the collar up around her neck. Despite the added layer of warmth, she felt a chill race down her back. So much of her wanted to charge into the forest and join the pursuit, it was the sharp end of policing that she loved so much. There was nothing more satisfying than tracking down and apprehending a suspect.

Officers searched in darkness, as the thermal imaging camera tracked the man.

"The person is in front of you, perhaps six to eight feet to your left. Officers on the ground please make your way in that direction," the operator added.

Karen bit her bottom lip and tapped her radio on her thigh to stop herself from screaming into it. Then she heard the news she had been waiting for.

"One suspect detained. I repeat, one suspect detained."

Karen raced to an adjoining street where uniformed officers were bringing out the suspect and manhandling him over the wall. The scene was calm but tense. A dog handler tugged hard on his lead to keep his barking dog at bay. A dishevelled-looking man was being restrained by three officers, a fourth patting him down for any weapons, needles, or personal possessions. Karen stood a few feet away and examined the suspect. He was a large heavyset man, slightly overweight, with short scruffy hair and a stubbly beard. His jacket and jeans carried the hallmarks of his pursuit in the undergrowth, with rips and tears.

The first thing Karen noticed was how scared the man looked. He was large and well built, but fear widened his eyes, like he'd been spooked by a ghost. Karen saw a wallet being pulled from a back pocket in his jeans. An officer thumbed through the various card slots before finding his driving licence.

"What's his name?" Karen asked with a sense of urgency that made her want to rip the card from the officer's hand and read it herself.

"David Simpson, boss. The address on the licence is from Ireland."

"Coleraine?"

"Yep."

KAREN STUDIED Simpson as he was booked into the custody suite. Her theories about the killer had been blown out of the water and she stood speechless as Simpson was led away to a cell where his shoes were removed and left out in the corridor without a word being uttered by him. All the evidence pointed to him being the murderer in their double investigation.

Karen raced to Skelton's office to see if he had returned, but his lights were off, and his desk was empty, suggesting he'd not been in at all. She flicked through her contact list and then dialled his number. She tried for a second time, and the call went straight to voicemail again. Karen stiffened in a mixture of frustration and concern. *Why is he avoiding my calls? And more to the point, where is he?*

49

Karen waited outside the interview room with Jade as they discussed what needed to be covered. Though she should have felt relieved at finding Angie Jones, discovering David Simpson added to the questions that piled up in her mind.

Jade had bought them two cups of strong black coffee, which they sipped whilst staring at the clock on the opposite wall. It was late into the evening, and their work had only just begun. They had twenty-four hours in which to interview David Simpson, gather all the evidence they needed, and present their case to the CPS or apply for an extension.

The door to the interview suite opened, and a portly-looking gentleman with glasses balanced on the tip of his nose poked his head around the corner and informed Karen they were ready to start. Karen rolled her eyes in Jade's direction. Simpson's legal representative was a man Karen had met on many occasions, as the duty appointed solicitor. They had clashed horns and never seen eye to eye.

Karen and Jade took up their positions on the opposite side of the table to Simpson, and his solicitor Charles Bridge. Jade did the introductions and presented the formal caution for the benefit of the tape recorder whilst Karen took a moment to cast her eye over David Simpson. He had a long face, with close-set eyes. She wasn't sure if it was the angle, but he appeared to be slightly cross-eyed, or at least his left eye tended to travel inwards towards his nose. He had a large forehead, partly due to a receding hairline.

Simpson cast a lonely figure as he sat opposite them in a white forensic paper suit. His clothes had been sent away for forensic analysis. He looked right through Karen as if she wasn't there.

"David, we've arrested you for the abduction of Angie Jones. Can you explain to us why you did that?"

Simpson remained tight-lipped, unflinching.

"David, we understand that you worked at the Lighthouse Children's Home between 1992 and 2001, is that correct?"

There was no reply. Karen followed this up with a few questions to break the ice, asking him to confirm his address, his date of birth, and how he knew Angie Jones. Each question was met with a wall of silence. She tried harder to get through to him by asking him if he knew Annette Buckley and Martin Shields. Karen hoped a mention of their names would spark a reaction, but the coldness continued. Karen needed to change tack.

Opening the folder in front of her, Karen removed pictures of Annette Buckley and Martin Shields taken by SOCO at both crime scenes. She placed them face down. It was a risky gamble, but she needed to break him.

"For the benefit of the tape, DI Heath is about to show Mr Simpson a sequence of photographs relating to a series of violent crimes that have occurred recently. We believe that Mr Simpson knows a great deal about these crimes."

Karen turned over the first few photos and slid them across the table and tapped each one. "These are the only pieces left of Annette Buckley. We never found her head. And this is how we found Martin Shields. Tied with rope, dropped into a sewer, his innards eaten by rats. They had nowhere to escape, so they chewed through his stomach and out of his side… just to escape."

Karen watched Simpson continued to stare ahead. She tapped the images again. "Have a look. Go on. That's all I'm asking you to do, have a look."

A few seconds passed before Simpson glanced down and studied the images. Karen watched for a reaction and noticed a slight tremble in one of his eyelids before he looked up.

"I fail to see what this has to do with my client, Inspector?" Bridges interrupted.

"It has everything to do with your client, Mr Bridges. We are investigating two horrific murders. Both victims were known to your client. In fact, he worked for them. We are merely attempting to learn the facts here." Karen glared at Bridges and leant back in her chair and folded her arms across her chest, before returning her attention towards Simpson. "Is there anything you want to tell us about these murders, David? When was the last time you saw Annette Buckley or Martin Shields?"

No reaction from Simpson. Karen sat silently, watching his face. She continued to sit without speaking and without moving for a few minutes all the time looking directly into David's eyes. It was impossible to read anything from his expression. Karen pressed on when no answer was forthcoming. "Did you enjoy working at the Lighthouse Children's Home? Did you get on with Martin and Annette? You see, we've spoken to a few of your colleagues and people connected to the children's home, and they didn't paint a nice picture of the place. It seemed to be quite cold, with a harsh regime. There were even allegations of bullying, harassment, and physical and sexual abuse towards the children."

Karen paused for effect before continuing, "Did you experience or witness any of that? You see, I'm curious. I wonder if you had anything to do with the deaths of Annette Buckley and Martin Shields. Were you directly or indirectly involved in their savage murders?"

Hopelessness crept inside her as the man remained tight-lipped. Every attempt to get him to talk had failed so far.

"David, we're going to suspend the interview and take a quick ten-minute break. I suggest that you have a conversation with your solicitor because we *will* get to the bottom of this, with or without your cooperation. And if we find that you are responsible for their deaths, you won't see daylight again."

Jade called the time and suspended the interview.

50

"He's not giving in at all," Jade muttered as she leant against the wall in the corridor and stared up towards the fluorescent ceiling lights.

"Nope. I am so tired. I want this interview over with so I can crash out," Karen replied, stretching her arms into the air and letting out a big yawn that made her eyes water.

"What are you planning to do?"

"I'm not sure, Jade. I think I'll go back to the photographs and try to open a few cracks in his defence. Considering Dr Rai said that people in his position often show very little emotion, everything I've thrown at him so far hasn't elicited a single response. I've not heard him mutter one word!"

They took a quick loo break before heading back to the interview room, grabbing another coffee en route.

"Boss!" came Brad's voice from behind.

Karen turned to see him jog up the corridor towards them, carrying brown paper evidence bags.

"We discovered these in a holdall in the boot of Simpson's car," Brad said, handing her the bags.

Karen shot Jade a look of excitement as she examined the contents. This could be the breakthrough she needed as she spun on her heels and pushed through the door to the interview room.

"David, have you got anything further to add before we continue?"

"No comment."

Karen raised a brow. "Well, at least you're speaking now, so I regard that as progress. I'll ask you again, did you have anything to do with the deaths of Annette Buckley or Martin Shields?"

"No comment."

Karen nodded, before placing the first evidence bag on the table between them. "You may recognise this item. For the tape, I'm showing David Simpson a brown evidence bag which has a bloodied meat cleaver recovered from a holdall in the boot of his car."

Karen waited a moment whilst David's eyes travelled to the table before she scooped up the second evidence bag from the floor by her chair. "For the tape, I'm showing David Simpson another brown evidence bag which contains a bloodied Stanley knife, also recovered from the holdall."

As agreed during their break, Jade leant in and rested her

elbows on the table. "David, what's the likelihood that once these are examined by forensic services, that they identify DNA that matches Annette Buckley and Martin Shields?" she said in a softer, appealing voice. "What would they be doing in your car if you haven't used them to kill Annette Buckley and Martin Shields?"

Karen noticed the slight tremble in Simpson's hands. "If you weren't responsible for the murders, then you're going to be taking the fall for someone else who will continue to walk the streets whilst you spend the next twenty years or more in prison."

The slight tremble had become more noticeable as Simpson's body twitched and shook. His solicitor placed a hand on his arm and shook his head as Simpson glanced across at him.

"It was me."

His voice was barely audible as Karen strained to listen. Surprised, she asked him to repeat it louder for the benefit of the tape.

"It… Was… Me!" he screamed. "I killed them. They deserved it. They deserved every ounce of pain. It was payback for all the pain they had caused."

Karen maintained her composure whilst prompting him to continue.

"Yes, I worked for them. I saw physical brutality and the punishment that Martin dished out to the kids. It was horrible. They didn't deserve any of it."

"Are you're saying that you witnessed Martin Shields physically attack and punish children under his care?"

"Yes."

"And did Annette Buckley have any involvement in this?"

Shields nodded. "She was there in the background on many occasions. She would stand there, soulless, with her arms crossed. Her eyes were as cold as the cold radiators."

"How long did that go on for?" Karen probed.

"Long before I arrived and probably continued after I left."

"Why didn't you stop it? You could have gone to the authorities?"

"I was silenced. I wanted to blow the whistle. I wanted to do something to protect those kids. But I was scared shitless of Martin and Annette. You see, I'm gay. And though it had no effect on my ability to do my job, Shields exploited that. He said that if I mentioned anything, he would spread rumours that I sexually abused the boys."

"And did you at any time interfere with any of the children, male or female?"

Simpson answered in a fit of rage, slamming his fist down on the table. His face contorted in anger, and spittle erupted from his mouth as he released a volley of obscenities. Karen and Jade quickly pushed back in their chairs, ready to spring from their seats if Simpson jumped to his feet. But a calming hand from his solicitor appeared to placate him.

"You left the country in 2001. You were arrested for being drunk and disorderly. You've been hospitalised for alcohol poisoning, and you've attended AA meetings. Why don't you tell us about your drinking problem?"

"You don't get it, do you?" Simpson blurted, jabbing his temple with a finger. "It's always there. The memories. The nightmares that haunt me. Those kids are like ghosts that won't leave me alone. Every moment of my waking day, I see them around me. When I go to sleep at night, they are there, tapping me on the shoulder, telling me to wake up, telling me to save them."

"Drinking is your way of blotting it out?" Karen asked.

"I guess," he replied with a shoulder shrug.

"Why now, David? Why after all this time?"

Simpson shook his head and shrugged, as his eyes tracked around the room, his mind searching for answers. "I've done my hardest to never go back there again. But then, a couple of weeks ago, I saw the sister of a young girl on Facebook marking the anniversary of her disappearance. And that's when it happened."

Karen narrowed her eyes, unsure what to make of Simpson's response.

"I don't understand David, what do you mean? What little girl?"

Simpson trembled again, his knuckles turning white as he gripped the table, his bottom jaw quivering. He shook his head and began to cry. "I'm so sorry. I couldn't save her. She's dead because of me."

"Who's dead, David?"

Simpson wiped the snot from his nose with the back of his hand and snorted heavily. "Claire Morgan. She died because of me."

Karen exchanged a quizzical look with Jade. The name Claire Morgan hadn't come up in the list of children at the Lighthouse.

"Was she a resident at the home? As the name doesn't ring a bell."

Simpson nodded. "You won't find her name. I'm not sure where she came from. It wasn't through official channels. She was there for about six months before Shields raped her and then strangled her to death."

"And how do you know about this?"

"Because I saw Shields carry her body to open ground at the back of the children's home before burying her. When I told him I'd seen it, he threatened to kill me. Then he changed his mind and said it would be better if I carried that image with me for the rest of my life. A living nightmare for as long as I breathed. If I said a word, he would spread those rumours. He said no one liked a paedophile in prison. I just left and tried to get away as far as I could. I wanted to distance myself from those memories… and that place."

51

The mechanical chugging of generators provided a rude welcoming as workers arrived at the offices at the location of the former children's home. With an ongoing police incident, workers were being turned away and the business centre was closed and sealed off within the outer cordon for the time being. Overnight, Karen and her team had travelled to the location where Claire Morgan was allegedly buried. The site had been converted into a business centre, with various firms renting office space. The grounds behind the centre formed the focal point for their search.

A specialist team of officers began the excavations under the glare of arc lights and temporary blue screens to shield their work. They took it in turns to remove the soil in layers. Every so often an officer would appear from behind the screens to take a break, their blue overalls streaked with mud. Each officer carried a look of respectful and sombre determination on their face. The importance of their work carried a heavy weight on the team as their uniformed colleagues looked on.

Whilst the officers painstakingly removed the soil, Karen and Jade had grabbed a little sleep in Jade's car.

In the cold light of day, Karen stretched and yawned as she paced up and down the car park. She had pulled many all-nighters whilst being a police officer, and though tired, felt relatively human. Jade wandered back from the local petrol station with coffee, which Karen cupped in her palms, savouring the warmth through her fingertips. She felt every sip of coffee trickle down her throat and warm her stomach.

"Do you think they'll find anything?" Jade asked, keeping her hands firmly tucked inside her jacket pockets.

Karen looked towards the blue screens. "I hope so. Simpson was precise in detailing what happened, and where the poor girl was buried."

"He could be buying time?"

"He could be. But all that would happen is that we would apply for an extension. He's already admitted that he killed our two victims. It also looks like we found the weapons used in both crimes, and with a bit of luck, forensics will confirm that for us."

"Other than clearing his conscience, he has nothing else to gain from bringing us out here?"

"Correct." Karen nodded, but also knew that it would bring closure on the poor girl's short life.

Mason Brophy, the crime scene manager pulled up in his car, followed by a white scientific services van. He exited his car and made his way towards Karen and Jade. "Morning, I thought you might need us once the search team found something."

“Morning. I’m hoping they find something as well, otherwise you’ve had a wasted trip and I’ve missed a night’s sleep,” Karen replied.

“You look tired, have you been out here all night?” Mason cupped his hands over his mouth and blew warm breath into them, before rubbing his palms together to heat them up.

Karen shook her head and rubbed her bloodshot eyes. “No, we apprehended and interviewed our suspect late last night, and his confession led us here in the early hours. I’m trying to keep moving, because I know if I sit down, I’ll probably crash out.”

Karen updated Mason on the outcome of the interview, and the progress of the weapons fast-tracked for analysis. Mason assured Karen that he would have her results later this afternoon.

Karen put in a call to Wainwright, asking him to be on standby should the search team discover any remains. She spent the next few hours pacing up and down the car park, breaking it up with moments sitting inside Jade’s car with the engine on, her hands resting on the air vents, enjoying the warmth that they offered.

“At times like this, I’d much rather be on a beach in the Canaries, than sitting in a car park freezing my tits off,” Karen grumbled as she looked at the bleak scene around them and tried to lift their moods.

“Oh my God, tell me about it. Just to feel some sun on my back, and that heat deep into my muscles. Can’t ask for much more...” Jade replied wishfully.

"I don't know. A fit waiter bringing me an endless supply of sex on the beach…"

"Karen!" Jade shouted, wide-eyed. "I wouldn't go that far."

Karen raised an eyebrow. "Don't tell me you weren't thinking the same?"

Jade shot Karen a playful look, which did little to hide her true thoughts.

"There you go. You're not all *posh* and innocent as you make out to be."

They both smiled and welcomed the moment of lightness in what had so far been a dismal morning.

The waiting ended not long after when one of the search officers beckoned her over. Karen slipped in behind the blue screen, followed by Jade. They both stood a few feet away from one of three sunken pits that had been excavated by the team. They were all in close proximity, with the first two offering nothing. It was the third inspection pit that stirred interest. Soil had been removed and placed on a tarpaulin sheet close to the dig. Karen noticed other officers conducting a fingertip search of it, looking for any evidence, whilst two further officers stood alongside the third pit.

Beside them on another sheet was a muddy, long, bulky black package. The package was wrapped in black bin liners. One end of the package was torn, revealing the top of a small skull. Karen felt the first waves of sadness wash over her as she stared at the remains. The emotions caught in her throat as her eyes moistened. A shivery chill raced down her back as if the temperature had suddenly dropped. She couldn't bring herself to look away, nor look up at the surrounding officers who stood in silent respect. Swallowing past the lump in her throat, Karen blinked a few times. A part of her wanted to thank the search team, whilst another part wanted to find the words to honour the young girl's life. But nothing felt right. How could she possibly articulate the discovery, the melancholy and sorrow she experienced? A young life taken too soon, her final resting place less than dignified. She had seen enough and with a heavy heart, walked away.

Simpson was right; Claire Morgan was murdered and buried in the grounds of the Lighthouse Children's Home.

Karen stepped away from the cordoned off area, blew out her cheeks and wiped away a tear with the back of her hand. "Mason, it's all yours. The information our suspect gave us sadly turned out to be true. It looks like the skull of a little girl."

Mason nodded as he made his way back to his car to fetch his protective clothing. "Are you okay?"

Karen shrugged and stared off into the distance. "Good question."

David Simpson could be charged with two counts of murder and withholding information about the death of Claire Morgan. It felt like a small victory, but one that didn't fill her with a feeling of success as she looked back at the final resting place for the young girl.

52

Karen sat at her desk, dominated by a profound sadness, and fatigue engraved on her worn face. The gloom of the morning's discovery crept into her like the damp into bare timber. It seeped into her pores, travelling to her heart, which beat more morosely. She rocked back and forth in her chair and reflected on what life was all about. She often wondered if there was any justice in the world. It felt like her job was a thankless task.

She should have been happy with a result. David Simpson had admitted to the brutal slayings of Annette Buckley and Martin Shields. But a sense of despair flattened her mood, and that of the team. They were busy compiling all the evidence and case notes, but there was little enthusiasm amongst them. The CPS confirmed that Karen could go ahead and formally charge David Simpson, but her thoughts drifted back to that muddied package, and Claire Morgan's remains.

Karen wiggled her mouse to wake her screen. The email

she was waiting for from social services hadn't arrived yet, but it was due any second. She opened the case records and reviewed the latest additions added by her team. They were awaiting further updates from forensics on the weapons seized from Simpson. Analysis of blood samples discovered in the boot of his car confirmed them as belonging to Annette Buckley. Forensics also identified fine clothing fibres that matched trousers that Martin Shields was wearing when found in the sewer.

A further piece of evidence that Karen reviewed confirmed Simpson as Annette Buckley's killer. Forensic footprint analysis matched the bloodied imprint left in Annette's bathroom with a pair of trainers found in the holdall. A unique wear pattern identified through their analysis matched the wear pattern on the left trainer.

With such damning evidence, the CPS couldn't ignore the clear-cut case. She felt satisfied on that front, but in her mind, justice hadn't been fully served.

She took a walk around the team, checking in with various members, doing her best to keep morale up, and getting them to focus on the good result. It was important for her to continue leading from the front and keep everyone's mind on the job. She had sent Jade, Steve and Brad home to get a few hours' sleep whilst she held the fort. Jade promised to be back in later that afternoon if Karen needed her. Jade had put in so much hard work that she wanted her sergeant to have the rest of the day off and come back in again refreshed. She relied heavily on Jade and didn't give her the recognition she deserved. Though Jade spoke about her wish to progress through the ranks, and Karen encouraged her, selfishly she didn't want to lose Jade. They had formed a great personal and professional relationship, and she thought they complemented each other well.

"Has anyone seen the DCI?" Karen asked, as she wandered through the desks. Her question was met with a sea of shaking heads and murmurs.

Karen spent the next few minutes looking for Skelton. It had been more than a day since she'd last seen or spoken to him. She had tried his phone again, only to reach his voicemail. There was no sign of him in any of the interview suites, the canteen, video suite or other offices that she passed. *Did he find out about Malik? Highly unlikely*, she thought. She felt both confused and concerned. He'd gone AWOL before, but never at such critical moments. He was always the one who liked to wrap up a case and take the glory.

Time wasn't on her side, and Karen knew that. She'd been occupied with the case, and that had stolen her away from tracking down and confronting Skelton. And now that she was ready to pin him down and throw the book at him, he was nowhere to be seen. As much as she wanted to go straight to the chief super and tell him everything, she needed to look Skelton in the eye first and hear it from his own lips.

Feeling shattered and confused, her body dipped as fatigue surfaced again. Hungry, tired and desperate for sleep, Karen shook her head to wake herself up. *Perhaps food and fresh air will help?*

Karen headed to her office to grab her coat and bag. She needed a break before heading to the PM.

The small Italian coffee shop hummed with noise, heat and rich coffee smells as Karen sat in the corner.

A coffee and bacon sandwich had never tasted so good as she licked the last of the brown sauce from the tips of her fingers.

Karen looked around the coffee shop. Groups, couples, and workers, all enjoying a brief break in their days filled the tables. Raucous laughter rang out behind her as two men struggled to keep the noise down over something they were looking at on a mobile phone. An elderly couple sat opposite each other, breaking little bits off their shared cake and nodding their joint approval with each mouthful. Every table appeared to be radiating happiness and contentment. Karen wished she could share a light-hearted moment, and laugh too, but not with the gloom of Skelton and the details of the case hanging over her.

Life carried on around her, and yet none of those she glanced at could ever know or understand what she'd witnessed in the past few hours. It was great getting a result, but the toll it took on her mental and emotional well-being left her tattered and drained inside.

Karen reached into her handbag to grab her phone after it beeped. Narrowing her eyes, she focused on the screen. An email she'd been waiting for had finally arrived. Karen had requested a report on Claire Morgan, and as she scanned through the details, it felt like her chest was being crushed. The report painted a sad and sorrowful short life. Though social services said that Claire was a bright, cheerful, and warm child, her upbringing had been painful, both physically and emotionally, and Karen tutted and shook her head in disbelief as she read the facts. An image of Claire's tiny and fragile remains flashed through her mind before she caught her breath. Karen glanced across to the window and beyond for a few moments, lost in despair, before dragging herself back to the email.

Claire had been abused by her mother and father in the last few years of her life before being taken into care. Repeated visits by social services had been blocked by her parents, claiming that Claire was either unwell, or staying with her grandparents. Both excuses were found to be lies. Teachers at her school noticed bruises on her back and arms. Once reported, social services had investigated. Again, when her parents were questioned, they claimed that Claire was clumsy, and was forever tripping and falling over furniture.

Protests from neighbours finally unearthed the truth. Frequent complaints of late-night rowdiness, loud music, and the smell of weed wafting over the gardens, led to visits by the police on several occasions. At that point, it came to light that her parents were known for having drug-fuelled parties whilst Claire was locked upstairs in her bedroom. Karen's heart tugged when she read that friends of Claire's parents abused her.

Just when it appeared that she had been rescued, her life took another tragic turn when she was taken into care at the Lighthouse Children's Home. But within two days of arriving, she was reported missing, seemingly having walked out and never found. Prosecutions were being bought against her parents, who also disappeared at the same time. It was assumed by social services that somehow Claire's parents had managed to take her unnoticed from the children's home and disappeared.

Karen rolled her eyes at the incompetence. Failings by the authorities had let Claire slip through the cracks, and Karen wondered the true extent of Martin Shields's involvement.

With him being dead, it was unlikely that the true facts would ever be known. Karen began to question whether there was a connection between Martin Shields and Claire's parents. *Did he know them before? Did he collude with them? Did Shields fabricate a story to put social services off his scent – allow him to indulge in his own perverse and sordid activities?* There were so many questions that Karen knew would remain unanswered.

Why are people so cruel? What did Claire do to deserve this?

53

Karen grimaced and pursed her lips. Seeing the skeletal remains laid out on the examination table did little to ease the wave of revulsion sweeping through her body.

What kind of disgusting fucker does this to a defenceless little girl? So young, and so much to look forward to if she had a better start in life. Far too many people let you down.

Since she'd only seen a portion of the skull in a muddy grave, it hadn't felt like a complete person. But in the mortuary, seeing the full skeletal structure of a young child left her speechless and dejected. She joined Wainwright as he was finishing up his inspection.

"As you can see, there's not much for me to go on. I can confirm that the remains belong to a young female child," Wainwright began. "I can also confirm that she was of average height for her age at the time of her death. But other than that, I can't give you much more."

Karen looked up and down the table before taking a few

steps back and folding her arms across her chest. "I don't suppose you can tell us if she carried any injuries?"

Wainwright picked up his metal probe and pointed to the left arm. "The victim did sustain a soft fracture to her ulna at some point in her short life."

Karen peeked over the table. "How can you tell?"

"Well the bones of children are more porous than mature bone, placing them at greater risk for compression fractures, termed buckle fractures. The tendons and ligaments in children are proportionally much stronger than the bones, leading to an increased incidence of avulsion type fractures. The increased flexibility of their bones makes them more likely to bend rather than break, termed plastic deformation. Are you with me?" Wainwright checked.

Karen nodded.

"A term that we call Greenstick fractures occur when the bone bends and partially breaks but does not extend through the width of the bone, giving it a tented appearance. And that was what this young lady was left with. You can see the curvature of her bone," Wainwright said, pointing it out with the tip of his probe.

Karen furrowed her brow. "Wouldn't something like that need to be reported by law?"

Wainwright reached for a printout that sat on an empty examination table behind him. "I took the liberty of contacting a few hospitals. Well I didn't, my assistant did. We found records that we believe confirm that this is indeed Claire Morgan. The child was admitted into hospital when she was three years old for a suspected fracture of her left arm. X-rays were taken, which confirmed there was a partial fracture. Matching the location and description of what we find now in front of us."

"Does it say how it was caused?"

"It does." Wainwright nodded. "Her parents were asked about her injury at the time, and they said they had left the stair gate accidentally open, and she'd fallen down the stairs."

Karen shook her head. Knowing what she had read in Claire's case file, she wondered whether the injuries were accidental or as a result of abuse.

They continued to discuss the remains for a few more minutes, before moving to Wainwright's office.

"It surprises me... and shocks me, to be honest, how so many children slip through the net and continue to be victims of abuse at the hands of their family," Wainwright uttered as he sipped his coffee and tutted.

"I know," Karen agreed. "We are talking hundreds of thousands of cases every year. So much of it goes undetected. Their parents or carers become masters of evasion, excuses, and deception. It beggars belief how many children go to nursery school, and their injuries are hidden from those who are closest to spotting them."

Wainwright pushed a plate of chocolate biscuits across the table in Karen's direction. She didn't hesitate in grabbing two and nibbling on the first one like a rabbit nibbled a carrot. Her eyes stared towards the ground, fixated on nothing but the brown carpet.

"Well, Karen, at least you're able to find some closure for the poor girl. She's finally been found, and now will be laid to rest with dignity."

Karen had tuned out minutes ago, as she continued to stare at nothingness, and munch away on her second biscuit.

"You look very tired and frazzled," Wainwright said softly as he raised a brow.

A shiver ripped through her. "I am. I am fucking shattered, and the day is not over yet."

"Well, can't someone else hold the fort whilst you go home and get some sleep?"

Karen shook her head. "I've already sent some of the team home to do just that. I've still got too much to do."

"A lack of sleep, and proper meals…" Wainwright quipped as he cleared his throat, and nodded towards the chocolate biscuits which were fast disappearing from the plate, as Karen continued a production line of hand to plate, pick up biscuit, place in mouth, rinse and repeat.

Karen snapped herself out of her trance, and blinked rapidly as she looked towards Wainwright, and followed his eyes towards the plate, and then towards her hand which had half a biscuit in it. She laughed as her cheeks glowed red in sheepish embarrassment. "Sorry, I guess I needed a sugar fix," she replied in her defence, placing her mug on the table and standing to stretch.

"Thanks for your help today, Wainwright, and for the coffee and biscuits. I promise I'll bring a couple of packets next time. I don't want you calling me a tight or greedy cow behind my back." Karen winked as she grabbed her handbag and left.

54

As the city overwhelmed him, Skelton pushed on, unsure where he was going or what he needed to do. All the tall buildings, the street lamps, the cars and the roads – they all looked the same. He glanced through his windows to get a bearing, but nothing looked familiar. One minute he was caught in stationary traffic, the next he was dodging busy junctions. Every time he nudged his car forward, Skelton seemed to have moved nowhere. He would stop, start, and then stop to see if that got him anywhere, but it didn't as he realised something he had denied for the past hour.

He was lost.

His mind was in tatters. If it had been anyone other than the Connells, he would have called their bluff. But the Connells were formidable, and Sally was ruthless. Yes, she was stunningly attractive to him, and he had never desired a woman more, but she had a darker side, which terrified him.

Skelton continued his journey, looking for distinguishable landmarks, but it all looked so alien. He thought he knew London like the back of his hand, after all, his whole family grew up here. But confusion clouded his thoughts. He didn't know if he was heading north or south.

The last twenty-four hours had been nothing more than a hazy recollection of thoughts and actions. He had so much to do, places where he needed to be, but he had to keep looking over his shoulder. Watching, waiting, and listening.

He perhaps had hours to make good his escape, he'd already overstayed his welcome.

Karen! He needed to see Karen. With one hand on the steering wheel, he rummaged through his pockets to retrieve his phone and dialled her number.

"Come on… come on, you silly bitch, answer the fucking phone!"

Eventually Karen answered. "Sir, where are you? I was trying to find you earlier."

"Listen, it doesn't matter where I am. Where are you?" There was a sense of urgency in his tone, but he resisted the temptation to shout down the phone as the traffic slowed in front of him.

A pause. "I'm in my office. I need to see you."

Skelton hadn't heard any of that as his eyes searched out a way to turn off and avoid the queue forming in front of him. "Shit!" he fumed, smacking the steering wheel.

"Excuse me, sir?"

"Listen, Heath. I need to see you urgently. Something has come up and I need to tell you face to face. I haven't got long. I'll explain everything when I see you. I'll call you when I get there." Skelton hung up and tossed his phone on to the passenger seat. He needed to think fast, and the first thing he needed was cash. He had a small lock-up in a Big Yellow Storage facility. He'd stop there first to grab his hidden cash and travel bag.

After meeting Karen, he would buy a one-way ticket to South America or Thailand. Anywhere where he could blend into the background and not be found. Dodgy deals had netted him a comfortable profit, so money wasn't an issue. He would have enough to keep him going. Either country would work for him. He knew the drinks were cheap, the women even cheaper, and that was all he needed.

KAREN STARED at her phone in confusion and narrowed her eyes. Skelton didn't sound right. He sounded jumpy and irritated. News had already spread about the arrest of Karim Malik; Karen had made sure of that. All she'd wanted was a name, and now she had that, so Malik needed to face justice too. That was one loose end tied off in her mind. She wondered if Skelton knew, which would explain the odd and frantic call.

Just hearing Skelton's voice irritated her. He had ruined her career, and turned her into a pariah, loathed by other officers. She had witnessed the killing of two police colleagues, and he had dishonoured them by choosing to protect criminals. Skelton had a lot to answer for, but she needed to figure out how to deal with him. Karen was angry, but above all else she wanted justice. The opportunity to confront him would make or break her.

Karen had risked so much in the search for the truth, and nightmares still followed her like ghosts from the past. Her sanity had been questioned by her bosses. So much had changed in her life, and she had changed as a consequence. As of today, she would take back control.

Malik was the first on her list.

Karen leant back in her chair and blew out her cheeks as she stared at the ceiling. *Stay calm breathe, focus.* But her heart hammered on her ribcage, desperate to escape. Adrenaline pulsed through her veins as she clenched her firsts. Her mind felt confused, shutting down her ability to think logically.

What would she say? How would she react? There was only one thing that felt clear in her mind.

Skelton would be next.

55

Karen stared at her phone, willing it to ring. All the reasons not to do this came flooding in, as if her body chemistry just sent them a blanket invitation. A muscle twitched involuntarily in the corner of her right eye. Her mouth formed a rigid grimace. With arms folded tightly across her chest, she tapped her foot furiously. Finally, the moment she dreaded was here and she couldn't halt the waves of nervousness that washed over her. Everything hinged on what happened next and once done could never be undone.

Though Karen had been waiting for it, she jumped when her phone sprang into life and rattled across the desk.

"Heath, it's me. Meet me downstairs by the entrance to the car park. I'm here now. Hurry. I haven't got long."

Karen stared at her phone as the line went dead.

Fuck. It's now or never.

"Jade," Karen shouted through the open door of her office.

The sound of hurried footsteps on the carpet signalled Jade's arrival. "Yep, what's up?"

"Shut the door a sec," Karen instructed, as she stood and readied herself to leave. "Listen, this doesn't go any further. But I've been working on the hijacking case in my own time, and I believe I'm getting to the bottom of who's responsible for it."

Jade eyes widened in surprise and intrigue.

"I'm about to follow up on a lead, and I need you to come with me and loiter by the back door just in case I need backup. I know it sounds all clandestine, and I get that. But just go with me on it."

Jade nodded her head and shrugged. "Sure, whatever. What are you going to do?"

"I'm going to meet someone downstairs, and hopefully I'll get a confession. I need you to listen, and if for any reason it gets out of hand, I need you to call for backup. Do not intervene otherwise… understand?"

Jade reluctantly agreed, as Karen ushered her out of the office and down the stairs towards the back of the building.

Karen stopped by the back door. "Wait here and stay out of sight. I'll ring you. Listen to the conversation that I'm having."

Before Jade could say anything else, Karen dashed out of the door and made her way towards the far end of the car park. She dialled Jade's number and held her phone in the palm of her hand, with the screen facing away from her.

Just seeing Skelton sent her from a mood of uncertainty to one of anger and resentment, as everything she had discovered in the last few days came rushing towards her like an express train. She wanted to run over and beat the living daylights out of him or jump in his car and run him over. Either would do.

As Karen scanned his features, he looked worse than she had ever seen him. His hair was messy and untidy, as if he had just got out of bed. His jowls hung lower than normal, his eyes were sunken with dark rings around them, and his movements appeared fidgety and uncontrolled. She noticed how jumpy he was, checking in every direction before he made his way over to her.

"Karen, we haven't got long. I need you to listen to me."

Though Karen wanted to listen, she was in no mood to be told what to do. "No, you fucking listen to me. I know it was you. I know it was you who manipulated the database, removed evidence, intimidated witnesses, and blackmailed Malik in IT to do your dirty work for you. I have the proof now."

Skelton wagged his finger at her. "I haven't got time to listen to your bollocks. I don't care what you've found. I've tried to do you a favour here. The people that you are messing with are very dangerous. If you carry on like this, they will kill you."

"Who? Who are you talking about?" Karen was desperate for Skelton to spill the beans. She knew who but wanted to hear it from his lips.

"It doesn't matter. It really doesn't matter. I've fucked up, and if I hang around much longer, I will pay the price with my life. I'm trying to save you. The last thing I want is for your body to be fished out of the canal."

"I can take care of myself. I've proved that countless times. I'm not scared." Karen tried to hold on to the bravado, even though her insides twisted, and her breath threatened to choke her.

Skelton paced up and down the pavement, slapping his hands on the sides of his face. "Karen, you just don't get it, do you? You can't win this fight. No one can. I can't save myself, but there's still time for you. If you carry on trying to get to the bottom of this hijacking, it's only gonna end one way for you," he shouted, spittle flying from his mouth.

Karen shook her head. "I can't do that. I took an oath to protect and serve. The bad guys come in all guises. It doesn't matter whether they are out there," she said, jabbing a finger towards the street and passing traffic, "or they serve alongside me," she added, staring straight at Skelton. "You have made my life a fucking misery since that day. I lost my job as a DCI… because of you. I've been plagued with nightmares… because of you. I now know that I was attacked in my own home… because of you. Questions have been raised about my professional competence and mental health… because of you. And the one person who should have been there to have my back and stand up for me was the same person who fucking stabbed me in it!"

Skelton threw his arms up in the air and let out a twisted squeal and laugh. "Oh, for Christ's sake Heath, get off your high horse. This isn't the time for speeches. Or a blame game. This is a matter of life and death. Yes, I'm a bad apple. I'm old-school. I'm from an era where you'd beat the confession out of someone, not find yourself wrapped up in PACE. I come from a time where we used to have a beer in the pub with the same people we were chasing. It's how the world worked."

Karen jutted out a hip as she struggled to control her breathing. "Exactly! It was how the world worked! Things have changed for the better, to weed out people like you. There isn't a place for you in modern-day policing, Skelton."

Skelton waved away everything that Karen said as he gestured and headed back towards his car. "I haven't got time for this any more. I've said what I came here to say. The rest is up to you. If you've got any sense, you'll drop this."

Karen looked over her shoulder as a Mercedes turned into the road. She headed over towards Skelton, closing the gap between them.

"You can't run forever. I've got to take you in," she said, grabbing him by the arm. "Detective Chief Inspector Skelton, I'm arresting you on suspicion of perverting the course of justice and concealing criminal activity. I also suspect that you used your position of power to influence the outcome of a criminal prosecution."

SKELTON HALF TURNED and violently pulled his arm from her grip, before shoving her in the chest and moving away from her.

Karen stumbled back a few steps before regaining her composure and ran after Skelton. She grabbed hold of him as they reached his car. But despite her youth, Skelton's strength was too much for her as they fought. He blindsided Karen with a punch across her face, which left her dazed.

Her phone fell from her grasp and clattered on the floor. She saw white speckles in her eyes, blinking hard to clear them. Karen felt a trickle of blood on her top lip as she held her grip of him.

She lunged forward again, throwing her arm around his neck, desperate to grab him in a neck hold, but Skelton leant forward, lifting her off the ground before pushing back and slamming her into the wall, crushing her between his weight and the brickwork. Skelton turned to lunge at her, making a grab for Karen's jacket, but this time she was ready for him, punching him hard in the windpipe. Skelton stumbled back, dazed. Seeing an opportunity, Karen hammered the base of her palm upwards as hard as she could into the base of his nose. The cartilage snapped with a satisfying crack. Skelton loosened his grip. Blood exploded over her arm and Skelton's face. A look of pure rage contorted his face.

Attracted by the commotion, several officers milling around their cars began to run towards the disturbance with Jade a few steps behind them.

From somewhere to Karen's left, loud snaps rang out, which sounded like firecrackers. Her heart raced in her chest, pounding, banging, trying to escape. She pushed away from Skelton as he staggered and screamed. Her limbs moved on their own, but she fumbled and tried to steady herself. Everything was disconnected.

Karen turned and saw the open rear window of the Mercedes. Her muscles froze, filled with a tingling pressure that made her want to run until her body ran out of energy.

Instead, loose forms in colour erupted around her as the Mercedes raced off, leaving her with the desperate need for the world to come back into view as her head spun. Karen fell to her knees, all the while gasping and trying to force air back into her winded lungs.

THE SOUND of heavy footsteps and shouting loomed closer.

"KAREN!"

56

Karen sat in her chair and leant forward, her elbows on the desk, and her face shielded behind her hands. The scene replayed in her mind like a broken film clip stuck on a revolving loop. It had happened so quickly that Karen struggled to piece it all together. No matter how hard she tried to think it through, it didn't make sense. *How did it go from words being exchanged to Skelton being shot dead?* The rumour mill was going full pelt as news spread of the shooting.

A room Karen had so often seen as her sanctuary, now felt like a prison. Following the shooting, she'd been checked over by the paramedics, before giving her statement and being confined to her office. The road behind the station continued to be an ongoing crime scene as forensic officers, and a murder investigation team from a different part of London conducted a thorough investigation.

Members of her team and others that she knew around the station were popping their heads around the door to check on her. Though Karen found it reassuring and thoughtful, she'd long since tired of repeating the story countless times. And such an explosive account wasn't confined to the station, as the news spread around the boroughs. Colleagues and friends were calling on repeat to find out what had happened.

Karen had just finished one such call when two officers appeared in her doorway and invited themselves in.

"Karen, I'm Detective Superintendent Paul Pascoe, and this is Detective Inspector Vicky Arden," the man offered as he stepped towards Karen's desk and planted himself in the first seat. He took a few moments to look around her office before returning his attention towards Karen. "We've been assigned to investigate the DCI's death. How are you holding up?"

Pascoe was of average height, with broad shoulders that barely fitted inside his suit jacket. Karen estimated him to be in his late forties, judging by the slivers of grey hair that skirted both sides of his head. The detective inspector who accompanied him had a round face and a stubby nose, with long mousy brown hair pulled back in a tight ponytail. She wore a smart two-piece grey suit, with a white blouse, and looked the consummate professional. Karen imagined that she wouldn't look out of place on a trading floor of an investment bank.

Karen shrugged a shoulder and took a deep breath. "I'm okay. A bit shaken up, but I guess I'm okay."

"We've read your statement," Pascoe began, "and I understand that Skelton had asked you to meet him outside?"

Karen folded her hands into a ball and rested them on her desk. "Yes, sir."

"And why was that?"

"It's in my statement, sir," Karen replied.

"Yes, I know. But I'd like to go over those details again," reinforced Pascoe.

"He wanted to meet, and to warn me off investigating the hijacking. The DCI implied it wouldn't end well if I continued to keep digging, and that he was involved with some dangerous individuals."

"And why were you doing your own investigation? You know the rules. Your case was being investigated by another team. There are procedures in place. With you being a victim of the crime, it would be impossible for you to maintain an objective view."

Karen raised her hand to pacify the man. "I appreciate that, sir. And there was no way in which I was impeding the investigation. Call it unfinished business on my part. It was a blot on my career, and I lost two good officers. I couldn't let it become another statistic."

Pascoe exchanged a glance with Arden who made notes. "And what did you find?"

"Sir, I noticed that vital evidence was being removed from the system. Key witnesses were either disappearing or being intimidated. The disappearing taxi driver, the shopkeeper with amnesia, and Barbara Murphy who has since become a key witness for me. As I continued my own investigation, it came to light that a member of the IT team was being blackmailed into removing vital evidence. Skelton was the blackmailer. I also believe that DCI Skelton was in the pay of the Connells crime family, and therefore responsible for the hijacking."

Pascoe raised a brow but offered nothing more than a nod to begin with. "Why has Barbara Murphy become a key witness for you?"

"Because she contacted me. She was initially paid off to keep her mouth shut. But the guilt got to her. She reached out to me, and following a series of discussions, I found that Barbara believes the driver of one of the vehicles that attacked us was Steve Connell as she saw him without a mask. She also recalled hearing the name Tel or Terry. If that is the case, and he was indeed one of the hijackers, then that links both of the brothers to the incident."

"Karen, if DCI Skelton was warning you off, do you think you were a target of that shooting?" Arden interrupted.

Karen turned towards the woman. She noticed that Vicky Arden had a softer tone to her voice than the Detective Superintendent. Pascoe appeared firmer and more direct with his intentions. Arden on the other hand came across like she was building bridges with her words and forming a connection.

"I don't think so, if I'm honest. I was near to the DCI when he was shot. It didn't feel like a random drive-by shooting, with a spray of bullets, and several victims. There were perhaps a couple of shots, and they hit the DCI and not me. If they felt they had missed, then surely they would have had another go?" Karen said, searching the faces of the officers in front of her.

Pascoe and Arden remained stony-faced, which did little to reassure Karen.

"Have we managed to trace the Mercedes, sir?" Karen asked, keen to fill the silence that sat uncomfortably between the three of them.

Pascoe nodded and curled up the corner of his mouth. "It was found burnt out in Tottenham near an industrial estate. We've got forensics going over it at the moment. I doubt they'll get anything, since it's a lump of twisted metal now. We've got local officers beginning enquiries, but they have not uncovered anything yet."

Karen bit her bottom lip. "Any witnesses over there?"

"Not at this time of night. Most of the units were already closed for the day. It was found on a no through road, so they picked the perfect spot."

"Sir, I've got Barbara Murphy staying in a hotel. I couldn't bring her in because I didn't want the DCI to find out. Until I confronted him, I didn't know how far the level of corruption went. And I know it's unorthodox, and not procedure, but I had to put Barbara's safety first. That's why I put her in a hotel out of the way until I could arrest DCI Skelton."

"No, it wasn't the right procedure, Detective Inspector," Pascoe fumed. "For a start, it's none of your fucking business. Conducting your own unauthorised investigation is a disciplinary procedure, and something we will deal with later. In the meantime, we need to identify who killed DCI Skelton, and place Barbara Murphy in protective custody."

"But, sir…"

Pascoe didn't let Karen continue as he stood up. "I've heard enough for the time being, Detective Inspector Heath. I need you to provide me with the address for Barbara Murphy. We'll also arrange for officers to take you home and remain outside of your property for your safety. We'll reconvene tomorrow morning."

Karen bowed her head, and slowly exhaled through a small

gap in her lips, as she listened to Pascoe and Arden exiting her office, and their footsteps fading down the corridor. It was only then that she lifted her head and blew out her cheeks.

Confronting Skelton should have made things easier, but it only left Karen's mind swimming with even more questions.

57

Karen rolled over in bed and pulled the duvet away from her face. Tired as hell, weary with the burden of long-closed eyes; she could have easily pulled off being a walking zombie, dead on the inside but subconsciously awake. She reluctantly opened her eyes, the light forcing her to squint. Glancing across to her bedside clock, her mind worked frantically to engage and figure out how long she'd been asleep.

Eleven hours. Karen groaned at the thought. It felt more like six, or so her body seemed to suggest as it protested, unwilling to move.

Having thrown her legs over the side of her bed, Karen sat upright and yawned, stretching both arms above her head. Her mouth felt sticky and dry, and probably smelt like a camel's armpit. Peeling herself off the bed and making her way to the kitchen, she flicked on the kettle and made herself a cup of coffee whilst putting breakfast out for the cat. Every part of her wanted to go back to sleep, but so much had happened in the last twenty-four hours, that she knew her mind wouldn't let her even if her body pleaded for more sleep. She made a mug of coffee and padded into the lounge.

The place looked a tip, with unopened letters, circulars and flyers scattered across the table. Cushions on the sofa hadn't been tidied up or plumped up, and still carried the impressions of where she had leant on them before.

Once she finished her coffee, Karen took a long shower to wake up, then hungrily downed a big bowl of porridge. Once she felt ready, she grabbed her purse and left the apartment. The officers who had dropped her off last night had been replaced by a new team who sat patiently across the road in a dark blue Ford Focus job car. As she approached, they looked thoroughly bored, and other than a cursory nod and brief greeting, they drove her back to the station in silence.

A MIXTURE of welcoming smiles and concerned looks greeted Karen as she made her way through the building to her office. Jade was the first to hurry in and check on her, swiftly followed by Brad and Steve, who equally expressed their concern. Karen batted away most of their questions politely, telling them that she was okay, and couldn't say much due to the ongoing investigation. It still seemed a blur to her, and in part, surreal. A sombre mood filled the building at the killing of a police officer, and rightfully so. But Karen knew that many who mourned Skelton's loss hadn't really known the man at all.

After Brad and Steve left her office, Jade planted herself

down in the chair opposite Karen and studied her boss for a few moments. "How are you feeling today?"

Karen rested her elbows on the armrest of her chair and formed a steeple with her fingers under her chin. "To be honest, I'm not sure. A part of me feels relieved I was able to confront the DCI, but another part of me feels cheated. I know the DCI lost his life, but I kind of wanted him to be around to face the music and be held to account for everything he'd done."

"I can't believe what the DCI put you through. To be honest, what he put us all through. I only wish we could have supported you more," Jade said.

Karen let out a deep exhale. "Yeah, he was screwing us all over, wasn't he? As much as I wanted help, I needed to do this myself. I wish I could have told you all, but I couldn't take the risk of getting any of you into trouble. Besides, this might not be over. It could be the beginning."

Jade's forehead creased. "I was really shocked listening to the way that the DCI was talking to you yesterday. I'm sorry I couldn't get to you quick enough. Everything escalated so quickly."

Karen cleared her throat, forcing the guilt away. "Yes, about that. Jade, I'm really, really sorry for dropping that in your lap at the last minute yesterday. It put you in a difficult situation. But my intention was to bring the DCI in. And it would have been his word against mine. I wanted you to at least listen to the things he said, so my accusations would carry more weight."

Jade's mouth twisted into a grimace. "It's a bit of a mess now isn't it, Karen?"

Karen nodded as a million thoughts tumbled through her mind. "Do you remember when we went over to Barking to visit my friend at the Ibis hotel?"

"Yup."

"Well, I told a little white lie. God, I feel awful for lying to you, Jade. I'm so sorry. A witness from the hijacking approached me. She needed my help. She had been paid off to keep her mouth shut by enforcers associated with the Connells. Well, in the end I met with her and she was able to potentially identify at least one of the Connell brothers as a driver involved in the hijacking."

Jade's eyes widened in surprise and consternation. "You're kidding?"

Karen shook her head. "I wish I was. I couldn't put her into protective custody because it would have meant squaring it up with the DCI, so I put her up in the Ibis. Detective Superintendent Pascoe who is investigating the DCI's death sent officers across last night to pick up Barbara and place her in protective custody."

"Christ. What's going to happen now?"

Karen rose from her chair. "I don't know. I'm just about to go and speak to the boss now. He's commandeered one of the offices on the floor below. I don't think I'm his favourite person. He was throwing his weight around last night, so it should be interesting. The DI with him… Vicky Arden seemed nice enough. But I got the feeling she was holding back in front of her guv and playing it cool and professional. Understandable, I guess," Karen added, raising a brow.

As they said goodbye, she promised to let Jade know the outcome as soon as she had met with him.

THERE WAS a flurry of activity around Detective Superintendent Pascoe as Karen entered the office. Vicky Arden was camped out behind her desk to his left and sifting through mounds of paperwork when she looked up and greeted Karen with a nod and a warm smile. "How are you doing this morning? Did you sleep much?" Vicky asked.

She's definitely more approachable than Pascoe.

"Yes, thanks. Though I could have done with more."

Karen noticed several other officers around Pascoe, taking instructions from him, before they moved away back towards their own desks, leaving Karen on her own in front of him. She felt like a little schoolgirl turning up at the headmaster's office, waiting to be bawled out for misbehaving or something.

"Morning, sir," Karen offered. Pascoe looked up from his paperwork and offered nothing more than a nod and simple greeting in reply.

Karen groaned inside.

"Sir, how did your team get on with picking up Barbara Murphy yesterday? Is she okay?"

Pascoe nodded. "Yes. Let's say she was a little uncooperative. For starters, she wouldn't open the bloody door, nor acknowledge she was inside the room. Despite us announcing ourselves, we had no choice but to get the duty manager to open the door. We found Barbara hiding under the bed."

Karen's stomach twisted. "Oh, okay. Where is she now?"

"We have her downstairs in one of the interview suites."

"Can I go and see her, sir?"

Pascoe shook his head in defiance. "I'm afraid not. We're just about to interview her."

"Sir, I'd like to sit in on the interview, if that's okay?" Karen asked.

"Absolutely not. If what you say is true, then she is a key witness in an incident involving you. It becomes hard for you to stay objective. And I certainly don't want your feelings getting in the way," Pascoe replied firmly, his eyes locked on Karen with a steely determination to ram home his point.

Karen lifted her hands, palms up. "But, sir, she trusts me. It's taken time to build up that trust, and we need to use that to our advantage. If she is interviewed by your officers, then she'll put up her guard, and we'll get nothing out of her."

Pascoe stood up and pushed his chair back, before stuffing his hands in his trouser pockets. "If that's the case, then we'll charge her with wasting police time and obstructing an investigation."

Vicky Arden remained a spectator whilst watching the exchange between Karen and her boss. She came round from the side of her desk to stand beside Pascoe. "Karen, perhaps stepping back to see what our officers can obtain from Barbara might be a good starting point. Everything is still raw and fresh in your mind, and I'm sure what happened last night hasn't fully sunk in yet."

Karen pursed her lips and nodded in resignation. It wasn't an argument she would win.

Vicky smiled. "Why don't you go and grab yourself a coffee in the canteen and wait to see how this pans out? I'll come and update you as soon as the interview is done."

Karen sighed, dropped her shoulders in defeat and headed to the canteen. She knew they were talking sense, but she feared the trust she had built up with Barbara would fracture permanently, and she would lose the only leverage she had in bringing those who had committed the hijacking to justice.

58

The noise of a dozen conversations about yesterday's events melted into a constant babble around her as Karen stared down at her cup. Her suspicions were confirmed as the odd glance was cast over in her direction. She felt helpless sitting there, unsure what to do next.

Karen's phone lit up and buzzed on the table beside her. She glanced at the screen to see Jade's name.

"Jade, hello. What's up?"

"A box has just arrived for the team, and, well… it's addressed to our team and it's about the DCI. Items belonging to him, I think."

"Where from?"

"There's no sender details. It was dropped off at the front desk by a courier. Shall I take a look?"

"Yes, open it and I'll be up in a sec," Karen replied, hanging up and preparing to leave.

"I think your hunch was right," came a voice from over her shoulder.

Karen spun around in her chair to see Detective Inspector Vicky Arden approach and come around the table. She pulled out a chair, the legs screeching across the floor. Karen's jaws tensed as the noise scratched through her.

Karen looked at the time on her phone, and then at Vicky through narrowed eyes, with a mixture of confusion and surprise. It had only been fifteen minutes or so since the interview with Barbara had started. "I thought you were in the interview?"

Vicky rolled her eyes. "We were. But you were right. Barbara has pulled the shutters down and is refusing to talk to the gaffer."

"I bet you that's gone down well with the super?" Karen wanted to laugh and say, "I told you so" but resisted the temptation.

"Well, bull in a china shop is a fair way of describing how the super often conducts interviews, so he didn't warm to Barbara. So you're up." Vicky shrugged. "Are you ready?"

Karen reared back in surprise. "Me?"

Vicky nodded. "Absolutely. All we need you to do is to convince her that we have her best interests at heart. I can fill you in on the things that you can tell her, and if she's up for it, the super and myself can continue the interview. All we need is for you to get her to talk to us."

Karen agreed as she pushed back in her chair and followed Vicky down to the interview suite. The burden of guilt sat heavy on her shoulders for putting Barbara in this position.

Barbara scowled at Karen the moment she entered the interview suite. The look of disgust and anger on the woman's face said it all. Tension bristled in the air as she took her seat. Barbara's hot and intense stare burnt through Karen as the other woman sat back in her chair and crossed her arms. Karen noticed Barbara's jaw tensing.

Vicky had already agreed that Karen would be allowed to lead, and that she would take a back seat until given the all-clear to take over the interview.

Karen offered a warm smile as she rested her forearms on the desk and took a moment to look at Barbara. The woman had aged in just a few days with weary, tired eyes. Her top eyelids sagged, and her cheeks drooped. Her hair looked untidy, and her clothes were crumpled. Karen imagined that the poor woman wanted nothing more than the warmth of a hot shower, and the comfort of her own bed.

"Barbara, how are you doing?" Karen asked.

Barbara offered nothing more than a cursory shake of her head, before looking away and staring at the blank, magnolia walls of the small room.

Karen sighed and tried again. "I know it's difficult for you, but we are so close to bringing those responsible for this hijacking to justice. Detective Inspector Vicky Arden," Karen said, nodding in Vicky's direction, "really needs your help. We all need your help."

"Why the fuck should I help you? Look where it has got me," Barbara hissed as she flapped her arms.

Karen shook her head and closed her eyes for a brief

second before opening them. "I know. I know. This is an awful situation that you are in. But you came to me, remember? And you wanted my help. Up until now, I've done everything to protect you. I've been working flat out to bring an end to this shitty nightmare that you and I both found ourselves in. Vicky is here to help us."

Barbara remained silent as her eyes danced between Karen and Vicky. The woman took hard, deep lungfuls of air as she fought to control the mixture of fear and anger that flashed through her veins.

Karen needed to work harder to convince Barbara. "Please. All you have to do is just tell them everything you told me. And they will look after you. They can move you to a new location so you're closer to your family. They can even give you a new identity and protect you as a witness."

Barbara slammed her hand down on the table. "I don't want a fucking new identity. I want *me*. I want my old life back. I don't want to go into hiding and be fearful of every new person I meet. I don't want to be looking over my shoulder when I walk along the street or be fearful of stepping out of my front door in the dark." Her voice strained with emotion. "Are you going to protect me then? When one of those thugs steps out of the shadows and points a gun in my face. Are you?"

Karen gave the woman a pointed look. "It's not going to come to that, Barbara."

"Oh, so you can promise that, can you?" Barbara added, throwing her head back in disgust.

Karen needed to tread carefully. She couldn't promise anything but wasn't about to let Barbara know that. "Our job is to bring those who were responsible for this crime to justice. We are this close," Karen added as she brought her thumb and forefinger to within just an inch of each other, "to getting those responsible. And once we have them, we'll be able to put them away for a very long time. They'll never be able to hurt anyone, including you."

Silence filled the room as neither side wanted to say anything. Karen could tell that Barbara was weighing up her options as the woman's eyes bounced from the table, to Karen, to the walls, and the ceiling. It was like she was watching an invisible ping-pong ball.

"Please?" Karen asked again, fed up with waiting.

Barbara let out a long sigh through puffed-out cheeks before she nodded. "Okay. I'll help you. On one condition."

"What's that?" Karen asked.

"I'm happy to talk to your colleague here, Detective Inspector Arden, but I want another officer in the room. I don't want your dickhead boss in here again. He's too full of himself for my liking."

Karen and Vicky exchanged a glance which morphed into a knowing smirk.

Knowing that Barbara would be in good hands, Karen handed over the interview to Vicky, and thanked Barbara, promising that she would try to catch up after the interview.

As Karen stepped out of the interview suite, she switched her phone on again, only to be confronted with several missed calls from Jade, and a few urgent texts, which had Karen racing up the stairwell at breakneck speed.

59

Conversations crackled amongst the small crowd gathered around one of the tables in the incident room by the time Karen flew through the door. Many glanced over towards the disturbance as the doors flew back and slammed into the walls.

Jade hovered over the box; her hands protected in nitrile gloves to avoid contaminating the contents.

She looked up as Karen approached, a look of excitement and surprise etched in her features. "You've got to see this boss, where have you been?"

"Sorry, sorry. I got dragged into the interview with Barbara Murphy." Karen stood opposite Jade and peered into the contents of the box. "What have we got?"

"I've not touched any of it other than this," Jade began, holding up a clear evidence bag with a handwritten note, "and a USB flash drive, which we plugged into a laptop that forensics offered us."

Karen took the evidence bag from Jade and read the short note. The writing was messy, but the message clear. Giddy with excitement, Karen wanted to run, to shout, to tell everyone what was going to happen... but it would have to wait. Her mind flittered like a butterfly, whatever distraction she chose, her mind kept drifting back to the note in her hand. Then she'd get that tingly feeling all over again.

Upon reading the note a few times, Karen felt like every fibre of her being was vibrating with anticipation as adrenaline coursed through her veins. Her hands trembled and her eyes widened. The note simply read that if Skelton survived, the information within this box and at his home address would be enough to make sure that DCI Skelton spent the rest of his life behind bars.

Jade nodded furiously as Karen looked up at her, seeking some form of confirmation that she had read it correctly.

"Tell me what we've got, Jade?" Karen asked. There was hunger in her voice, a sense of desperation in wanting to know every single detail.

"Inside the flash drive was a video showing the DCI meeting three people in a property owned by the Connells. Other than DCI Skelton's clear image, the others present had been obscured out. The DCI was handed a white package. Also contained within the box were pictures of a young female with injuries to her face, mainly bruising."

Karen's heart whomped against her ribcage. "Who was she?"

"Her name is Greta," Steve added. "There was a copy of her passport highlighting her date of birth. She is sixteen years old. Apparently, the injuries sustained were as a result of an assault by the DCI."

Karen's mind swam with those implications. "Do we know where she is?"

Steve shook his head.

"But it gets worse," Jade continued, scrunching up her nose. "There was a used condom in a plastic bag, and a sticker on the front which said it has both Greta's and the DCI's DNA."

Karen felt her stomach flip again as another wave of nausea hit her for completely different reasons. The prospect of Skelton having underage sex against her will repulsed her. The sentiment amongst the team appeared the same as Karen shot them a look.

Jade went on to explain that the flash drive contained dark grainy footage of Two-tone Charlie's execution. An empty shell casing reportedly recovered from the scene was included in the box.

Jade opened her phone, and flicked to her gallery of photographs, where she showed Karen a picture of a handgun.

Karen took a good look. "Where's that from?"

"It's from the DCI's property. A search was conducted at his place yesterday, and this was found under his bed. Forensics ran a ballistic analysis overnight, and they've confirmed the weapon was used to murder Two-tone Charlie, and… Anne Woodward in the hijacking."

The revelations left Karen reeling, and her mind in turmoil. She wondered about Skelton's involvement in the hijacking? *Was he present? Or was he storing the gun for someone else?*

Karen instructed Jade to get all the items over to forensics for them to do the detailed analysis for fingerprints, DNA and fibres. She also put in the request to have handwriting analysis conducted on the note before she shot out of the incident room and went downstairs to the evidence store.

MASON BROPHY the crime scene manager, was recording and cataloguing the final bits recovered from the search of Skelton's property. He smiled as Karen came through the door. "I wondered when you'd turn up…" he teased.

"Mason, you have no idea just how important these discoveries are."

"Oh, I think I do. I know this has been a big deal for you. Let me show you what we've found," Mason replied, pointing to one corner of the storeroom.

Karen gathered around the items that Mason had laid out on the table. Each item had been labelled, photographed and recorded before being added to the HOLMES2 database by the exhibits officer. Karen noticed several small bags of white powder, that appeared to be cocaine. Along with a handgun, a brass knuckleduster had also been discovered. There were several large bundles of cash which had been counted and totalled to the sum of five thousand three hundred pounds.

"Firearms officers made the gun safe. It had a full magazine of ammunition, and a second half full magazine allowing them to trace the empty casing," Mason said.

Karen peered at the wealth of evidence. "Do you think we'll be able to extract anything from the cash?"

"I should imagine so, Karen. This will be more interesting," Mason said, pointing to a scrap of paper with six rows of numbers, each row having eight digits per line.

Karen leant forward and examined the numbers. They didn't look like telephone numbers to her and carried no distinguishable pattern. "Any guesses?"

Mason shrugged. "Your guess is as good as mine. My first thoughts were that they could be bank account numbers, but we'll be hard-pressed to find their origin. That will be for the financial investigation unit to look into."

"Okay, Mason. Thanks for all of this. Even though I can't be involved in the investigation around the DCI's death, can you let me know if there are any developments?"

"Sure. But don't you dare say where you received the information," Mason replied with a small wink.

THE HOURS SEEMED to drag as Karen waited for news. A nervous energy pulsed through her that left her agitated. She hated hanging around at the best of times. There were two kinds of waiting in her book. The kind of waiting that felt like a gentle onshore breeze that lapped the shore. It offered a sense of calm, of things expected. Which left the kind that felt like the head of a medieval club was loose in her guts and her head had taken a beating with a hefty plank of wood. As she poured hot water into her coffee cup, she decided this waiting felt more like the club than the breeze.

"Ah, there you are. I wondered where you were."

Vicky poked her head around the corner, shaking Karen from her reverie.

Karen smiled. “Sorry, I was miles away. This whole thing with the DCI has knocked me sideways. It sometimes feels like a blur. I’ve waited to get to the bottom of this for so long, and to find the DCI was always there, finding ways to trip me up or hold me back… well…”

Vicky leant against a kitchen unit and studied Karen for a minute. “You’ve had a close call. A stray bullet could have hit you. You’re in shock still, so things won’t make sense.”

Vicky was right, but Karen still found it hard to accept.

“Besides,” Vicky continued, “you’ve got a great team, and I’m yet to find anyone with a bad word to say about you.”

Karen laughed, welcoming the moment of light relief. “That’s because they know I’d kick their arses if they did. By the way, thank you.”

Vicky furrowed her brow. “For what?”

“Dunno. For listening, I guess.”

“My pleasure. Listen, we’ve finished with Barbara. We believe we have enough to arrest the Connells in connection with the hijacking.”

The excitement rose in Karen again. “Do you mind if I go with you as an observer? I’d like to be there when they’re arrested. I want to see it with my own eyes.”

“Sure. But we need to find them first. There’s nothing you can do for the time being. So get yourself an early night, and we’ll see where we are tomorrow.”

Karen concluded that Vicky wasn't too bad after all. Without Pascoe around, Karen had seen her in a different light.

An early night sounded perfect as she poured away her freshly made coffee and called it a day.

60

Karen shook the sleep from her tired body as she crawled out of bed and stood in her bedroom for a few moments. Her body felt exhausted, her mind felt in tatters, and her thoughts felt like they were bouncing off the walls of her skull. She headed to the kitchen and flicked on the kettle and reached for the Nurofen and a glass of water. Though she'd only been awake for a few minutes, the beginnings of a headache were already squeezing her head to the point where she thought her eyeballs would pop out.

After a quick shower to revive herself, Karen dressed and collected her belongings, anxious to get back to work. She gave a sigh and a little eye-roll that only Manky saw. Time to head back to her office again in stilted silence.

Officers had remained outside her apartment all night, as they had done for the third night in a row. With Pascoe's team closing in on the Connells, Karen had accepted that she'd have a police tail for the time being.

Slipping into the back seat, she gave the usual cursory nod to the two officers up front. The time alone with sparse moments of conversation with those in the car gave Karen an opportunity to press the pause button and watch life pass by. Very little entered her mind as they passed through Loughton, then Woodford and on to Stratford. She noticed how leafy suburbia morphed into tighter, busier streets as they neared inner London, with a higher density of low-cost housing and a plethora of mini marts, Asian and Caribbean food stores, and knick-knack stores.

By the time Karen arrived at the station, Vicky Arden was waiting by the back door, her arms folded across her front and a nervous energy in her movements.

Karen smiled as she stepped from the vehicle and made her way towards Vicky.

"Morning, is everything okay?" Karen asked, as she slung her handbag over her shoulder.

Vicky nodded and smiled. "Morning. Yes. It's looking promising. We've had plain-clothed and intelligence officers searching London for two days now looking for any sign of the Connells. It's been like they went underground. We've been following the movements of many of their associates to see if we can build a pattern of their activities. And we had a breakthrough late last night."

The news spiked Karen's interest as she followed Vicky into the building and up several flights of stairs until they reached Pascoe's commandeered office. As Karen entered the room, Pascoe was in discussion with several officers around the table at one end. Karen wondered what they were talking about as Pascoe appeared more animated than normal.

Vicky dropped into her chair and swivelled it around to face Karen. "Intel has confirmed the location of the Connells's bolthole. Officers on the ground followed some of their associates to a house in Leytonstone."

"And the Connells were there?" Karen asked.

"Not to begin with. The three men that they followed entered the property and didn't come out. About an hour later another car pulled up and two men exited. Officers identified them as Steve and Terry Connell. So far, no one has left the building. The boss has given me the authorisation to do a targeted raid there this morning."

Karen perked up at that information. "That's bloody brilliant news. Hopefully, we can nail the bastards."

Vicky agreed with Karen's sentiment as she grabbed her notebook and dashed off towards the briefing room, with Karen in tow.

KAREN TRAVELLED in a convoy of vehicles towards the location. She was in the same car as Vicky, who received constant updates from the intelligence officers who continued to observe the property. A mixture of heightened anticipation and nerves twisted Karen's innards. Everyone involved in the raid knew the importance and the need for a result. This was the deadly and serious end of the job and not taken lightly. Every angle had to be covered, and every precaution taken to protect all the officers.

After sitting in the back of the case briefing, Karen had listened to Vicky providing a background to the gathered officers. She'd gone into detail about the suspects that they were looking for and stressed how everyone needed to be vigilant as they were considered armed and dangerous. Vicky had discussed how they would conduct the raid, which point of entry they would use, and where officers would gather.

Now they drove through the streets of Leytonstone in a silent convoy. The tactical entry team led from the front, followed by another armoured carrier of officers, and then two unmarked job cars. Approaching from a different direction was a dog unit, and two units of AFOs. Because of the propensity for the Connells to use firearms, authorised firearms officers needed to be deployed, and would form the first wave of officers who would swarm the building once the tactical entry team had gained access.

They arrived with minutes to spare for their scheduled eleven a.m. strike time.

As they pulled up around the corner, Vicky glanced around for any signs of activity or lookouts. None had been identified by her intelligence officers, who continued to update her, but she wanted to check for herself.

"I don't really want to hang around here for too long. The sooner we get in, the better. We are already attracting attention," Vicky muttered as she looked at the faces of those who walked by, their beady eyes staring into each of the vehicles that were parked in line. Vicky knew from experience that such a large police presence would bring residents out on to the street, many of them driven by curiosity, their mobile phones poised ready to record any action. She checked her watch and reached for her radio. "All units, two minutes, ready to go."

Karen listened as the supporting units replied in unison,

confirming that they were ready to go. She could hear the faint whining noise from the rotor blades of an NPAS helicopter circling high above them. Her heart thundered in her chest so loudly, she thought Vicky would hear it. Tension crackled in the air like an angry thunderstorm. Karen clenched and unclenched her fists to relieve the pent-up adrenaline that pushed her breath out in short and sharp bursts.

Vicky gave instructions for all officers to leave their vehicles. Doors swung open, shields were unloaded, and the tactical entry team readied themselves. She checked her phone again just as the AFOs arrived and unloaded. They crouched behind the wall of an adjoining house and hunched up like coiled springs ready to go.

"Go, go, go!" Vicky barked into her radio.

61

The team moved off on Vicky's command, the heavy rumble of boots breaking the uneasy silence.

Karen held back towards the rear. Though she had her stab vest on, it was no defence for a machete or firearm.

The entry team raced to the door, followed by the AFOs. One officer gently pressed the door in certain places to decide the weakest points, before pointing to the officer at his side. A large burly black officer carrying the "red enforcer" stepped forward and swung it back before launching it at a precise spot on the door frame. The door shook but held firm. He swung again, and the first cracks appeared.

The line of officers behind him crept forward and fidgeted, desperate to get in. The officer hit the door with all his might, and on the third try, the frame splintered. Annoyed that it hadn't fully caved it, the black officer shoulder charged the weakened obstruction and tumbled through as it flew off its hinges and crashed to the floor.

An organised and aggressive storming of the building followed as the AFOs streamed through the house, their guns aimed at any moving targets. Dog handlers held back, their four-legged companions straining at their leashes, desperate for a slice of the action.

Explosions fractured the air as Karen ducked behind a garden wall. Flash bangs deployed by the AFOs from somewhere within the building signalled an aggressive escalation in their tactics, followed by a cacophony of shouting and swearing.

Karen bit her bottom lip as she listened in on the commentary coming through on Vicky's radio as they both crouched for safety. "One suspect detained!" screamed one officer.

Just as Karen thought they were taking control, her eyes widened, and her breath caught in her throat when shots rang out. Karen strained to see anything, as further shots and shouts came thick and fast. This felt more like the ending of an embassy siege by the SAS than a police raid as a gun battle raged inside.

"Two suspects detained, one suspect down."

Desperate to know who had been detained or shot, Karen strained her ears. She hoped the Connells were the former. With one person unaccounted for, her eyes scanned the windows in the hope of seeing any movement.

"One suspect detained!"

Karen kept a mental tally of the numbers. By all accounts, there shouldn't have been anyone else inside. It was a tense wait that felt like hours as AFOs searched the entire property for any signs of others still hiding out.

"All clear. I repeat, all clear," came the response from the lead AFO.

"Come on, Karen. We've got the all-clear to go in now," Vicky announced as she stood up and made her way to the house, with Karen trailing behind her.

A smoky cloud hung in the air as Karen followed Vicky through the property. No one had been detained downstairs, so Karen assumed that all the suspects were on the first floor. As they headed upstairs and reached the landing, a mass of bodies confronted them. Firearms officers mingled amongst their tactical entry colleagues. One of the officers pointed Karen and Vicky towards the rear bedroom, and as Karen stepped into the room, carnage confronted her everywhere her gaze landed. The bullet-ridden walls carried the scars of battle and the crumpled body of a man slumped against one wall. Shots to the face and chest riddled the corpse. A handgun lay by his side. Though his face was contorted and bloodied, Karen recognised him. Steve Connell had decided to take on the best of the Met's firearms unit and had come off worse.

As Karen moved through the other rooms, she found the four other occupants, three of which were face down, with their wrists secured by cable ties behind their backs. Karen felt a shiver race through her body. The fourth was Terry Connell. He carried chest injuries, from where he had launched an attack at police officers with a club hammer, resulting in the use of deadly force. Paramedics were being summoned to the scene as a matter of urgency whilst AFOs provided immediate medical attention. If there was one thing that Karen wanted more than anything else, it was to bring that particular suspect in alive.

As Karen stepped out on to the pavement, she met a sea of onlookers, being kept at a safe distance by a police cordon. She noticed many were aiming their phones towards the scene as she paced up and down the road. Normally, Karen conducted raids of this nature. On this occasion, she felt like a spare part. Though Vicky had allowed her to join them as an observer, Karen wanted to be in the thick of it. She wanted to be back in the house, quizzing the suspects, seizing evidence, and locking down the crime scene.

Karen didn't care for the helpless feeling of not being in control of an investigation where she held a personal stake in the outcome.

"You okay?" Vicky asked, joining Karen on the street and scanning the crowd.

She pointed towards the scene. "Yeah, I guess. I kind of want to be in there. It feels odd watching from the sidelines."

"I bet," Vicky replied. "Officers seized evidence from the basement."

"Oh, yeah?" Karen asked, now interested again.

"We've found another handgun and two sawn-offs, a substantial quantity of a substance we believe is cocaine, balaclavas, baseball bats, chains, the lot."

"You're kidding…" Karen said, as excitement once again raged through her veins.

Vicky nodded. "Nope. The sawn-offs were wrapped in a jumper within a carrier bag, along with a decent stash of cartridges. We've got the AFOs making the weapons safe before it's all bagged up for analysis. We also found a knuckleduster. It's a right Aladdin's cave of criminal gear."

"That's a great result, Vicky, well done."

"Cheers. We have you to thank for it. Well, Barbara too. She ID'd the Connells."

Vicky was right there. Despite her terror, Barbara had given them the break they needed. But one question remained in Karen's mind.

Where is Sally Connell?

62

F*ive days later…*

Karen swivelled in her chair, moving from a pile of paper to her monitor. She was going through all the evidence compiled and submitted in the case of David Simpson. Her team had pulled it off, and she'd rewarded them with a few rounds at the local pub last night. Her head thumped and her mouth felt furred up, even though she'd brushed her teeth twice so far this morning.

With all of the recent events, it felt good to get back to her work and plough through the hundreds of emails that had gathered in her inbox over the past week. The outcome of her unauthorised investigation still hung in the balance, but Detective Inspector Vicky Arden had promised to put in a good word in favour of the help and cooperation that Karen had offered.

Karen accepted that there would be repercussions, but a large part of her felt relieved. She'd finally got to the bottom of the hijacking, uncovered a corrupt senior officer, and provided a breakthrough that resulted in the collapse of the Connells. Sally Connell was still at large, but intelligence suggested she had slipped out of the country and was being protected by associates in the Sierra Nevada hills of the Andalusia region.

That will be a battle for another day.

Karen leant forward in her chair and clicked open a follow-up email from Vicky. The first bit of good news was that Steve Connell's DNA had been found on the recovered cash from the search of Skelton's property. What surprised Karen further was that the labs had discovered microbes on the notes.

Tiny creatures uncovered on the banknotes helped her forensics and financial crime colleagues to locate stolen money buried in a secret location underground. Karen's brow furrowed. *What the fuck!*

Vicky continued by explaining that in 2019 a criminal gang in Spain with links to the Connells made off with at least half a million euros, which they took abroad and buried for safe keeping. But forensic analysis of microscopic organisms found on the money allowed the specialist officers to pinpoint the real location of the money – in Thailand.

Karen's mind was blown. She hungrily devoured the contents of the email as Vicky revealed further details. Forensic specialists found dozens of dead Rhizoglyphus howensis Manson mites on the notes, which aroused suspicions because the species wasn't found in Europe. The size of the colony indicated they had infested the banknotes whilst they were buried underground. Moisture that made its way into the plastic bags containing the money whilst in the soil allowed the growth of fungi that provided the best feeding conditions for the tiny creatures. Tiny microscopic soil samples matched those found only in a region of Thailand.

Karen leant back and whistled. She continued to scroll down the lengthy email.

Terry Connell had been charged with murder following the hijacking. His voice had been recognised by Barbara Murphy. Hair fibre analysis also linked him to one of the balaclavas. His DNA was discovered on a baseball bat, along with DNA from one of the murdered officers from the hijacking. Karen nodded, feeling a surge of satisfaction swelling within.

Firearm analysis conducted on the weapons confirmed that one shotgun had been discharged in the hijacking. Scattered shotgun pellets recovered from the hijacking scene were a match for the weapon, and Steve Connell's prints were all over it. The evidence just built up as Karen continued to read on.

"Thank God for forensics," Karen muttered as she punched the air. Fragment and particle analysis confirmed the presence of gunshot residue on the balaclavas, which matched residue traces recovered from one of the police cars attacked in the hijack.

Terry Connell won't see freedom ever again!

The final section of the email finally sealed the Connells's fate. Sixteen thousand pounds found in a sports holdall in the basement had been seized under the Proceeds of Crimes Act.

Karen nodded to herself as she entertained a small smile.

At least in this case, her extreme focus and diligence had tied up all the loose ends. Justice had finally been served.

CURRENT BOOK LIST

Hop over to my website for a current list of books:

http://jaynadal.com/current-books/

ABOUT THE AUTHOR

I've always had a strong passion for whodunnits, crime series and books. The more I immersed myself in it, the stronger the fascination grew.

In my spare time you'll find me in the gym, reading books from authors in my genre or enjoying walks in the forest… It's amazing what you think of when you give yourself some space.

Oh, and I'm an avid people-watcher. I just love to watch the interaction between people, their mannerisms, their way of expressing their thoughts…Weird I know, but I could spend hours engrossed in it.

I hope you enjoy the stories that I craft for you.

Printed in Great Britain
by Amazon

59741071R00236